Paper Tiger

Paper Tiger

Tigre en papier

Olivier Rolin

Translated by William Cloonan

UNIVERSITY OF NEBRASKA PRESS

LINCOLN & LONDON

Cet ouvrage, publié dans le cadre d'un programme d'aide à la publication, bénéficie du soutien du Ministère des Affaires étrangères et du Service Culturel de l'Ambassade de France aux Etats-Unis.

This work, published as part of a program of aid for publication, received support from the French Ministry of Foreign Affairs and the Cultural Service of the French Embassy in the United States.

Publication of this book was assisted by a grant from the National Endowment for the Arts.

A Great Nation
Deserves Great Art

⊚
Library of Congress
Cataloging-in-Publication Data
Rolin, Olivier.
[Tigre en papier. English]
Paper tiger = Tigre en papier /
Olivier Rolin ; translated by
William Cloonan.
p. cm.
ISBN-13: 978-0-8032-3955-5
(cloth : alk. paper)
ISBN-10: 0-8032-3955-6
(cloth : alk. paper)
ISBN-13: 978-0-8032-8999-4
(pbk. : alk. paper)
ISBN-10: 0-8032-8999-5
(pbk. : alk. paper)
I. Cloonan, William J. II. Title.
PQ2678.O4155T5413 2007
843'.914—dc22
2006016231

Set in Adobe Garamond by
Kim Essman.
Designed by R. W. Boeche.

These stories were dozing in thirty-year-old newspapers, and nobody knew about them anymore.

Marcel Proust, *The Past Recaptured*

I

Emerald green against the blue night. INTERIOR BELTWAY CLEAR EX-
TERIOR BELTWAY CLEAR. Emerald, you love that name, who knows
why. Because of Esmeralda, the first girl who turned you on, under
the features, or rather the curves, of Gina Lollobrigida? Or maybe
because as a child you spent summers on the Emerald Coast? No
windsurfing, no outboards, nothing on the water, the sea empty like
it is in paintings. You had to watch out for drifting mines; the tide still
brought them in, big balls of death, patient, rusty. Just waiting. The
end of the war was so recent. You were born exactly halfway between
the Mother of Defeats and Dien Bien Phu. Just your luck. The sadness
of history, you sucked it in with your mother's milk. She used to take
you and your brother to see the sunset from a cliff close to the house.
Seated on the bench, you'd wait. It's not the sun that's going down,
she explained, but the earth turning, toppling, pushing itself into the
night. On the other side of the world, in Asia, in Indochina, as we
used to say, day was breaking. Hard to believe. You hoped to see the
green flash, but you never did. You would go home silently, confused
and disappointed. You like the name of the night, also *navire* night,

noche triste, notta continua. In German, you won't say it. Glistening highway, black with golden flecks—BOBIGNY LILLE BRUXELLES PORTE DE BAGNOLET—black towers whose tops are lost in the fog—PORTE DE MONTREUIL HYPERMARCHÉ AUCHAN green and red, NOVOTEL blue 550 METERS to NATIONAL 302 CAMPANILE green SANT-MACLOU PEUGEOT PARIS NORD. First days of the twenty-first century. You lived up on the right over there in the dark night, at the top of the street . . . what street was it? How many years ago? The night of time . . . with Judith. Maybe it's too much to say, "living there." You slept there. How long ago? Let's see . . . maybe thirty years. Could that be? The Internet didn't exist, not even computers. No beltways, no high-speed trains, no laptops, no cable, no Walkmans, not even answering machines, can you imagine? The Baltard Pavilions in Les Halles were still spreading their umbrellas over Paris's stomach, the TV was in black and white, just one channel or maybe two, you can't remember, so long ago, so deeply buried in the night of time . . . Supermarkets were a novelty, the Socialist Party a tiny group, the Communist Party—we used to say, "the Party"—got 20 percent of the vote . . . Judith, did she still have the long hair you loved? Soft fur rolled up on one side of a thin neck, which side? Sliding forward over her breasts. Like a small silky animal perched on her shoulder. A joyful, small, silky animal. Didn't she used to take a lock and put it in her mouth? Now she has short hair, hedgehog style. You were living in the house of an anemic blond guy, or rather his mother's. She sold needles and thread, a notions seller, a trade that's pretty much disappeared. Blondie lived with his mother and you with them; they were friends of The Cause, she made you dinner, later you or Judith did the dishes, well, not always but often, then you unfolded the cot in the "living room," as we said at the time. There must have been a sideboard with some porcelain, a TV on a little table, President Pomp on the screen, dark red-velvet double curtains, floral carpets, a silk doily on the table, you get the picture, it was before Habitat-Ikea. Boy, you must have pissed those people off . . . Being a friend of The Cause was no picnic. It must be said that being

2

part of The Cause wasn't that easy either. A water pipe ran through the cellar: that stream from Ménilmontant most likely, which turns into the sewer through which Jean Valjean fled. Judith's now selling apartments. She used to dream of being Rosa Luxemburg or Tamara Bunke, known as Tania, that young woman killed in Bolivia alongside Che, or even Tina Modotti, photographer, secret agent, lover — that beauty that a taxi carried off dead into the night of Mexico City. In short, she used to dream of an adventurous life. LA GRANDE PORTE red CARREFOUR blue 700 METERS to NATIONAL 34 PORTE DE VINCENNES PORTE DORÉE DÉCATHLON blue ÉTAP'HOTEL green 245 FRANCS LA NUIT HOTEL FORMULE I STATION SERVICE 700 METERS. Shit! All of a sudden, a big truck swerves without warning, your heart in your mouth, you jerk the car to the left; luckily the breaks aren't locked, just slipping a bit. Asshole! Thirteen's daughter didn't blink, she's got nerve. From her father. And you still got your reflexes. Reflexes, they come from the time you were driving on icy roads in a stolen Mercedes, with a small sheet-metal rectangle cut out behind the rear armrest so you could talk to the prisoner in the trunk, a politician who had been a collaborator, what was his name, that bastard? You think it was a cardinal's name. You had ripped off the car at the Vesoul station; it was the only time you went to Vesoul, except in the Jacques Brel song. The water was frozen in the Vesoul gutters. The departmental roads were like ice rinks, to plan the job you had one car connected to the other by makeshift radios. You wore vests and incredible velvet hats to look like notaries or country doctors, at least you thought you looked like that. Twenty-year-old notaries! You could probably get away with that now, only the desire's gone. That's it, "now": gray hair, a middle-class look, and the desire no longer there? But then, all around you, snowy expanses, ruffled by the wind, clumps of black woods, with buzzards perched on the boundary markers; they took off painfully when we passed. The freezing cows seemed to really take you for notaries; they looked at you with no emotion. Old-fashioned cows, the kind they had thirty years ago, you tell Thirteen's daughter. They were dinner a long time ago. Never heard about mad cow disease. That's all people care about today: you've noticed that? Safe eating. Precaution Principle. Death prowls at the edge of the plate. Assholes. Do you think that's what the "present" means: the fear of dying from eating? This ambience of the "Splendid Spud," which is what the draftees used to call the Haute-Saône, reminded you of a bizarre Western, *The Great Silence*: Trintignant, the good guy, the upholder of the law, silent because bad guys cut his throat when he was a kid, gets himself shot to pieces at the end, in the snow. A little like Brando at the end of *Viva Zapata!*. The Revolution always gets killed at the end. Rosa Luxemburg gunned down in the snow, on the edge of the canal where they threw her body. Che executed at la Higuera, laid out naked, hairy, glassy eyed, like he was being readied for dissection, his hands cut off, the death mask that tears the skin from his face. Tamara-Tania, riddled with bullets at the Vado del Yeso ford, her body drifting in the Rio Grande. Your head was stuffed with these tragic images. Making the Revolution was not so much preparing to take power as learning to die. It seems worth it when you're very young. At the time you were no longer going to the movies; the Revolution couldn't waste its time with those tricks and jokes, but you were living like you were in a film, a low-budget cops-and-robbers. You would have liked to see Trintignant in the role of you playing your role. In the end, you never did manage to holler anything through the prompter's hole at that collaborator-pol with the bishop's name, because that gallows bird had disappeared by the time you were ready to nab him; it often happened like that.

VINCENNES DORÉE SERVICE STATION JOHNNY WALKER KEEP WALKING BELTWAY CLEAR bridges yellow lights Paris on the right under a somber lilac sky emerald signs in front METZ NANCY PORTE DE BERCY DISNEYLAND 32 KM the tires tear up the night's silky golden black dress A4-A86 CLEAR, A4-A104 CLEAR. Everything is clear, even you, red MR BRICOLAGE. Two in the morning. BERCY 2 green CARREFOUR blue BERCY EXPO red. On the right the great phosphorescent rod that is the

4

Ministry of Finances 300 METERS to NATIONAL 19 the sky lightens as we near the Seine. The rivers spread this sort of phosphorescence in the darkness of the sky. When you had gone to My Tho you had made out the Mekong from this glow in the clouds. You didn't go down there, to the Cochin-China Delta, for Marguerite Duras, not for a moment; you wanted to see the place from where the lieutenant left one morning, the year after your birth, to get killed in an inlet, what the Viets call a "*rach*," of the Mekong. The lieutenant was your father. You see Marie, you say to Thirteen's daughter as you pass by the Gare de Lyon's shiny iron beams, the orange and blue-gray train cars soaked with dew, you see, I don't know any more about my father than you do about yours. If I went there, it was because only these distant places could tell me something, maybe—not teach me anything, no, it wasn't that; it was to talk to me, the way rivers and woods, intense heat, the lazy flights of butterflies, cockroaches and the damn snakes, the dog days at noon, speak, those unchanging witnesses. All the other voices had been silenced: dead. That's often the way: you really only want to hear about stuff when the voices that could tell you something are stilled. For example, in this decrepit photo there's a woman's face, next to your father on the edge of a river; you can't tell whether the river is from around here or over there. Nobody can tell you anymore, and this face, even if it's nothing special, will have the dignity of the forever silent. Me, I'm still alive, so you're lucky, you tell Thirteen's daughter. So use it. In the south suburb of Saigon that's now called Ho Chi Minh City, you had gotten on a sampan that went up and down the delta. The boat's deck was cluttered with bikes and big wicker baskets; the passengers in the steerage were peasants returning from selling their vegetables in the markets at Ben Thanh and Cho Lon, they looked at you with frank curiosity and without much sympathy. In a birdcage was a monkey that the hicks were having fun annoying. The wind was making the tarps sheltering the deck snap, the sky foamed in gray and white above a narrow strip of land gnawed by the water. At a turn in the river, beyond the mangroves, beyond the roofs of sheet metal or palm, you had glimpsed the buildings of Ho Chi Minh City topped with red flags and advertisements for Jap, Korean, and American brands, DAEWOO HONDA HITACHI SUZUKI CANON IBM HEWLETT-PACKARD TOSHIBA, the same as here along the beltway, or anywhere else in the world. Ho Chi Minh City, of all the cities you had seen, was perhaps the one where the obsession with money was most nakedly apparent. Later, you passed through the plain of Joncs: aquatic villages, looking like baskets of bamboo, thatch, reed, teeming with life, geese, ducks, and black pigs splashing about under the pilings, green fluorescent rice fields, green like beetle wings, or a peacock's tail, in the middle of which there would sometimes be a white tomb. Iron bridges guarded by blockhouses dating from the Americans, or even from the Phap, the French. Swarming along the waterways were potbellied sampans whose prows sported an appeasing eye, whose sides were riddled with portholes sprouting toothless, louse-ridden heads, slow barges whose name you don't know, propeller shafts fiddling with the water, barges groaning under piles of plants whose damn name you, pathetic intellectual, didn't know, and then some sort of gondolas loaded with the same plants, radiant green and mauve in the descending night, and on the poop deck, the jerky motion of women in Tokinese hats glided the boats smoothly along, thrusting forward, in a movement rather like a lunging fencer, pushing forth the oar, then hauling it back to the point where it floats in the wake, their arms bending in rhythm with it, then starting again (the eternal story of Asia! What a stereotype!), and so on.

300 METERS CRÉTEIL MARNE-LA-VALLÉE METZ NANCY QUAI D'IVRY PORTE D'IVRY we should have got off here, but you missed the exit, already too carried away by the inertia of the story, should we continue? you asked Thirteen's daughter. Unless you're in a rush to get home? No. Me, I'm fine. A little drunk, but not much. So we continue. We are going to turn this story over and over, like a stone in a slingshot so that it would travel far. On the right, the spangled plains of light from

the Bibliothèque Nationale de France look like launching pads. To the left, the great incinerator's chimneys spit out exhaust from the space shuttle. Feel like a little orbital tour? OK? No sooner said than done. Five, four, three, two, one, blast off! Zoooom! A Molotov cocktail. You step on it, you're flying above the tracks of the Gare d'Austerlitz, the turbine pumps purr like cats, ignition of the second stage; you let loose the booster rockets, fantastic crackle, normal trajectory, beltway clear; you climb into the black velvet sky, you overcome the attraction from the big globe on the right: below the world of sleepyheads. Now you're an angel, an old angel at the commands of the vessel, Remember, you have things to do, Thirteen's daughter and you, experiments on memory in a state of weightlessness. The earth spreads out below and behind you NANTES BORDEAUX ORLY RUNGIS ÉVRY LYON CASINO red CASTORAMA blue HARDWARE DECORATION VOLVO blue JACK DANIELS (Hi there, Jack!) PORTE DE GENTILLY HOTEL IBIS ÉTAP'HOTEL NOVOTEL blue, we deploy the solar panels, golden petals in the night, already the Porte d'Orléans is coming into view, and the Montrouge bell tower planted in the rind of the red sky. You remember a scene that took you a long time to laugh about. Years in fact.

Here's the story: you're seated in the entrance of an apartment a friend loaned you in one of those cheapo brick buildings at the Porte d'Orléans . . . maybe 1967? You're seated at a table writing a tract. It may well become the longest tract in the history of agitprop because: to your left the door leading to the bedroom is open. What time can it be? One, two in the morning? Back then, night didn't exist; the night for sleeping was a bourgeois invention (you still think that). Night was for meetings (the day too: incredible how much time you spent in discussions. You had to "dissect the sparrows," according to the expression of the Great Helmsman — an elegant way of saying "fuck yourself with your own folderol"). Morning would find you dozing on crummy mats, foam mattresses, in sleeping bags, surrounded by coffee cups crammed with cigarette butts. Old, cold Nescafé and cigarette juice — one of the most disgusting memories of that era. No doubt there was a "meet" that night at the Porte d'Orléans; anyway, there you are, writing a tract. A tract, Internet users ("a tract," you explain to Thirteen's daughter), here's how it was done: somebody types on a sort of onion skin called a stencil. If you use the machine without a ribbon, it makes holes in the stencil, OK? Then you put it on the ink cylinder of a Roneo (*tech.*: a copying instrument, first half of the twentieth century), and turn the handle—on some luxury models, you just pushed the switch; the tracts would glide along and pile up, sticky with ink, black with vitriolic words, ready for the "distrib" at that awful moment when workers slouch off to work under a dawning sky. A tract can't be more than double sided, and even a single side is much too long because at that lousy hour when workers slouch off to work in the windy early morning, eyes still black with sleep, nauseous, acid stomach, the hour for a black coffee at the bar, a stinking little coffee with some bubbles on top that you could easily mistake for detergent, as dead leaves swirl around in the street (even in the spring leaves are dead when you head off to work), the hour when the street lamps, as well as the illuminated ads on buildings flicker; at that particular moment, my friend, nobody reads. You blink again, the lighting is crummy, you turn off the lights, no desire to rouse yourself, maybe just lights out once and for all, a wretched coffee chased with a shot of calvados in those tiny trumpet-shaped glasses at dawn. "Protecting the mercenaries of American imperialism," you wrote, "the fascist cops raised a big stone, only to let it fall on their feet." Although, all in all, you are partisan of a purely national style, a Chinese expression, here and there, can do the trick. Pick up a big stone to let it fall on your feet; it's a good joke from the Great Helmsman. In the "propaganda organs" of The Cause, there are admirers of the vulgar "Père Duchesne" style, but you're not crazy about this supposedly common-man language. Of course, you could write "son-of-a-bitch cops, we'll hang you by your balls." That might please the powers that be, but, no, that gets on your nerves. You prefer a certain decorum. You are a sort of Malherbe of revolutionary

8

poetry, a potential social traitor, so to speak. You are not against the heavy irony of Marx the pamphleteer. Even the bourgeois can read that, especially the bourgeois, the university types; in a word, it makes a serious impression, reassuring. Aragon the patriot, *French Diana* and all that, now there's somebody who, according to you, creates popular literature. "I will never forget the lilacs and the roses," "Death does not dazzle the eyes of the partisans": Wow! That makes you cry, flatters your pathetic side . . . a real sentimental fool . . . While "son-of-a-bitch cops," . . . no, forget it. "Our task," stated the resolution (adopted unanimously!) at the last conference of the Vietnam Committee, "is to speak of the Vietnam people's just struggle in the language of the broad French masses." Fine, but what language do they speak, these "broad masses?" And why does one say "broad"? First of all, it's an adjective that the masses, as for them, use to qualify highways and pant legs. Troubling questions, subject to various opinions. "While protecting the so-called embassy of the South Vietnamese puppets, the coppers . . ." Stop, nobody says "coppers" anymore. "Flat-foot," then? No, too slangy, almost friendly. Pimp's parlance. The "fuzz." Nope. Maybe in a Bourvil film. The real French comic. (Why not "the law," while you're at it?). "The cops?" Boring, but good enough. The cops. "The cops have clearly demonstrated they're merely an auxiliary militia . . ." "Clearly," there's an adverb you like. Everything has to be clear. All the time. Otherwise, how can you avoid dying from stress? Gideon is the master of clarity; he gets his clarifying power from the Great Helmsman. Who's Gideon, Thirteen's daughter wants to know. Wait a minute, I'm getting there. Our Great Leader. "The cops have clearly demonstrated they are merely an auxiliary militia of the American B-52s." Or even U.S. Maybe "Amerikkkans?" No. They won't get the reference. The B-52, you bring to Thirteen's daughter's attention, is one of the rare things that has not changed, not much anyway. It comes right from the era I've been telling you about today. The B-52 and Johnny Hallyday, so to speak. Impressively long-lasting, from the Golf Drouot theater, where Johnny started out, to his triumphs at the Zenith and the Stade de France, from *Doctor Strangelove* to Desert Storm. They've both been done over, been tightened up a bit, but all in all they're the same, rustproof: the same rock star, the same planes carpeting the Vietnamese jungles with their bombs and layering the greenery with their defoliants. The right stuff. The stencils, the Roneos, the broad masses, the Red East, the Great Helmsman—all gone, the world turns and everything disappears: not the B-52, you tell Thirteen's daughter. "The cops have clearly demonstrated that they are merely the auxiliary militia of the American B-52s. But they are only paper tigers, and the partisans will give back as good as they get." No, cross that out. "Will give back as good as they get" sounds farcical. "Will pay them back a hundred times over the interest from their exactions." Nope. "Exactions," too complicated. Intellectual petit-bourgeois language. And then, "interest," not a great image. "The partisans . . ." well . . . While you're writing that . . . it's already tough . . . while you're trying to write that, you get distracted, really terribly distracted, by what you see on the left, in the bedroom doorframe.

FLAT TV PHILIPS ROUEN PORTE DE CHATILLON PORTE DE MONTROUGE ITINERIS 2 A.M., TEMPERATURE 12, all's well on board, the instruments glow softly, the earth slides by, from one moment to another, you are waiting to see sidereal dawn's electric arc burst forth from behind the mighty sphere in the night. Quietly, on the radio, lalala lalala lalala la . . . do-mi-la do-la-sol si-sol-la mi . . . : *The Appassionata*. At the time, music was also counterrevolutionary. Several years after the notions saleslady and her son's apartment, you rented—naturally under an assumed name—a little dump near the Buttes-Chaumont. There was a sort of cot that folded up against the wall, and a sideboard with, incredibly enough, what we used to call a "record player" on it. Judith had gotten from her father, a Russian Jew whom the ups and downs of the century had turned into an import-exporter in France, two or three records, including that sonata played by Richter. What a wonderful moment! When you would be listening to it, in the evening, after a day of tough, subversive work, you felt like you were yielding to a guilty pleasure. If the Great Leader had only gotten wind of that! He would not have liked it, for sure. Do-mi-la do-la-sol si-sol-la mi . . . Lalala lalala lalala la. HOTEL MERCURE FORD ARISTON ÉLECTROMÉNAGER PARIS EXPO BIOMER THÉRAPIE SOFITEL SHARP PORTE DE SÈVRES SECURITAS the black star on your right streaked with lightning bolts of neon, with bursts of red, green, white, sometimes a lighted window watches over the night. This enormous swirling darkness consists of piles of History, History that collapses under its own weight, you tell Thirteen's daughter; the city is a ball of string that knots and tightens the threads that are lives past and present, lived and dreamed; somewhere in this inescapable muck is my story, as well as Thirteen's, and all the others whose lives were entangled with ours: Gideon, Judith, Chloé, Angelo, Fichaoui-called-Julot, Jean d'Audincourt, I sense them deep in the darkness, Juju, Amédée, Roger the Belgian, Momo whom we called the Lock-Eater, Hairy Reureu, a guy known as The Shits, another called Pompabière, Klammer, the saints and the stool pigeons, the brawlers and the gutless. Also greater, more tragic stories we were part of in our dreams, Saint-Just at the guillotine, the wall of the Communards in Père Lachaise, the February barricades and the June ones, Colonel Fabien shooting the German officer in the Barbès subway stop, Aragon's *Affiche rouge*, all these stories jumbled together in a gigantic tangled line, some glorious and rough, others fragile, but the weaker ones drawing from the former a naive strength. All this muddled, mixed-up past, piled up in the shape of a city; you just have to take the right string and pull it gently to unwind the past, that's what you say while signs flow by in this garrulous night AQUABOULEVARD NANTES BORDEAUX BELTWAY CLEAR BELTWAY CLEAR QUAI D'ISSY PONT DU GARIGILANO 200 METERS, the Garigliano Bridge, who remembers what Garigliano refers to? The lieutenant was in that bloody Italian stream in 1944. A young man driven by a nameless, wordless revolt to run away from his middle-class, provincial family to equatorial Africa, it was called the "colonies" then. Listen, you new generation of the self-righteous, you maniacs of "repentance"—eunuchs who dropped God but stayed drunk on the worst in Christianity, the genuflecting, the mortifications—you grumble as you fly over the river for the second time—listen, down there was more than sadistic noncoms and blood-sucking planters. There were hotheads, apostles, scientists, utopians, sad sacks. Rimbaud, he dealt in rifles in the Horn of Africa, didn't he? That pisses you off, right? You would have preferred that he remain a "poetaster," that he had his little Tuesday gatherings where he would give readings with his elbow on the fireplace, right? And that he signed petitions? And Conrad, you would have doubtless liked him to be anticolonialist. Well, sorry, he wasn't. Not for a minute. And another revolt, the same one in truth, against the cowardice of the bourgeoisie, had pushed the lieutenant, in the autumn of 1940 to join the Free French: a great name that has almost become an oxymoron. He was also at Bir-Hakeim, the other bridge you can make out over there on the right, across the shiny water, that misty, iron form. You, for whom Nazism is truly a filthy beast, you try in vain to think the way you're supposed to, the way you're encouraged to, but you stay convinced the fighting Resistance was more honorable and useful than Sartre's or Breton's, or Aragon's (etc.). It always struck you as strange that it appeared strange to think like that. It's this amazement, among others, that made you back then join The Cause: what pushed you was not so much the love of the proletariat as disgust with the bourgeoisie, and the distrust of those slicker sorts of bourgeois, phonier than the others, that intellectuals often are. It seemed to me, to us, me and Thirteen, you tell his daughter, that the poor were less false. We wanted to think so, in any case. One night at the Bir-Hakeim metro station, you had stolen several thousand tickets to protest the rate hikes in public trans-portation. At the time, they were sold in little sewn booklets. This was the era of Gainsbourg's hit "The Ticket Puncher of Lilas." A hundred booklets, a thousand tickets, made a compact little stash, not bulky at all. Thirteen was in on it, of course. For a lookout, while you were playing around with the jimmy in the station, you had positioned a comrade fellow-student at the Polytechnic School—you forgot his name—under the windows where *Last Tango in Paris* was set; the guy was in full uniform, cocked hat and all that, with a striking, big-busted brunette. They were supposed to be kissing passionately, a sort of return from the debutantes' ball, all the while checking out the surroundings. You figured if the cops passed by, they would be favorably impressed by the couple, maybe even salute. The next problem was to give them away, the thousands of tickets I mean, in the train stations or in front of the factories. The tracts, people were used to them then; they grabbed them automatically, crammed them in their pockets. But tickets . . . second-class tickets, well alright . . . (second-class ones were pale yellow, you explain to Thirteen's daughter, the color of . . . well exactly the color of Greek books in the *Belles Lettres* collection, the color of Plato or Aeschylus, you see?). But the first-class tickets?, reseda green . . . They were afraid of a trick.

EDF GDF FRANCE TELEVISION TFI, buildings all in glass port and starboard, SABLIÈRES MORILLON-CORVOL hoppers, trains of barges loaded with night, ROUEN PORTE DE SAINT-CLOUD NATIONAL 10 BOULOGNE 100 METERS. The cheapo housing in brick on the quay called Point du Jour, the Daybreak quay. You had a servant's room there. You were active in a Vietnam committee named after the neighborhood, Point du Jour, and you would never exchange that name for another; the word transported you toward the place of all birth and rebirth, the Red East where the revolutionary sun would rise to dissipate the shadows, once and for all. You used to try and interest the locals in the success of the "people's war." You'd stick handwritten posters on the walls, writing them out in longhand at night with the help of multicolored felt pens didn't bother you, all the while drinking beer, the smell made you slightly high; but what you really liked was grinding razor blades into the glue you smeared on the posters, for the imperialist lackeys who never failed to try and tear them down: young little fascists, from the Occident Movement, old shits from Action Française, who tried to hawk their rag at the market where you were selling, printed in black and red on lovely airmail paper, *Le Courrier du Vietnam*. Once you chased one of these crummy royalists inside the church at the Porte de Saint Cloud, knocking over chairs and prayer stools in the process. There's another thing your life will have shelved, or so you think: razor blades. Like the old-fashioned locomotives straining under the glasswork at the Montparnasse station, their long black steam generators mounted on the sun-red wheels, they towed the trains as far as the Emerald Coast, like the stencils and Roneos, the typewriters, the pen holders, the big, shiny nails of the street crossings people still call "studded crossings" (Or maybe it's just me? you asked Thirteen's daughter; now they say "pedestrian crossing," she replies. Fine, sure, of course): all that stuff hadn't lasted as long as the B-52. Those razors, little cobalt-blue serrated steel leaves, weirdly crammed into containers with Mr. Gillette's head on them: a quite irritating mug of a New England gentleman, or so it seems now (but you could not swear to it), arched eyebrows, a thin moustache, and of course a perfectly shaven chin, rising above a wing collar. Sort of a Boston version of Faulkner, if you remember correctly (but that's not sure). The nightly poster outings, club under the car seats, brass knuckles in the glove compartment; those forays also had their own charm. You felt like you were on patrol in 1917 Petrograd, like something out of Alexander Blok's "The Twelve"—which you hadn't read. Odd as it may seem, quite often housewives came to our public meetings in a room above a café in the Avenue de Versailles; before their puzzled glances, you used to spread out maps where lines and arrows represented fronts and offensives; you had made symbols for rivers, roads, and hills with exotic names, Khe Sanh, Tây Ninh, Dông Khê . . . These jungles seemed close to you, or rather you were convinced that the world's axis passed by there, and that the places where you were, Europe, France, Paris, the Porte de Saint Cloud, were merely the distant outskirts of this center. You thought the history of the world had been written there before you were born, and it continued to be written far from where you were. You hadn't the slightest idea of what you could be, except for shadows of the past, shades of somewhere else. You were living as if deprived of what you could be, in a place that had ceased to exist, you tell Thirteen's daughter (you try to make her understand). But why were you like that? she wants to know. Didn't you love life? Of course we loved it. Allow me this too-well-known phrase, but we used to think that true life was somewhere else, an elsewhere that in Maoist gibberish was called the "tempest zone," the Third World surrounding the imperialist strongholds. And we were too intransigent to be satisfied with a phony life. There are generations born in the midst of History, right in the bull's eye. And others who are off to the side. That's where we thought we were. We had missed the great moments. Such a pretentious thought! The housewives, what were they after on the first floor of the café? Big, strange terms like "the dry season," "the national liberation," "the rainy season," "a carpet of bombs," "the Red River's dikes," maybe these words made them dream, just as they thrilled you. Maybe too they came to your strategy lessons because they were abandoned, alone, dissatisfied. How many Madame Bovarys among them? At the time you would not have dared to ask yourself this question, or rather asking it to yourself, you would not have dared to ask them if they were sad. Simple things seemed so much more complicated to you than a battle on the other side of the world. You suddenly remember, as the Porte Saint Cloud tunnel swallows you up, that the specialist in composing and discussing these didactic cue cards with the housewives of Point du Jour, with the passion of Proust's Saint-Loup at Doncières, was a philosophy student whose red face and pointy head made him look like an alcoholic mosquito magnified a thousand times. Strikingly thin, puny in fact, he did not enjoy the street fights the way you, Thirteen, and the others did. His intensity, which was no less than your own, went into the making of those maps, and what he said about them. But the cause of his passion was no different: boning up with the crude brochures in foreign languages published by the Hanoi Press, as if they were by Thucydides or Clausewitz; he got high going in the opposite direction his training had destined him for—the way you did in learning to be tough guys. Later, pressured by The Cause to work in a factory despite his puniness, he chose a light-bulb manufacturer, Claude's Light Bulbs: so that, he said with a grin, he would only have to carry the vacuum inside the bulb. Later he would write a book; it seems to you it was on the pre-Socratics.

PORTE MOLITOR PORTE D'AUTEUIL A3 — A12 CLEAR A13 — A14 CLEAR everything's going smoothly: the vast spiral galaxy of the Parc-des-Princes versAILLES SAINT-QUENTIN-EN-YVELINES ROUEN, over there on the left is the Rhine and Danube roundabout and farther along the bridge and highway now called A-13, perhaps in honor of Thirteen, you say to his daughter. Back then, it was the highway to the west. I don't know if I'll manage to talk to you about your father who was and remains my friend (since real friendship can only be eternal), but at least I want you to understand that we were perhaps the last—that's right, us, as ridiculous as we were, half Don Quixote, half Sancho—to be interested in eternity. Yes, that's it, you assure yourself after a moment of reflection (because all the same such a claim is pretty strong): more than anything else, we believed in eternity. Thirteen and you had planned to ambush the security police, called the CRS on the highway to the west. Those were the dark days of June '68. The reactionaries were winning, the red flags were continuously disappearing from the roofs. The factories, one after the other, were opening up again. You were at an age where you had too much imagination, and certainly not enough background to give it a coherent form; you readily saw yourselves as resistance fighters, or even as "Marie-Louises," those young draftees in 1814 who doubtless thought they were defending the remnants of the Revolution against the dismal army of the kings. You had fought with the police near the Renault factory at Flins. The countryside, the sun glittering off the enemies' helmets, in the middle of fields where clouds were casting blue shadows, the wreaths of smoke that the wind tore apart in the branches of the trees—the contrast between the explosions, the droning of the choppers in the sky, and the slow crawling of an emerald-winged insect along a shaggy stalk of rye—all this gave these skirmishes the appearance of a real war (what thrilled you as well, you realize now, was the unacknowledged certainty you were fighting for a lost cause). On the surrounding hills, some of the farms could have been the Haie-Sainte or the Mont Saint Jean at Waterloo. We could see in the fields the poppies' blood-red crests, just like in a Monet painting or a song by Mouloudji. A young student was killed that day; you had spent the night before his death with him and some others from the elite college at Saint Cloud, sitting around the bivouac fire. The whole thing was perhaps a bit like the Boy Scouts, one could say that, but you were convinced you could see the great curtains of History moving in the darkness. You were expecting to see the bullies from SAC show up, the auxiliary militia of the party in power: bouncers, Corsican pimps, noncoms. Those bastards had the wind in their sails; at the time they were "cleaning up" what remained from the terrifying month of May. Because you know, Marie, you say to Thirteen's daughter, these days the well-off claim to find this incident funny, a real farce, a student happening in the streets, slapstick, not even five killed, think about it, not even a single real shootout, what a joke! They would like to be compensated for their fear: because at the time, I can tell you, they were really scared. Those who were hoping for glory, for power, for money—and who have them now—they were as scared as those who had those things then. Part of their current hate comes from that time: to be so frightened despite so few deaths! Rigged out, helmeted, leaning on your ax handles amid the darkness of the trees that flickered in the campfires, you imagined yourselves doing guard duty in the trenches of the university campus at Madrid in 1938. That's how it was: it was as if the world out there, where you lived, became more profound, transfigured by a power that linked each event, each individual to an age-old chain of greater, more tragic events and individuals. Sure, this can seem silly; all the same, it was a kind of poetry. Today it seems there's only the present, just the instant; the present has become a colossal hustle and bustle, one big stimulus, a permanent big bang, but back then, the present was more modest, modesty itself in fact. The past had a powerful presence, the future as well. The past, History, was the great projector of images of the future. The young student, Gilles, had been killed; actually he drowned in the Seine trying to escape the police, the first man you ever saw cut down like that, the sound of his voice still in your ears, all his familiar and even childlike gestures dancing around him: it was the first time you would die. You had run, you and Thirteen, to the elite school in the rue d'Ulm, which was like the Great Leader's stronghold. A closed but unguarded footbridge spanned the highway of the west, which was used by the CRS relief troops. An all too easy assonance made for a nice insult: CRS = SS. We thought that after dark it would not have been too complicated, equipped with bolt cutters and a crate load of Molotov cocktails to clip the padlocks on the entrance gate and attack the convoy from above, then quickly disappear. While you were laying out the revenge plan you and Thirteen had concocted, the Great Leader, stroking his goatee, was listening to you without the slightest hint of approval or disapproval, but we suspected, both of us suspected, you yourself suspected, that the inalterable condemnation was forming in his head, was cogitating along like gears in a machine.

Tunnels, rows of pale neon lights, black trees on the left, the Bois de Boulogne at seven hundred meters straight ahead, the Porte Molitor, then the Porte d'Auteuil where you got into a tight spot once, in a light van loaded with all sorts of arms, smack in the middle of high school kids demonstrating. All that paraphernalia, the obviously stolen Fiat van (some said it was a Renault Estafette), and the popguns were supposed to help "arrest" (the word you used at the time!) the retired general Chalais, the CEO of the company that had laid off the strikers. That morning you were all set, ready to go, equipped, disguised for the occasion, but the guy didn't show. Must have been on a business trip. You had waited over an hour in front of his door; by now the tension started to increase, inexorably, then Thirteen had to piss. It was sort of funny . . . And you started laughing out loud; the guy at the wheel, disguised as a delivery man, could barely contain himself, you were going to wind up calling attention to yourselves. And the more you tried to get a hold of yourselves, crouched up in the back, invisible, armed, all flushed, the more Thirteen had to piss. The counterrevolutionary laughter increased until finally it was unbearable; you had to raise the siege. The guy who was driving was Fichaoui-called-Julot, a little Tunisian Jew with nerve enough for anything, funny too. Now he runs a hardware store near Mutualité. Following the established escape route, he suddenly found himself surrounded and blocked by a crowd of high school kids pouring out of Jean-Baptiste-Say to protest I don't know which of the educational reforms that were starting to get trendy at the time. Unless it was against police violence; that was trendy as well. Naturally you agreed with them in principle; surely in this howling crowd were some members of The Cause, nonetheless, the situation was getting sticky: there you were, cut off, with your false moustaches, wigs, and muskets, in the middle of a bunch of riled-up kids; the cops, as you knew from experience, wouldn't be slow to reach for their clubs. Once again, Fichaoui-called-Julot was great, you tell Thirteen's daughter, just as, smack in front of the vessel Remember, appears a kind of gigantic, Queen of England–style hat, mauve, shaped like a trapezoid, sparkling with golden flecks, swept with wavy spotlights, wow! The Palais de Congrès, the new bleached look, old lady lovely. Fichaoui-called-Julot emphasized to the high school comrades that he was a comrade worker, and that his boss would fire him if he did not make his rounds on time. In the back of the van, you held your breath. The matter was settled amid enthusiastic fraternization, and the protesters, juvenile fists in the air, opened a passage in front of us just before the appearance of the first helmets of the riot police.

FRANCE TELECOM PORTE DE CHAMPERRET right ahead the comet HITACHI glowing in the fog LECLERC blue D911 600 METERS PORTE DE CLICHY PEUGEOT white CASINO red; you lower the window for a little fresh air, a little excursion in space would do you good, the stale tobacco is starting to stink in Remember, the first space shuttle without a "no smoking" section, CONFORT INN yellow PORTE DE CLICHY PANASONIC white PENTAX red SUZUKI, HERTZ yellow LOCATION DE MATERIEL, PAPERMATE blue-red, Remember is racing into a hurricane of color, an aurora borealis, a magnetic storm. How long has your father been dead? you ask Thirteen's daughter. I've already told you: it was twenty years ago, I was four, she replies looking at you from the corner of her eye. Of course, if you say so; you know I'm not good with dates. In my mind the text of the past is completely deformed, crumpled up. And what was behind the portal, at the Porte d'Orléans? she asks. What, what was behind the Porte d'Orléans? Uh, Montrouge, or Malakoff, I don't know anymore. As usual. That's not what I'm asking, she replies, don't be stupid, you were telling me that you were writing a tract, and that something behind the door . . . anyway you always stop in the middle of your stories. It's the effect of weightlessness on words, you say. Then you add, a little alcohol too. Not much. I'm almost sober now.

"The partisans warn." No, cut that. Bombastic. "We inform the henchmen of the imperialists that their skullduggery will not go unpunished." Yeaah . . . "skullduggery." Obviously that's not used much anymore, but it's one of those old words that contains some anger, some defiance: maybe worth resurrecting? You are, you always have been in favor of uniting the old and the new; you don't see much difference between Joan of Arc and Louise Michel. That makes you suspect, could cause you trouble, but what can you do? Anyway, at that time, in the friend's borrowed apartment, Porte d'Orléans or around there, you were far removed from worrying about the eventual trouble your ideological fantasies could cause. You were struck—struck, no, fascinated, yeah, obsessed rather, by what you saw, all the while pretending not to look. On the left, just after the bookshelves piled with a collection of books on the Spanish Civil War, the Resistance, Cuba, the October Revolution, the Black Sea Mutiny, the Algerian War, China, Vietnam, anarchist-unionism and other edifying subjects (not Venice, for sure!)—after this quite typical preamble, or vestibule, well (Do you know, you ask Thirteen's daughter, Queneau's song about the guy who swallowed a clock? No. And the clock ended up in the vestibule of his cock. What I would like, she insists, is the rest of the story. ok), after the vestibule is an open door through which you can see in diagonal half a bed on which are Chloe's naked legs, not the rest of her body. The legs are moving. That's the half of it; the legs twist around each other, untwist, slide, rub up against one another. Stupid as you are, even you know the legs are speaking, talking to you, quite frankly. You're at once fascinated and terrified by what they're saying. They're not speaking the stuffy language of the "meets," nor the one you use in your tract. Those legs got balls. You don't imagine those legs have to bother with politics. Of course, that's not what you really think: in the heart of your pounding, truthful heart, you believe that bodies, particularly the ones you want, and most particularly the parts of them that are signs of their strangeness, are pure masses of terror. And it frightens you to realize, well, to guess, that if you disguise or deny that thing that stammers inside you, claiming "the priority of politics," if you use for instance this tract you are writing, or claim to be writing, seemingly forever, to hide your fear, then more and more all the rhetoric that encompasses your life, all the elements tied together like the threads of an espalier, would be nothing other than a gigantic fraud. You think you understand that what's most important to you, most frightening to you, is exactly this: the place around which Chloe's legs are moving, what those legs are pointing to, and what the wall prevents your seeing. You're not afraid of getting beat up or going to jail, but you're scared of Chloe's sex: that's the truth. And just suspecting that is terrifying. All the jungles of the "tempest zones," the whole Red East, you would find them there, in the V made flesh, V like Vietnam (and which you now imagine resembles the curving folds of a book's pages). The Plain of Joncs, the Mekong Delta, the Ho Chi Minh Trail, the Tsingkang

Mountains, could they be anything else for you? Your so-called courage, might it be nothing other than a front for this enormous, ridiculous trembling? You dive back into writing your tract. "For an eye, both eyes, for a tooth, the whole puss": a bit vulgar as expressions go, but effective, historical. One that worked in the past. Get back to it. You would like to pass the whole night with it, with the tract.

BELTWAY CLEAR PORTE DE SAINT-OUEN GSM NETTOYAGE INDUS-TRIEL BOUYGUES TELECOM SON DIGITAL CASIO SONY CITROEN. Claudia Schiffer in the snow LA NOUVELLE XSARA red blue green red blue blue, tunnel, that night from the past, it was . . . it was more than thirty years ago. The night of time. The snows of yesteryears. Thirteen's daughter wasn't even born. Fewer years separate that era from the end of the war than today from then. You had to get old to begin to realize that your youth, your generation's youth, had been completely thrown off course by the proximity of the mass of death, the world war, the defeat, the collaboration. That recently struck you, merely by driving a little way on route 175, which goes to the sea, toward Mont Saint Michel looming above the fields where sheep graze: toward the pink kilometer markers punctuating the "Route of the Liberation," markers that evoked for you as a child strawberry ice cream; you recognized what used to be the "summer vacation" road that led to the distant Emerald Coast, passing through what seemed to be immense numbers of hills, woods, small sleepy towns. A world still under the sway of nature, deliberate. A world of scents and silences, murmurs, a France forgotten, limited (yet believing itself a continent), a world of hunters, horse traders, café owners, teachers, and priests, where figures from the Middle Ages, figures from the church of Saint André des Champs would meet on every street corner. Percheron horses pulling carts. Suddenly you were overwhelmed by the self-evident: when your uncle used to drive you along this road, with your mother and brother, in his Frégate Renault (the road only paved in places, you could still see gas bubbling in the cylinders of the Avia or Caltex pumps), those markers were new, the destruction from the fighting they commemorated must have still littered the countryside. It's from there you come, my friend, from this enormous disaster, without having been part of it. Your generation is born of an event it never knew. SAGEM LOGICIELS DE GESTION PORTE DE SAINT-OUEN JVC SIEMENS ELECTROMÉNAGER HOLIDAY INN HOTEL FORMULE UN red green white yellow red, at the time I'm telling you about, you say to Thirteen's daughter, whose sullen profile you catch against the flashing lights as you turn slightly toward her, at the time this stuff didn't exist. Of course. The "clear" beltway. The boundary between the city and the suburbs was still the way, so to speak, that Cendrars or Céline had described it, a zone at once decrepit and poetic, a shaggy wreath, a pile of oddly assorted dwellings, bungalows, workers' lodgings, old, broken-down villas, traces of villages, slums too, and then factories, studios, warehouses, and scrap iron, empty lots, even vegetable plots, shacks, all of it sinister, sometimes funny, all of it mangy, disorganized, without rhyme or reason. The smell of fortresses in ruin, the nineteenth century, industry, revolutions. And concerning slums, The Cause had decided to defend—over there, you stick your arm out the open window into the night, beyond that ring of concrete, those orbiting trailer trucks, beyond those blazing neon comets, beyond anything you see from the corner of your eye, and beyond what you can't see, but which must be farther over there, a loop, an iron bridge, then another one, the dog cemetery, the memory of Impressionist regattas—The Cause had decided to protect a very large slum that the mayor wanted to level. And don't kid yourself that the mayor's office was conservative, no, not at all, they were communists, retros, revisionists we used to call them—since then the word has come to mean something else. It was war between them and us. Those guys, they loved the Soviet Union, and we thought we loved China, OK, it was a bit more complicated than that, but I don't want to get into it. In any case, at the time, we were not talking about those decent fellows, a little nuts, who organize fashion shows in the Central Committee's headquarters; if they could have shipped us to Siberia, they would have done so with pleasure. And while wait-ing for just such an occasion, they had no qualms about handing us over to the cops. The slum consisted entirely of Moroccan and Alge-rian proles who busted their butts at Chausson or at Simca-Poissy, great guys, dignified and reserved, serious and generous, nothing like today's lowlife. You notice that Thirteen's daughter gives a start. Right, you had forgotten, it's her age, she's stuffed with the ideology of the trendy middle class, "inner-city youth," put more simply, "youth," they're sacred pure victims, so forget about the knife and the pit bull, the dealer and the racketeer, the rapes, the burning down of synagogues, the threatening of profs and proles; they're the consecrated host, the Agnus Dei of limousine-liberals. In the past, when we were Marxists, not progressives, and not humanitarians for two seconds, you tell Thirteen's daughter, we used to call this crew the lumpenproletariat; that meant more or less the same thing as thugs, henchmen, snitches, SA men, paramilitary, terrorists, dictators' lackeys. We did not feel any obligation, not any at all, to admire the lumpen. But I don't know why I'm talking to you about that. In any case, we'll not understand each other. Ideology is the cult of false witness, a very imperious passion. Let's talk about something else. I was telling you that at the time the beltway didn't exist. And when they started building it, this'll strike you as strange, we were convinced that it wasn't just for cars and trucks, but for other stuff too . . . We were sure it was to seal off Paris, the revolutionary Paris where we still thought we were living, Thirteen, me and the others; they wanted to imprison that Paris, that rebellious, pugnacious Paris in the ellipse of a giant stadium. They wanted to position up there—where we are at this very moment and every-where—assault tanks, cannons, floodlights—all aimed at the city of revolts. They wanted us to experience again the shock of the Brunswick manifesto—a Prussian prince, maybe Austrian, I don't know anymore, an aristo who threatened to destroy Paris at the time of the Revolu-tion—is what you quickly add because your references are not those of Thirteen's daughter. But he missed his chance. The belt, you see, was to prevent Paris from breaking out, from exploding, from becoming Paris-Berlin-Moscow and Shanghai—and all cities. I know that seems crazy, but that's what we suspected. Getting back to the story of that slum, it was . . . I think it was a few months after the first man on the moon. We didn't give a damn. Getting to the moon wouldn't save the imperialists from being paper tigers. In the slum, the people liked us. Not so much because we reassured them, but I think because we took their minds off their boredom, which is the most sordid of misery's mantles. We were interested in them, and that changed them. They had that mixture of sad reserve and almost naive curiosity so typical of exiles. Sunday mornings we used to whip up a crowd in support of them at a big market along the Seine. We would carry red flags along with strong clubs and protective helmets. The mayor's office confronted us with their regulars, guys from the sports clubs and the boxing club. Merovingian melees. Stalls knocked over, skulls cracked. Teeth were flying all over, spread around on the asphalt along with change from cash registers. Once, after a fight, Angelo was getting himself back together in a bistro when he saw coming in a bunch of the boxers, frothing with rage; their throats were parched too. He had just enough time to hide in the shithouse before they could notice him, but then, what to do? From behind the door he could hear the jocks getting fired up just imagining what frightful things they would do to the first leftist they would be lucky enough to catch. Angelo couldn't stay there forever with these guys who, courtesy of the beer, were beginning to shake and pound the door with their fighters' fists. There was a small window, but too small to even hope to squeeze through. Then Angelo pulled something completely crazy that had one chance in a hundred of working; he suddenly threw open the door and came flying out, pale as death (no need to fake that given his own fear), and screaming to the others not to go in for any reason because a snake was in the hole. It was, of course, a Turkish toilet. Stupor. A what? A snake, just like a viper, only bigger. No question about it. Maybe a rattler. What? Where? In the shithole's hole. Frenzy, hypotheses, arguments, all the tough guys immediately in a semicircle around the door of the place, overexcited, but prudent all the same, everyone proposing a strategy: Just gotta get its attention, Wait a minute, I'm tellin' ya, and during this time Angelo was quite calmly slipping away. The show-off even claimed he left a tip.

You explain to Thirteen's daughter that at the time Angelo was taking advanced courses; he was The Cause's head high school student. With his troops he would interrupt the profs with jibes or curses; depending on their mood, they would stroll naked in the corridors, slip stinking animals into the administrative offices, they would answer the comments of the "teachs" with homemade bombs; when the weather was good, they'd organize swimming parties in the main courtyard's fountains, they invited whores to the philosophy courses, created a "people's prison" in the study hall where they claimed to lock up alleged fascists; in a word, they never got bored. They founded an open competition for inventors of new cocktails; Nessim headed the jury. It was what used to be called "the anti-authoritarian revolt." Thirteen's daughter wants to know who are these guys, Angelo and Nessim? You don't know how to tell a story, you mix everything up. Just the opposite, little lady, you respond: confusion is part of the story. Angelo, Nessim, and the others, I'm getting there. Just have to drive a little more. The teachers back then were not used to insults; several had heart attacks. Since then, obviously, they've become more robust. Improvement of the species. Angelo's father, a French Algerian with Spanish roots, had been in the Resistance, a Communist, then a member of the fascist Secret Army Organization; his mother was an Italian whose anarchist convictions never quite replaced her fierce Catholicism, so in his background was a predisposition to disorganized extremism. One year — it could have been 1970 — you had sent him in your name to Peking, to some conference or other where emissaries from Uruguayan, Belgian, even French cells were supposed to represent the peoples of the world's support of the Chinese line against the Russian line. After endless speeches they got all the bit players together on the steps, behind a first row of dignitaries in Mao pajamas, everybody waving the "little red book" (abbreviation: LRB) and sporting the silliest grin, then click! a photo that would appear in *China in Construction* under the rubric of "We Have Friends Everywhere in the World." The leaders of China-red-for-eternity didn't like The Cause (or rather the bureaucrats who dealt with these minor matters from a cubbyhole in the Forbidden City); they were not wrong to see in us a hodgepodge of irresponsible anarchists quite capable of complicating their business with President Pomp's France. Our ambassador Angelo's behavior didn't risk making them change their opinion. They had begun by ordering him to the barber shop; they thought his hair was too long. Angelo protested in vain, his ears had to show. Then, in the presence of Marshal Lin Piao, the heir apparent at the time, he laid out the plan he had developed to establish, within the perimeter Saint Jacques-Soufflot-Sainte Geneviève-Saint Germain, an armed-student, insurrectional commune. The marshal, who looked like a servant in a comedy, rightly noted that makes a lot of saints; several years later he would disappear in the sky over Mongolia. Finally, Angelo, as part of the delegation, "Friends from the West," was presented to the Red Sun Incarnate: bursting out of his linen suit, his little feet covered with black varnished sandals and crossed between the ironwood dragons of his throne, the warty tyrant incessantly puffing blond tobacco cigarettes he brought to his mouth with that little hand so pink that it looked boiled, the very hand that had made such a strong impression on Malraux. With the other hand he was nonchalantly playing with his fly. No doubt the old Minotaur had just done one of the high school girls he had delivered to him on a regular basis. At the moment when the delegation entered the room (a place that, Angelo would tell you later, seemed more like a Chinese restaurant in Belleville than a site of power), the squeaky sounds of "The Red East" rang out: *Dong-fan-ang hong, tai-yan-ang sheng* . . . "The East is red, the sun is rising . . ." It was too much, overwhelmed by emotion, Angelo passed out.

Your own Great Director went by the name of Gideon because of the initials of his function, GD. Gideon could speak for an hour without notes or hesitation, without a single grammatical error. His steady voice, which indulged in no change in tone or rhythm, no slip of the tongue, and certainly no jokes, was literally hypnotic. The only details you could seize upon, in a fruitless effort to resist the growing desire to agree totally with everything he said, were the glare from his little metal glasses and the slow gyrations of his delicate, ivory-colored hands, index and middle fingers extended; but pretty soon these distractions, given their repetitive nature, just reinforced the feeling of beatitude overcoming you. On the face of the Great Director, while he was pouring into your ears the honey of his words, was a look of disgust, as if he were a little tired of teaching dunces like you. Whenever he became silent, the most complicated matters suddenly appeared simple; luminous paths opened through the world's morasses, everyone knew what he had to do. If Gideon had decided — and it wasn't rare — to break the pride of one of The Cause's chieftains, the accusation he pronounced so softly, so calmly, allowed the sinner no recourse except confession and complete contrition (once however, one of them, named Robespierre, because he was active at Arras and also because he displayed an intransigence akin to fanaticism, held out for two days before giving in; no question that it was hunger that made him collapse, the supply of rice and tomato sauce that was your staple had run out the night before). You remember that now, and also his somewhat round-shouldered bearing despite his youth, and his thin, well-cared-for goatee, yet for a long time you couldn't figure out what he looked like. You only knew that he developed powerful ideas somewhere inside the walls of the "School" in the rue d'Ulm. In your eyes, that place's only value came from his being there. You had comrades who knew him, or at least had seen him, listened to him. Nothing prevented you from going up to him, only respect, a sentiment that your own teachers could no longer awaken in you. You tell Thirteen's daughter that the first time you saw him was that day in June of '68 when you and Thirteen had come to lay out your ambush scheme for the highway of the west, today's A13. For nothing less than a dead comrade would you have dared to request a meeting; this contributed greatly to intensifying the aura around him, a sort of Pluto or an Anubis of the Revolution. While you were speaking, you were even more impressed by Gideon's impenetrable silence, by the anticipation of his decision, than by the eventual consequences of what you were proposing. You were speaking, he was stroking his goatee, his chest thrust slightly forward, looking disgusted, and you felt your words getting jumbled, drying up, becoming literally frozen with fear. Lost, you turned to Thirteen, let him try, shit. Maybe he can be more convincing. "We thought. . . ," he began, but Gideon raised his ivory hand as if it were a scepter. His round steel glasses threw off a brief spark. Enough. In a few, almost disdainful sentences, he condemned your plan. You hadn't understood anything about the laws of symbolic violence. You still had progress in theory to make. You suspected that a little.

You see, Marie, you say to Thirteen's daughter while you pass through meteors of red white blue neon BOSCH AUTOMOBILE PARTS AUDI KOREAN AIR VOLS DIRECTS PANASONIC SAINT-DENIS CH. DE GAULLE A1-A104 FLUIDE SANYO SAMSUNG red blue large nebulous orange on the left, you see we were both tough and childish, ready to kill without hesitation and to get ourselves killed for sure, at the same time scared as hell by sex, and also terrified by the authority of a leader who was never more than a student a little more learned than us, older as well, maybe two or three years, but just as distances that seemed immense in childhood become minuscule when you travel them long after (for example, the road we had to take on the Emerald Coast, between the family's house and the beach, which ironically my mother called "Eden Rock"), in the same way back then several years seemed a vast stretch of time, and so Gideon possessed in our eyes a formidable seniority, as if he had been anointed by History, and also by "The Theory," as we used to say. Because he had been a favorite student of the philosopher whose name the public only learned the day he strangled his wife, but you had read his books, which seemed to restore to Marxism the dignity of a science. Lives are forests filled with shadows and mysteries, Marie, you tell Thirteen's daughter; enormous things rot, hideous, nightmarish animals caterwaul in the darkness of each life. All the while you were stupidly wondering what was keeping him from joining The Cause, this mentor who was for you the image of rigor was going nuts, imagining he was hijacking a nuclear submarine or stealing gold from the Banque de France, he was trembling on his knees at the feet of the woman he would wind up killing. On one of the first days when the red flags were invading the Paris streets, at the beginning of that long ago month of May, he was crossing the city in an ambulance from a psychiatric clinic. He had never believed that could ever happen, the avenues transformed into poppy fields. And him, haggard, fleeing. What good had been "The Theory?" You had no idea how completely men are woven from darkness, scarred by fear; literature would have taught you that, but you had rejected literature, you only believed in "life," "life," and "experience," clarified by the Theory, and by Gideon's analyses and instructions, which were of a terrifying simplicity. You were intransigent and frightfully ignorant—and it would have done no good to tell you that. But wait! you say to Thirteen's daughter: you were also reckless, so passionately sure that one day the world, maybe not very soon, but not very far away either, would be re-created, freed from the inevitable, from the infamous old scars of inequality and scorn, and that, just like in the time of our great forebears, all that was necessary was audacity, more audacity, always audacity. Don't let the cynics, a mob stuffed with ads and polls, don't let them insult us later on; we were ignorant, but audacious, you tell Thirteen's daughter as you get ready to complete your first circumnavigation around the black star, the black sun of melancholy, around Apollinaire's anemone and columbine, around Cendrars's city of the Great Gibbet and the Wheel, the nocturnal sphere alive with a past that still haunts us;

you are jumping through the wreaths of tracks at the Gare de Nord, through there you fled with Thirteen in the postal train after the . . . but hold on, let me start over from the beginning. METZ NANCY PORTE DE LA VILLETTE emerald green like the coast of your childhood. N31 150 Meters DAEWOO radiating red in the fog STATION-SERVICE TOTAL, PÉRIPH FLUIDE PORTE DE PANTIN CASINO VILLAGE HOTEL 240 FRANCS CLIMATISÉ CAMPANILE IBIS HEINEKEN ABBAYE DE LEFFE blue green blue red white HOTEL MERCURE, then the tracks from the Gare de l'Est and the Ourcq Canal, which resembles the Landwehrkanal where Rosa Luxemburg's body was thrown on a snowy, bloody day (What do you want, Marie, that's what a canal brings to mind. Not a TV channel like Canal+), then in the park the shimmering green houses of the City of Science, the blue beacons, the Zeppelin Zenith, and on the other side the towers of the Grands Moulins, a Hollywood-Gothic chateau worthy of Victor Hugo N3 PORTE DE PANTIN we had our little studio there, at the Porte de Pantin, where we made false papers in a quiet little street, right behind the animal sellers' bistros. We hid the silk-screen printing frame used to reproduce the watermarks under a diaper table; obviously it smelled too strongly of trichloracetic acid for a baby's room, even though there was one, a real baby, OK, not exactly living there, but he came with his father who made the phony papers. His mother worked in a munitions factory; she used to rip off blanks for our armory; when all this was over, she joined a sect. It's strange to think that baby is alive somewhere, how old must he be now? a little older than you, you tell Thirteen's daughter, maybe he's a young executive in advertising, or something like that, probably he hates our guts, then maybe not, it's not sure, probable, but not sure, things aren't so simple. Now what was his name? Can't remember, a first name of a member of the Resistance, comrades' children always had names like that . . . while to starboard the City of Music's observatory cupola with its radarlike tower shoots by . . . music of the spheres . . .

2

You met Thirteen's daughter at Judith's birthday. The fiftieth. In a fairly
trendy bistro in Belleville. The owner is a former member of The Cause,
Pompabière, indeed a Beer Pump. He used to be a clever little hood,
now transformed into a soda salesman. OK, "soda salesman," it's just
a way of speaking. Pompabert is his real name, his legal name. There
really is a courtesan named Pompadour and a President Pompidou,
called Pomp. All the same, a name like Pompabert creates an aura. In
the old days, for such a brutal guy to possess such verbal agility and
almost unimaginable flamboyance separated him from his associates
in the Issy-les-Moulineaux gang. A great inventor of elaborate insults,
served up with spin and topspin, pretentious, scorching invectives that,
taking the adversary by surprise, left him stunned even before getting
knocked flat. A goldsmith of the complicated, a practitioner of that
popular art form that mingles a smooth tongue with a hard fist. Seated
on the edge of the pool table at Pompabière's (busy making bubbles in
your whiskey glass), you tell Thirteen's daughter that one day you saw
him, in a working-class bistro in the fifteenth arrondissement (because
back then in Paris there were these sweatshops, you can't imagine, you

tell her: for instance, there were enormous Citroën factories in the fifteenth, and workers' bistros all around them; get the picture?) in a bar at the Porte Brancion, one day you saw him order a glass of beer with a big foamy head, then go over to this guy, part of Citroën's own union, a cop for sure, and say to his face: "Little shaver, I'm gonna shave myself with you," blowing the foam in the guy's mug. Right after that, he rammed him with his head, of course. But you have to hand it to him. "Little shaver." Right out of a working-class Homer. So this Pompabière, a little later, when he saw you, rather when Judith introduced you, Martin, what do you mean, you don't recognize Martin? He put his hands on his hips in the classic pose of an incredulous barman and cried out, no kidding, he could not get over it: Martin, it's really you? No, really, he never would have realized it, recognized you. Wow, man you've changed, unbelievable. And since he got started again with the no, never, the it's not possible—billing and cooing like a pigeon in heat, with his dishtowel on his shoulder, this ruddy guy, calling on the others to witness, to acknowledge that this marvel, this Martin, was me—you ended up getting a little annoyed. As for him, he hadn't changed a bit. Lost nothing of his elegance. The chic wrestler, ruddy as ever, handlebar moustache, hairy fingers.

You expected it to happen, this sort of unpleasant melancholy, always the same, every time you get together, which is less and less; you'll always be for each other what you'd been together, impassioned youth, intolerant, ascetic, but time has gently enveloped you in old wineskins. There you are, comically trundling along in these sacks, in death's direction. Some errors you can't avoid when you're a young, slightly romantic man, for example, imagining your funeral. Your girlfriends and mistresses are there, pale and beautiful; they are leaning over an ivory visage, creased like Chopin's or Shelley's; no way! when the day comes, the ones that remember you will be waddling, not doing too well themselves, around a mug looking like an old, rotting pear. But this sarcasm that bodies direct toward the image of what one used to be, what matter conveys to memory, up till now you had more or less escaped it; rather, what was astonishing was the fact that you had "changed so little." And you, naive as ever, having always been on the margins of everything, even, you thought, the passage of time, you did not see yourself as an aging man. One day, you thought (or rather you let the moronic inertia within you think it for you), one day you'd be grown up; maybe then would be the moment to think about getting old, to vaguely envision such an extravagant thing, so removed from everything you had ever imagined—although death had always been strangely possible, in its own way a companion. All the while you search for your image . . . discreetly, in the bistro's mirrors, and my God . . . not much to see, it's true, compared to the famous photo of Che . . . that face with the curly hair under the beret, the dark eyes, that face, the dark angel of revolutions in a low-angle shot, bouncing between so many young breasts all over the world, since that day in October 1967 when the death mask, applied in a rush by Alberto Quintanilla, lieutenant colonel in the carabiniere, left it skinned, like a rabbit in a meat market, red and bleeding, no eyelids, no flesh, in the morgue of the Vallegrande hospital. As for you, none of this beauty, this fragility, this tragedy, as you gingerly eye your reflection in Pompabière's trendy bistro on the heights of Belleville. Damn! Instead just a growing resemblance to Daladier. The pasty, waxy look of age. You remember experiencing a sort of sadness staring at portraits illustrating a biography of Nabokov: photos of a young man possessing a slightly demonic beauty followed by those of a self-important man of letters, then a granddad decked out in shorts and long socks, chasing lepidopterons in Swiss pastures. A sadness and a curiosity; where, how did this happen? This degradation, this betrayal of self by the self, that one does not notice on the occasional photos, too dispersed in time over the course of a biography; you didn't see it happening either, but for opposite reasons: too many snapshots in your own lifetime, and then Pompabière's crude outbursts make you suddenly discover your own image in the mirror, the image of a jerk who chases after death's black butterflies. We see friends marry, then our friends' children, and we don't know what it means, so says the narrator of *The Past Recaptured*: because of fear, because of laziness. You look liked who? asks Thirteen's daughter, her little butt perched on the edge of the pool table. Daladier, prime minister of the Third Republic, a blowhard who trembled before Hitler at Munich; you've heard of Munich at least? Anyway, a guy you don't want to look like.

However, around your motionless face that you no longer recognize, flanked by the smaller, pale, younger, and certainly prettier one of Thirteen's daughter, ironic caricatures of a distant youth come and go; there they are, in the mirror, amid a cloud of cigarette smoke, slightly, mercifully blurred by the wearing out of the tain and the filth on the glass. And Judith, who still moves you, but a prickly person, no longer foxy, talking to Foster; why did she invite that bore? A minor Socialist dignitary today, getting a paunch, with a leftist teacher's beard. There are cravings, money and honors for instance, that increase over time, to the point that one tells oneself that death, which normally occurs through the slow shutdown of circuits, terminal breakdowns, and disgust, must, on the contrary, in cases like this, result from circuit overload, a Chernobylian surge in the reactor; Foster's like that, more and more radioactive with age. You tell Thirteen's daughter that this guy makes you think of Victor Serge's remark about the delegates to the First Conference of the International: "How happy they are to finally see parades from the official rostrums." What do you mean, Victor who? Victor Kibaltchiche, called Victor Serge; I gotta explain everything to you, a magnificent anarchist, whose relatives dumped potfuls of dynamite on the czars' carriages, exile, jailed in France as an accomplice to the Bonnot gang, insurgent at Barcelona, Bolshevik at St. Petersburg, deported to Central Asia as a Trotskyist, in a word, a real life. There's a scene in his *Memoirs* where the Whites and the Reds are firing at one another from the roofs of St. Petersburg during a springtime evening in 1919; they're taking potshots here and there, hiding behind the chimneys; he remembers the whiteness of the city in the arctic night, and the color of the sky reflected in the canals. There are people you love for a sentence, an idea, a smile. This bearded guy, stuck with a rifle, a bad shot without any desire to kill, even the "class enemy" — he's marveling at the beauty of St. Petersburg by night, for me he's part of my portable Pantheon. I would love to see Whistler paint that, what Victor Serge sees. Have to say that St. Petersburg, or Petrograd, did a lot for the theatricality of the Revolution. Somewhere, in an Isaac Babel story, there's a description of the Nevsky Prospect at night, deserted, cluttered with dead horses, frozen stiff, legs straight up against the sky; when I was young, this was one of the images I had of the Revolution: abandoned palaces, the glow of several candles glimpsed through dark windows, and the cavalry horses upended, manes welded to the pavement, hooves pointed to the clouds. OK, Foster, despite everything, he only managed to become an assistant to someone, to some sort of minister. Maybe that's what's worst about him: he's ambitious without the stuff to succeed. Back then, when he was the leader of The Cause in Normandy, you could recognize his foam mattress in the collective's apartment because just above it there was always a portrait of Stalin tacked to the wall. His own pinup. Fichaoui-called-Julot has a white mop of hair now, but twenty years ago, wasn't it prematurely gray? Small, lively, cheerful, clever, with a turned-up nose, throwing back a lock of hair, fists deep in his pockets, he hasn't changed a bit — or are you inventing what he was then because of what you see now? No. It's a pleasure to see him, from back then; he's one of those you really like, the flat opposite of Foster. One could even wonder (you have wondered) why you don't see him more often? No, the passage of time has not made you strangers to each other, but it has nevertheless made you irrevocably distant. Time does that. Among other things, Fichaoui had been responsible for pirate radio broadcasts, have to admit it wasn't his greatest success. He had unearthed a ham radio operator near Amiens, an old snipe hunter (maybe it was teal) who had been in the Resistance and promised to build you a transmitter. In the end the thing filled three chests. Two strong men were needed to move one of them. If it had been a machine to disintegrate Paris, the relationship between quality and weight would have made sense. However . . . you tried it out one night on the roof of a new building at the Porte de Vanves. It wasn't much fun lugging this stuff to the top at seven in the evening without attracting too much attention and without breaking the antique glasswork in the radio tubes rattling around inside. If anyone had asked you anything, you had planned to say you were moving dishes. In the end, you got lucky; everything got there in good shape, just in time for the apéritif amid the chimney pipes. Then you had to set up the antenna, dozens of meters of copper or brass wire—enough to dry wash for the whole building. Was Thirteen there? asks his daughter. Sure, Thirteen was in on everything, or almost everything, but that time he was with me, in the car, several blocks away. On the spot, I mean the roof, Fichaoui-called-Julot was in command. Thirteen and me were in the car, chain-smoking, the radio tuned to the wavelengths we were supposed to pirate. A beautiful blue house nestled on the hill . . . the people living there have thrown away the key . . . Choose well, choose Cent . . . A beautiful novel, a lovely story, a ballad for our time . . . Shit like that. We had dreamt up a stirring appeal to refuse rent hikes in the projects. Stirring but concise, for once: it had to be done quickly to elude the cars with direction finders the cops were sure to use to trace us. Our hearts were racing. We were waiting for our powerful voice, the voice of the "New Partisans" to rise above Paris. At least Paris, because given the size of the installation, it wouldn't have been hard to flood the whole region. The snipe hunter seemed a serious guy, someone who knew what he was doing.

Of course, that wasn't true for everyone. There were proles, more than one, that you didn't trust. For instance the guy from Flins, who insisted you stuff cast-iron tubes with powder and screws and then throw them at the Mureaux police station (maybe it was Meulan?). He personally, due to family obligations, regretfully would not be able to participate. He would have loved to, but we can't always do what we want, sad to say, yet after the Revolution it would be different, right? But he did offer the plumbing and nuts and bolts. No thanks. Or that nutcase from the north, a tall, melancholic fellow that Victoire and Laurent had consulted you about. Victoire and Laurent, it must be said, the most beautiful couple in The Cause. That's her over there; doesn't she look like Fanny Ardant? They made the front page when they were arrested, OK, maybe not the front page, but anyway large photos on the inside pages of *Nord-Éclair* and *La Voix du Nord*; nowadays, were they getting out of prison, they would have been offered contracts in modeling, advertising, and TV . . . Their beauty bothered some of the comrades. You find that odd? You're right, Marie, it's strange, even monstrous, this suspicion of beauty, the prelude to the hatred of beauty, a type of moral leprosy that had infected our souls. Why? Well, listen, even now, so many years later, I really can't explain it. Maybe just because beauty resists that terrible desire we had to level everything out, make everything equal. Because beauty's the opposite; it's what distinguishes, it's what's unfairly given to some and refused to most people. But in this case, it is human beauty, but we scorned as well the beauty of a country church, which is there for anyone who wants it, or the beauty of a sky filled with clouds, city roofs—we weren't like Victor Serge, we wouldn't have been moved by the spectacle of Petrograd on a green night (I've seen that since, that opaline night on the Neva, the canals, the golden crests); and that's what's wrong. What was wrong. And the beauty of art, forget about it! We detested it without knowing it. Beauty throws you off track, confuses you; as for us, what we loved were "the masses," as we used to say. No exceptions. And then, there was a quite disgusting deification of unhappiness. During those months you lived with Chloe (several months, long enough for her to get fed up with your bullshit), you remember you were intimidated by her sparkle, which seemed so contrary to . . . to what, Tartuffe? To propriety, that's it, to decorous

38

modesty. A militant couldn't have a girlfriend who turned heads. You weren't far from thinking that her seductiveness was satanic, right? Right, you little Taliban? She was starting a career as a model that politics first of all, then the drugs and alcohol, would completely destroy; her profession embarrassed you (now you'd like it fine, you old sleaze?). You were afraid, poor bastard, that Gideon would have something to say about it. During the short time you lived together, you insisted that your liaison, like a fault, stay secret, that, for example, you never left a "meet" in her company, no way; you'd whisper to her a place to rendezvous, on a street corner, two hundred meters away. What a lowlife! Remembering this makes you ashamed, the same way you would have felt shame if you had tried to show her off everywhere with that ridiculous male vanity. You're an idiot, Thirteen's daughter opines out loud, in the way young people have of ostentatiously bursting through doors already open. Thanks for the information. Her manner, a bit contrived, of swinging her crossed legs, while sitting in her little black skirt on the edge of the pool table . . . Nothing more striking, in general, throughout the vast universe than this form (not even that of her lips): full, extended, smooth lines of flesh under the edge of the skirt, suddenly sinking around the knee's shiny flatness, then spreading out, one leg crossed over another, tightening again around the ankles, and the light sliding over these killer forms, these fuselages that insult words . . . Mad desire to stick your hand in . . . Hold it! Don't touch! She's Thirteen's daughter, your dead friend, dead and buried! Such a long time ago . . . What's she doing here, at the old folks' ball — what are we doing? Taking Thirteen's place? Representing him amid *les natures mortes*, the calmed-down lives, the half-dead, *the still lives*? No. She told you just a while ago: wants to know about him. Learn from us who the father she scarcely knew really was — dead before they had a chance to talk. You, obviously his "best friend" . . . the first witness called to the stand . . . right there, on the edge of the pool table. Tell me what he was like. Look, Marie, I can't talk about him without telling you about us. I don't know how to make you understand this, but we were not so much "individuals"; nobody was an "I" at the time. It had to do with our youth, most of all with our era. The individual seemed negligible, even an object of scorn. Thirteen, your father, my friend forever, he was one of us. One strand in a ball of string. I can't disentangle him, separate him, tear him from us. If I did I would kill him a second time. Without us, his image would fade away; without "us," all our memories disappear. We were together, even to the point of absurdity. We were not History, but we were little her and his stories, real, imagined, intersecting ones that we created, piles of them. I get it, she responds, I'm not an idiot. Tell me about you guys. All the while hoisting her little butt on the pool table, two bare arms stretched out on each side, hands flat on the wood. Yow! Now this leg, the right one, crossed on the left, which is swinging . . . foot taut, high heels . . . what a fantasy . . . And then, her nice way of telling me I was an idiot with Chloe. Thanks for the info. Swinging her shiny leg. Those first moments of your life with Chloe, sure, you remember them, but you're not about to describe them to this silly kid who's starting to annoy you; let her leave you alone with your stories, and invent the father she wants, it won't be you in any case. You were going to attack the South Vietnamese embassy. You wanted to overrun the "so-called embassy of the South Vietnamese puppets," that's how you phrased it then. You had advanced toward the dark, sparkling wall of helmets, visors, shields, shin guards, from which burst forth the exhilarating fireworks produced by the grenades; what were you brandishing . . . what did you have in your hands? Oddly enough, you recall quite clearly the certitude you had, racing in front of the first lines of the demonstration, that something would happen to you; you remember the shock, the smash, the fall and the pain, the grenade's pin busting your teeth, the stupor and at the same time the sort of satisfaction in realizing that something had in fact happened, those bloody particles, the salty taste in your mouth, and the almost simultaneous obsession with getting up to flee the *pigs*, that's the word you used, in homage to the Black Panthers in the States, when you weren't calling the cops ss; all that happening in the instant of a detonation, in the flash of a tear gas launcher, but you've forgotten what your right hand was getting ready to throw: a cobblestone, a Molotov cocktail? And next thing you know, that hand, Chloe's holding it; you're stretched out in some son of a bitch of a doctor's office who's sewing you up as brutally as he can, telling you you got what you deserved; the bastard doesn't seem to understand that you couldn't dream of anything more beautiful than that: to be lying on his fucking table, stinking like someone wounded in a real war, blood all over your face, and Chloe's hand holding yours. Sorta like paradise. God were we romantics, you tell Thirteen's daughter (because all the same, with the help of the whiskey that loosens the tongue and literally makes words pour forth, you can't help yourself from relating this story in rhythm with her leg swinging in the half-light), and at the same time you admit to yourself that for sure you wouldn't have taken off so absurdly against the helmets and shields if you had not read *The Iliad* or seen Robert Capa's famous photo of the militiaman hit right in the head by the bullet near Cordova, and that young people's minds produce strange Molotov cocktails, explosive caroms, short-circuited images.

Victoire and Laurent, for whatever reason, were caught up in the case of the melancholy prole whose obsession was to derail the TEE Paris-Brussels (do I have to translate that too, TEE, for the generation of the high-speed train: Trans-European Express, a normal train, right? With cars, compartments, whistles, OK). Lucien, who worked in a hosiery factory (they still existed back then), convinced himself that the TEE was filled exclusively with plutocrats, rich guys smoking cigars, wearing pearl-gray morning coats, white ties, and top hats, just like that Baron de Rothschild whose photo he had seen at the weighing-in for the Arc de Triomphe prize in one of those racing magazines he was crazy about. The rumbling, whistling passage of this tedious convoy through the middle of mining villages, slag heaps, mining frames, and beet fields seemed to him an outrage as intolerable as the daily profanation of a slum by a Rolls-Royce. He imagined the sarcastic remarks of the well-to-do in the train, contemplating the world of the poor, his world, through the smoke rings formed by their chicken-ass mouths, and the champagne bubbles rising up as they clinked their flutes. Their fucking gloves, the color of fresh butter, on the edge of their fucking hats. Victoire and Laurent had tried to give him a more realistic notion of the average passengers on the TEE, but nothing worked. These rich people must "stop believing that everything is permitted," a phrasing whose brutal simplicity corresponded nicely to the philosophy of The Cause. Besides, Victoire and Laurent felt embarrassed trying to moderate a social hatred so naively and poetically pure. This guy, Lucien, was a douanier Rousseau of the class struggle, while Victoire and Laurent saw themselves as trying to emasculate him with banal considerations drawn from bourgeois sociology. So, giving up on trying to divert him from his crazy obsession, pretending they approved of his scheme, they contented themselves with trying to sabotage it secretly. However, that got exhausting. At least once a month, to satisfy his dark mania, they pretended to make a bomb out of modeling clay. Lucien, obsessed, pale as a ghost, hovered over the operation. You're sure it's good?, he used to ask, sipping a glass of beer. Yeah, of course, don't worry, top-of-the-line plastic explosives, delivered by Thirteen, a comrade from Paris, an important guy, Martin's number two man: it's like he bought it at Fauchon's. Lucien had a gigantic and suspicious wife — she didn't like "this screwing around," as she used to say (Victoire and Laurent agreed with her on this point, but dared not admit it) — and a Mongoloid child, as we still said at the time. The wife paced back and forth with what was called "a knowing air"; the Mongoloid moaned softly in a corner. The TV was on all the time. The child would be moaning, the wife would be lugging around her enormous body, her slippers slapping the floor, Lucien would be knocking back his liter of Valstar (or maybe Dumesnil?), smoking his Gauloises, livid, coughing, burping; Victoire and Laurent would pile the modeling clay in a jelly jar, stick in a detonator to which they would attach, with a quick bite, the Bickford line, then jam all that into a workout bag, and take off in the night for a war as feigned, but for different reasons, as the one in *Così fan tutte*. Lucien, no more than the guy from Flins, would not push class hatred to the point of considering lending a hand personally to the derailment. This time, they'll not make it to paradise?, he would ask quietly on his doorstep. Each time they had to concoct a reason why it did not work; once, too much fog, impossible to mount a lookout, another time, too much rain that was going to put out the fuse, or again, a dog had barked and windows lit up on the Wassingue road. We could give the mutt pellets, he suggested; he had a proven recipe: chopped meat with steel slivers, no poison, just good, natural stuff, the dog's sense of smell wouldn't warn him; at this thought, a Buster Keaton smile contorted his face. On another occasion, the gendarmes were in the area, searching all over in their blue 4L. They seemed to be on to something. You don't suppose your wife would have . . . without meaning to, of course? . . . That was a good idea: that suspicion, with all the consequences it inevitably entailed, had bought them several months of peace. Nevertheless, the life of Victoire and Laurent had become an exhausting fiction. Constructing false bombs, inventing false reasons for false failures (all that to prevent a true prole from committing, through intermediaries, a true massacre); sucked into this whirlpool of lies, they wondered from time to time, if this was really it, the Revolution for which they had sacrificed families and studies, the Revolution that they had thought would show the true nature of the world, would be the Great Exposer. Not a good beginning . . . But why did they do that? Thirteen's daughter asked. Because they loved the proletariat, Marie, so they did not want to hurt Lucien; don't you understand? And it could have been that the aforementioned Lucien was an informer; it might have been the police who asked him to trick them in order to catch Victoire and Laurent placing a bomb on the tracks; in any case the business with the modeling clay was driving them all nuts. But it could have also been that he was just a little perverse, a guy who really wanted to blow up the TEE, and then

43

hadn't been taken in by Victoire and Laurent's act, that he got pleasure from just seeing them getting tangled up in their own lies, exhausting themselves dreaming up cock-and-bull stories—and all for him! For his pleasure! As if they were dancing around in front of him, in other words. That's the explanation I prefer.

Anyway, the snipe hunter (or maybe teal) had seemed like a serious guy. Sure, he hit the beer a little hard, but that's the custom in the northern swamps, a land of little light, low lying and mournful, a place of world wars; but this guy wasn't crazy. So it was with a certain confidence that Thirteen and you were waiting, chain-smoking in the stolen, disguised Citroën, for the call to strike against the rent in the projects to resound all over Paris. Time passed. Nothing happened. Mondays in the sun . . . Cut the shit! Electrocute yourself! The sergeant's laughter, the regiment's nutty girl, the one the captain of dragoons prefers . . . Asshole! Don't ever forget, oh no, never forget that you looooooooveee me. What the hell are they doing up there, damn it? Then the news bulletin jingle (you had chosen to pirate a working-class station): President Pomp is meeting with Leonid Brezhnev at Minsk . . . New rumors . . . North Vietnamese offensive in Cambodia . . . American bombardments in the Delta . . . b-52s spreading sheets of Agent Orange . . . in the My Tho region . . . Heart skips a beat. The lieutenant was killed down there, on the other side of the world whose images you see on television, villages of bamboo and cinder blocks teeming with life on the edge of the canals, right under the bombers' wings, yokes, buffaloes, red trails the tanks move along, scared faces under Tonkinese hats, a little pile of stereotypes, a ready-made Asia . . . Squealing, children, pigs, ducks splashing under the pilings . . . swollen corpses in the Mekong current . . . Your father, the lieutenant, killed in a rach, a tributary, several months after your birth. Barely begun, your life was already marked, like meat in the butcher's, with death's violet ink, in this place you don't know, those jungles on which today (then) rain down slanting mists of defoliants. You would like to tell that to Thirteen, you say to his daughter, but you don't dare. You inherit death, nothing to do about it; you would like to refuse it, this legacy you sense will poison your life, but you can't; I didn't dare tell your father because mine, after all, had been a "colonialist soldier," his death weighed less than a feather, as the Great Helmsman used to say, no reason to make a big deal. But you vaguely wonder (you dare not, and doubtless cannot, ask the question directly) whether all the same it's not because of this stupid death that you inherited, that you were unable to refuse, that you were born into so to speak, whether all that doesn't explain why you find yourself now (then) sitting in a white, stolen Citroën, chain-smoking Gauloises, waiting for a pirate broadcast that never comes. Because it was never coming. You had to get out of there. Later we found out, you tell Thirteen's daughter, I don't know how, that our program had been heard in the building, but nowhere else. It was a big building, a high-rise, but still . . . Wouldn't he have understood, if you told him? she asks. I don't know, how do you expect me to know? But I think so. That's why he was and remains my eternal friend.

And while you tell these stories the metronome of a young leg beats time to the rhythm of the kinds of music played at old people's parties, Cesaria Evora or Paolo Conte, or Alain Souchon to appear more with it, or a good old Rolling Stones to recall that we had once been young too, or perhaps Richard Anthony or Françoise Hardy for the irony of it, "All the Other Boys and Girls My Age" (and maybe you intend these stories for that charming leg, and for the other one as well, over which the first leg is crossed, beating time for nothing and nobody; maybe these legs, which cause so many sparks of light to shoot forth from the short black linen skirt, are the distant reflection of Chloe's legs, signs of a parenthesis that is closing, and in which you have spent practically all your life), and while you're talking, the masks continue their slow carplike dance in the depths of the mirror, cloudy, like waters that have not been changed for a long time. Swim, old squama! These people make you think of fish, nervous vivacity under the scales, in

45

the jaw, yet bellies soft and white, protruding eyes, pockets, folds, and rictus of a carp. And your lazy swimming spreads clouds of excrement in its wake. Over there is Amédée, who will only stay a few moments; now he's too important a man to hang around, but it's nice of him to have come (everyone, not just Judith, felt a secret twitch of self-satisfaction); Amédée would be a pike. Boney mandibles, hydrodynamic, look out roaches . . . You haven't seen him for quite some time; life, as they say, separated you, however you really like him; he spoke well of one of your books. Today he's a famous journalist, someone who cultivates a capo-mafia look: hair slicked back, twill suits, signet rings. His guttural voice has become one of the republic's. We dreamed of such unreasonable things, you tell Thirteen's daughter. That we would kill, or be killed. And then, you see, in the end Amédée impresses us because he's an important person; it's as simple as that, even though no woman of the world will blow him away with a pearl-handled revolver, the way it happened to Calmette in the past. Who? A boss at *Le Figaro*, doesn't matter. And for sure he'll not provoke someone to a duel, like Clemenceau did, or later Defferre. He might be capable of it, maybe. It's the times. Me, if I were involved in politics, you say to Thirteen's daughter, I would put the authorization of duels on my platform, even the encouragement of dueling. Tax reductions for every appearance on the field. You see her stiffen on the edge of the pool table. Death is the Great Satan for these youngsters. Sure as hell she won't vote for you. Too bad. Go fuck yourself. Vote the Green Party, if that does it for you, kids. I vote Pushkin, damn it! And the other fish, over there, stickleback, all bones with a little mask of tender skin jutting out, crackled, waxy, darting nervous eyes: Chloe, right, your first love. Now she's a waitress in a bistro next to the Porte de la Chapelle. And the grouper who swims in big eddies, potbellied, paunchy, unshaven; that's César, the famous architect, the most vain and generous guy in the world. Over there, Max, he's an editor, with a mug that didn't get that way from mineral water; sure, he looks half asleep waiting for another drink, but don't believe it, he catches everything, the old scorpion fish, his little half-closed squinty eyes, his ears bristling like antennas, watch it if you're near him. All these amphibians still have in their bodies, in their aging faces, lingering marks of their youth; a distinctness that's become a little blurred. Some of these faces, not too removed from the original, have become caricatures, while others, completely remodeled by the approach of death, only retain a concealed detail of their former appearance—often in their way of looking—yet discovering that detail suddenly leaves you flabbergasted, embarrassed—as if you had been the unwilling witness to something obscene. And you never know which one of the memory's prejudices is the strangest: the one that chooses, in spite of everything, to recognize the youth in the bloated body who usurps his name, or the one who refuses recognition, despite the proofs provided (like Pompabière just a few minutes ago, as incredulous before this sort of Daladier—you—in his own bistro, as was Marcel discovering, in the salons of the Prince de Guermantes, that the haughty d'Argencourt had become a "benighted dodderer"). Thirteen's daughter curls her lips and exhales a perfect smoke ring. Hum . . . she smokes like a guy. And you quit about a year ago because of too much rumbling in the chest . . . You're at the prophylactic age. The time of workouts in the gym and colon exams . . .

The voices seemed to have changed the least: Judith's high and piping, Amédée's guttural sound, Foster's squeaks . . . Fichaoui-called-Julot seemed to speak through a pillowcase. However, it can't be. Someone you don't know, whom you have never met, you can still figure out his age within five years on the phone; so it must be the same for us too. Absolutely. Still, you think you are hearing their voices from the past; Fichaoui's discussing the failure of the pirated program with a casual humor that was not often encountered at The Cause, running his hand through his hair, which must have already been gray, white, no gray, no doubt about it; Foster's voice announcing God knows what "struggle-critique-reform plan" (useless to try and explain to you what that was, you say to Thirteen's daughter, anyway, I don't know what it was, some stuff inherited from the worst forms of Christianity, the Christianity of mortification. You take a comrade and don't let him go until he made his auto-critique); Judith's voice telling you . . . you don't remember anymore what she was saying, nor what you were saying to her, whispering to her back then, what words, did you know words of love back then? Passing your hand through her long hair as it slipped onto her shoulder, which one, you can't remember, then cascading between her breasts; you've forgotten what her breasts were like — they had to have been pretty. And now, just a minute ago, she's telling you she's going to have her knees operated on, and you, not to be left out, in an effort to say something nice that shows you're in the same place as she is, you start chatting about your herniated disks . . . Lord . . . You think you're hearing your voices from the past, but in truth what you are listening to is the breath of time. The great sperm whale! Suddenly a new vision imposes itself on the aquarium: You're a living collection of ex-votos. In each of you is an organ, a faculty where the sickness of time is concentrated and displayed, like broken arms, clubfeet, blind eyes, the tin-plate goiters that common people display in church to beg God's mercy. Part of your body is image and prayer; a part of each of you is nailed to the wall of life, in silent supplication. This withering away, you saw it emerge in the mirrors where you shave, where you put on makeup, on the surface of your bodies: incredulous at first, then intrigued as well, and finally almost honored, at least in the beginning, like children happy to be sick; it's Time, History's old protagonist; in the end it's not just anybody who visits you, you personally. Pretty soon, the laughter's over. This leprosy moves in, takes over inside you, screwing everything up. Runny eyes, swollen, streaked eyelids looking like sagging canopies . . . eye shadows the color of old ham, blotchiness . . . hairy twists curling from the nose, from the ears . . . tufts of hair comically sticking out . . . pancake batter covering your features . . . dewlaps, scabs . . . wrinkles, crow's feet . . . all this crap, this create-a-corpse-kit . . . and that's just the face . . . forget about the rest, catarrh, varicose veins, flatulent gut, flabby skin

48

hanging off the arm, creaky vertebras, forcing you to walk bent over like a lackey; all this pathetic jumble, it's you. The whole set . . . The voices seem the least changed, but that's not possible. Once, you tell Thirteen's daughter, we set up this impressive loudspeaker to scare the screws at the Santé Prison, where some comrades from The Cause were being held, including Foster (pity they didn't keep that guy). Actually, the comrades had it pretty easy behind those walls, much better than before their arrests; in any case, they had visits and books to read, no more explanations and auto-critiques to make, or punches to take; it was as if they were in a psychiatric clinic; a little austere, to be sure, yet nonetheless they only had one fear, that we'd be crazy enough to try and free them, and lucky enough to manage to do so (they overestimated us). And then there was Beatrice, the lawyer with the yellow eyes. Foxy. We were all in love with her, but only those locked up had the right to see her several times a week; the rest of us, on the outside, could only dream of her . . . I'm sure some got arrested for no better reason than to spend time with her. Of course, it wasn't Foster who told me all that, he never had enough of a sense of humor; it was Danton, you see the chubby guy over there talking to the pretty redhead. I like Danton. Nobody knows Mozart like him, nor Schubert. He's not a cruel fellow. Rather a sensualist, like his illustrious homonym. He would have been guillotined in Paris in 1794, shot in Moscow in 1936. At the beginning of this whole story, we happened to go with him, Angelo, Thirteen, and me, to Harry's Bar. If Gideon had heard about that, we would have been hit with a stiff auto-critique. Not to mention what would have come after. You don't get out of Souchaux-Montbéliard; the Peugeot factories were our Siberia. That made the cocktails we were downing all the more potent, Blue Lagoons, Alexandras . . . the stuff you drink when you're young and want to seem an old star. Once, all four of us, no, Nessim was there too, of course, he knew a lot more about cocktails and all that went with them than we did, so there we were, all five of us crouching over and puking into the gutter of the Avenue de l'Opéra, the flat fronts of the sanitation department's garbage trucks slowly moving toward us under the dawn's carbon-paper sky; all around the trucks were the cries of the garbage men, the thud of the metal garbage cans and the snorting of the electric compressors, and Angelo claimed we looked like geese on the Capitoline Hill watching Hannibal's elephants pass by; that might seem ridiculous, you say to Thirteen's daughter, it's a smart kid's joke, but I still would like to laugh one or two more times in my life the way I did that morning between two hiccups tasting of bile, just above a stream reflecting the violet-blue sky beginning to turn pink in the direction of the Grand Boulevards . . . Nessim, his father, a Lebanese banker, had a garish chateau, quite ugly, near Fontainebleau. At Montargis, I think. In the park was a pond with moor hens; once you saw Nessim's father coming back from fishing; a servant was following him, carrying his rod and a pike on a silver platter. If TEE Lucien had seen that . . . To tell the truth, you yourself didn't believe your own eyes. You didn't think that rich people like that could actually exist, quite expressionistic. Flesh-and-blood plutocrats right out of a Grosz painting. Why was Nessim screwing around with The Cause? He must have felt himself vaguely attracted by that great event, terrible and chic: the Revolution. Because there was a time when it was "in" to be part of it. The university was involved, and by contagion the intellectuals and the trendsetters. Proust's Mme. Verdurin would have been a leftist. Listen, Marie, you say to Thirteen's daughter, some of the people who insult us today, distinguished people, academicians, guys with ribbons, that sort of crew, they don't think we're worth the rope to hang us, that we were just novice assassins, and ridiculous to boot; but at the time, their much-admired mentors were our friends: philosophers, moviemakers, novelists, better believe they cooled their heels waiting to see us; they wanted to sign, to petition, to march, to climb onto the barrels, to distribute the newspaper, to appear part of the movement; just as today, the times having changed, people now want decorations, embassy postings, tax exemptions, or just invitations to dinners . . . They didn't think we were all that repugnant back then when we were a little dangerous. They paid their dues . . . Nessim was not the only heir hanging around you. You recall that once you organized a big meeting, a central committee or something like that, in a house belonging to a branch of the Rothschild family. No kidding. The daughter, a student at Vincennes, was sympathetic to The Cause. It was near Saint Cloud, you could see golfers passing by in the shaded blue distance, unreal figures way in the back of the lawn with flower beds the size of tropical islands. When he's not filled with hate, the petit bourgeois is scared stiff; you were shocked and impressed, afraid of breaking something. Shaking in your shoes. But not the proles. Pompabière, Momo Lock-Eater, Hairy-Reureu, the Issy gang—were all there. Completely at ease. Doing their business. They had forced the door to the wine cellar (Momo got his nickname from his talents in that area) and stolen dozens of bottles. Mouton-Rothschilds, Pétrus, Haut-Brions, nothing but incredibly expensive Bordeaux, but they had no idea what treasures they had in their hands. They thought that all these dusty bottles were "badly maintained." The bottles dirtied the fingers of these delicate guys. In their opinion, moneybags like these people ought to have been able to pay someone to dust them . . . They suspected that, to accompany the morning Camembert, this stuff would be better than the cheapo Grévéor (or the Kiravi) in starred liter bottles that they regularly knocked back, that's all. So, as I was saying, you tell Thirteen's daughter, Foster had begun a hunger strike at the Santé Prison. Danton also went along with it, but half-heartedly; he used to sneak a little sugared water. In his mind he was inventing phenomenal recipes. To support their action, we had bought two loudspeakers, the biggest we could find; not as gigantic as the ones the North Koreans used all over the demilitarized zone to celebrate the beauties of their great socialist deathtrap, but ours were still pretty loud. The idea was to install the sound system on a roof near the prison to send messages to everyone, our guys and the guards. Earlier, we had gone to test it in the country, in Normandy. Blitz had lent us his house. The famous producer. OK, at the time he was not that well known. He made films about strikes, but that didn't mean he was a radical activist. We had found a deserted place nearby, on a little road that dated from the horse-and-buggy era, and there we gave it a try. Thirteen had recorded the message. A direct, efficient style, no flourishes. Screws, watch out for your balls, that sort of thing. Boy, could we hear it! Nothing like the pirate broadcast. It was Big Brother! But then, something unexpected happened: all the local cows heard it, and in a flash went into a gallop! We saw them bearing down on us from the far horizon. Jumping hedges and ditches! Hypnotized by our loudspeakers. The ground was trembling under their hooves. We were scared out of our minds. We cut the sound off, and they stopped in their tracks, as if we had unplugged them. Instantly, they were all grazing, moping about, like nothing had happened. Apparently there was something in our howling, a wavelength or a frequency, that turned them on. Or it could have been Thirteen's voice. Maybe your father was the Orpheus of cows.

At that moment Winter walks by, hesitant, holding a wineglass by the stem, and giving you a sickly smile. In the old days Winter was a thin, handsome young man with delicate, feminine features. It would have been easy to imagine him in the role of Saint Sebastian (or Saint-Just, for that matter). Something, a painful fragility, seemed to evoke the martyr. A pale and transparent skin, a girl's skin others jeered. He dropped out of school to "establish himself," as we used to say, at the wool factory in Roubaix. He lived in a furnished apartment in a brick house along the canal with an ex–high school student who had established herself in a cookie factory. It appears, it appeared (you never saw her), that she had a nineteenth-century sort of beauty: melancholic, long dark hair held in place on a fragile neck by a rubber band, slender, ivory skin under which you could make out blue-green veins, a reserve found at the two ends of the social ladder, in certain aristocratic families and certain working-class ones, that was her case; her parents were miners. And you know, you say to Thirteen's daughter, what is more beautiful than anything else in a young girl is a slim waist. One where your two hands can almost touch. We age by the waist when it begins to be called a stomach. She had that kind of waist, slender as a cane, Cosette. Yes, Cosette, the name her parents gave her. Because it used to be that some books help us believe in a future for humanity. You can't understand that anymore, can you, you say to Thirteen's daughter. You're already too removed from books, right? She sticks out her pink little triangular tongue, between lips over which you would like to run your finger, under a nostril pierced by a shiny stud. Fuck! OK, she's right. Every morning after unbolting the lock on the Mobylettes, they used to embrace for a long time amid the canal's yellow fog — the air in the morning was like a grease stain. Their naive love, solemn like all young loves, got a little on the nerves of the others: those who, having nobody, were jealous, those who pretended to be cynical, those already tired of disappointing loves. A day came when Gideon, inspired by some Chinese silliness, introduced a measure with the ridiculous name of "the red pair": each young "intellectual" would be placed under the guidance of a sort of worker-preceptor (or political commissar). Foster and some others set out to preach this sermon to the provinces, adding, as is almost always the case with coadjutors, extra rigor. In the north, certain people found in this an opportunity to separate Winter from his high-schooler. Maybe not really out of nastiness, rather to see, to test their discipline, with a little malice all the same. They demanded that she move to Valenciennes to serve under the authority of a semi-illiterate: Barouf was not even a prole, but the head of a section at an Auchan supermarket (or maybe Intermarché?). He wore with pleasure something strange among you guys: wide, multi-colored ties under fitted jackets; he was proud of his sideburns and hated "the intellectuals." What now seems incomprehensible is that they obeyed. But, you know, we were like Jesuits, *perinde ac cadaver*. Cosette left the house on the canal. Winter thought he was going mad. At first, they managed to meet. But on a scooter Valenciennes is far from Roubaix. And then, in yielding to this stupid order in the name of a revolutionary abstraction, they suspected they were betraying each other; shame and rancor infected their love, began to corrupt it. At Valenciennes, Cosette lived in a collective apartment; they would meet in noisy, cloudy bistros. Drunks were stumbling around, insulting them: the two girls . . . The vulgarity of this life suddenly left them on the verge of tears. They would still kiss, but furtively, unhappily, with an embarrassment they had never felt before. It was raining; the world was narrow and dark, enclosed in smoke. While they had been together, Winter told me later, this old industrial landscape in the north had not overwhelmed them; in a confused way they had felt they were living in an uncouth, ugly shell that protected their love; but now that they were separated, these grim horizons only filled them with agony and disgust. She got sick; they did not see each other for two months, then they never saw one another again. Winter is presently an aging prof, not quite yet an old prof, but soon, he knows it and doesn't give a damn; he awaits it with indifference. He is supposed to be teaching literature in Lille, to little hoodlums more interested in martial arts than Baudelaire or Apollinaire. He's still pale and fragile, and that doesn't help him win his students' respect, but the alcohol has swelled his silhouette. Winter drinks a lot, without joy, without rage either. He imbibes that stuff like medicine, and that's probably what it is. He started a new translation of *The Aeneid*, which, as he says himself, he'll never finish. He talks like he's in a dream, always with the same tone, a little smile on his lips, dragging softly on his pipe, puff, puff. His eyes seem to look at you from behind a little veil. Look at his eyes, you tell Thirteen's daughter: you'd say they're glazed over. Or that they have been boiled. Winter's a ghost. He never forgot Cosette, never forgave himself for having let her leave. And, look, he's right to not have forgiven himself; you can pardon others if you wish, if you're given to that, but not yourself. He was afraid of life, like a lot of us, and tried to cloak the fear in gaudy heroics. This story, this love, might have seemed to him too beautiful, too terrifying. It's strange, but we were not brought up to accept happiness without having to discuss it. But why? she asks you. That, I don't understand. Maybe because, I don't know, suppose for example that at any given moment humanity only has a certain amount of happiness available, let's say a billion megawatts — the number doesn't matter — if you take too much for yourself, you're stealing from others, you're depriving them of their portion, get it? And then they have trouble lighting things up, because of you. You can see things that way. That's completely stupid, she says; in fact, if you're happy you can help others to be happy. Can you prove that, I answer, hoping to annoy her. Your little smugness about happiness is just too simple. OK, who cares. Winter's been screwed up for a long time. That's why I like him. Your father as well, after all, let me remind you that he was really screwed up (I don't know why I can't control this rudeness). There's a pile of things I'm not sure how to say well, you tell Thirteen's daughter, I don't know how to say them, because I really don't know how to think them; I'd need to live a lot longer than I will live, I'm not a quick study, just somebody dying faster than he thinks. But among those things, there is one I know: there must be a relation between your naive cult of individual happiness, I mean you, the ultramoderns, and your fucking ignorance of history. Because there's tragedy there, Prometheus and the rest, sorry, but that doesn't fit in with the blossoming of the individual. But your models, you find them in ads, that sort of third-rate eternity, the contrary of History. Sure with that stuff, there's happiness all over the place. But humanity doesn't work that way; shit, we're not all supermodels . . . the saints, the heroes, the revolutionaries were not all necessarily the well-balanced ones . . . models of good health . . . early risers . . . well-shaven and with manageable hair . . . You're starting to pontificate, she shoots back, pissed off, shaking off the ash at the end of her cigarette butt . . . Maybe she's right. Look out, or you'll turn into an old fart. Easy does it, as they used to say in the old films, the detective ones with Gabin and Lino Ventura when they were breaking into the safes with their hats angled over the cigarette butt . . . Or even better: Take it down a notch, guys! Your uncle saying that, raising his index finger, raising his right hand from the Frégate Renault's imitation-ivory steering wheel, en route more or less toward the Emerald Coast, your mother seated next to him, between Avranches and Pontorson, Mont Saint Michel in your sights, just above the salt marshes, saying that when you and your brother begin making too much noise in the back. Yellow and black plastic seats (we used to say "straw and black," it was ritzier). Your mother in "the death seat" (but your uncle more truthfully in the place of the Dead One, *Dead* in capital letters), chain-smoking English cigarettes. The strawberry ice cream–colored mileage markers filing by, quite slowly really, on the "Route of the Liberation." On the dashboard, to hold your mother's packs of Players, sort of a little fence of corrugated plastic. "Plastic": this word means "modernity." Your mother's against it. Thinks it causes cancer. For her "modernity" is more or less everything that has happened since the lieutenant's death. Modernity is a raging torrent in whose waters she's lost her footing long ago. Be careful not to drown as she did in the current of time, is what you think today. Your life barely begun yet already marked like meat in a butcher store with the death's violet ink, in a place you don't know, whose name you have no idea of, a river in the Far East whose name people hide from you, a shameful name since it means "colonial war," and a colonial war, from that time on, is something you don't brag about, something not scheduled on the program of life and death "for France" in certain families at least, a river in the Far East on whose delta where, twenty-five years later, slanting sheets of defoliant and bevies of cluster bombs will rain down; you don't dare say to Thirteen, in the white, stolen Citroën, that in a sense you were born there, born into a crazy life that his daughter, or so you think now, on a day as far in the future as was your father's death in the past, could never understand. Died for France . . . Died for nothing. Sure. Or died for greenbacks. Even more, killed by his own shell. But obviously you didn't know that then. Your mother's smoking, silent, nervous, destroyed forever: having absolutely, rigorously decided she would be, no doubt about it. Your life barely begun, yet already marked . . . But why marked? The girl, Thirteen's daughter, after all; her father died when she was a kid, for reasons she doesn't know, yet she's decided not to be marked, decided that happiness would be her response. Good luck! The uncle, a real Frenchman, no way a hero; it annoys the hell out of him, his sister's dramatic side. Concerning his brother-in-law, he's had it up to here with him. More of a pain in the ass dead than alive. Having to drive the kids around too . . . Go ahead and ruin the gears (the gearbox was the weak point in the Frégate Renault). Griiind . . . garbage gears! The "white-walled" hearse for the postliberation bourgeoisie nevertheless continues hiccuping, shambling along to the west, grinding its gears. You and your brother, you are pulling one another's hair, pretending to puke on the "straw and black" plastic seats in the back. "Take it down a notch, guys," intones your uncle, raising his right hand from the middle of the imitation-ivory steering wheel. The smell of burnt rubber permeates the car. Back then the cars always smelled of burnt rubber. Or even (at the same time) of a wet dog. Wet dog is normal, the No Big Deal smell; on the other hand, burnt rubber was the start of problems. When quite by chance we couldn't pick up a hint of burnt rubber we still had such fear of smelling it that we wound up smelling it. Your mother smokes cork-tipped Navy Cut. "You don't think that smells like burnt rubber?" she asks your uncle in a tone of voice that shows how little she cares about all this mechanical stuff. And everything else, for that matter.

What are you thinking about? asks Thirteen's daughter. Nothing. Childhood memories. Winter bought the house on the canal. Furnished it, made it attractive. He lives there, alone, or from time to time with a young colleague, or one of his students, I really don't know. He gets drunk there alone, waiting for Cosette to come back. He translates Virgil, watching the rain fall on the canal; he translates until the drunkenness clouds his eyes, his mind. Her return, I don't think he really hopes for it, but he waits for it; not exactly the same thing, is it? You can wait for something you no longer hope for—that's really human, in my opinion. I know what I'm talking about. What are you talking about? she asks. Later. I'll tell you later. Look, take death for instance: you await it without hoping for it. I mean, more or less. Who was I talking about? Before Winter, I mean. She's at a loss to say. Everything's too jumbled together. But that's the way life is, Marie, this tangled ball of string . . . When you no longer understand anything, when you get everybody mixed up, then you'll have an idea how it was, what your father was like, along with other people. That's exactly what I want to tell you, what your father was like, with other people, with us. Group portrait with Thirteen. OK, I remember, I was talking about Nessim. He wasn't part of the inner circle, nor even the second. Too rich and also too cowardly. The street-fighting part was not his favorite chapter in The Cause's serial novel. He took part every so often, to participate in the effort, armed with some sort of ivory-knobbed sword-cane bought at the flea market. He used to manage to arrive late, after the brass knuckles and the clubs had settled matters. Was nice of him to come. Nobody forced him. He embarrassed you a little, with his ox-hide jackets and silk scarfs, trying to look tough . . . You liked him fine; he was your buddy in the secret drinking bouts, even paid the bill, but still he was someone you called with a little scorn a "sympathizer": a guy not really trustworthy, but at your beck and call. He had an old Bentley from the '50s; you had made him sell it to replenish The Cause's coffers — except for the toolbox that you kept, a small box with a collection of screwdrivers and pliers that were really useful for working on revolvers and machine guns. It was especially helpful that he rented a little house in the sixteenth arrondissement, not far from the home of the retired general Chalais, the CEO of Atofram. One day you had announced to Nessim that he had been chosen to accomplish a great deed. This annunciation took place in his house; you had come with Thirteen to add to the importance of the occasion. Nessim was wearing a garnet dressing gown and Turkish slippers. He served you bourbon, ice and glasses tinkling on a silver platter. Well, what's it about, he asked as he stroked the fringe of his beard. He had a tendency toward solemnity that came to him from his education with menservants. He was flattered, but nervous. Were we going once again to pressure him to sell something? . . . You didn't know where to begin. We have decided to arrest an enemy of the people. Naturally, we can't reveal his name. A good start. Nessim would have the honor of putting his house at your disposal as the departure base. Useless to remind him that he was henceforth bound to the strictest secrecy under pain of severe punishment. He could still refuse, but it had to be done at once. Nessim went white. With a flap of his garnet robe he rubbed compulsively the steel-encircled lens of the glasses he had just removed from his sweaty brow. He hadn't imagined that his occasional drinking buddies would one day play him such a dirty trick as to let him into their confidence. He put on his glasses and stared at you as if he doubted that his tormentors could really be you and Thirteen. No mistake. And what would be . . . what would it consist of . . . his role? If he went along . . . For the details, you turned to Thirteen; in your opinion the assignment of responsibilities seemed quite professional. Nessim was panic stricken, yet at the same time this was the type of emotion he was expecting you to evoke in him for a long time. To go and get plastered at Harry's, he didn't need you. He agreed. And what ever happened to him? Thirteen's daughter asked. Is he here tonight? Oh, he's dead. Killed in an ugly way. Thrown out a window of the Murr Tower in Beirut. That's how all this ended for him. A guilty conscience had made him a sort of revolutionary. Disgusted by the injustice his family's money represented. To come right down to it, selling the Bentley was no big deal for him. Wheels, he got rid of them like shirts. He had his first, an Austin Healey, when he was fifteen. When you're a rich kid in Lebanon, you can drive a Ferrari while you're still in short pants. He went back to Beirut in the middle of the war. On the "Palestine-Progressive" side, of course. Don't ask me what that means; it doesn't mean anything. What Nessim got from us was that you had to be at war with your deepest self. And he was ashamed of being happy at the expense of others, ashamed of always having the silk dressing gowns, the convertibles, the governesses, and then the mistresses that come with all that, and was it really bad, this shame, you're supposed to think so, you say to Thirteen's daughter, but me, I don't know, I'm not so sure. Do you have to be at war with yourself, and not just if you are a rich heir? Anyway, he got involved on the side of his worst enemies; oh, he didn't become a sniper, not his style, but he did favors, I don't know what kind. He joined that side precisely because it was his enemies' side. To put it more precisely: because they were the enemies of the part of himself he wished to fight. Muslims, because he was Christian, so-called poor, because he was rich. Of course all that's stupid. The head of the "Progressive" Party was the biggest warlord in the country; while he was idly liquidating members of Nessim's family, his horses were running in the Arc de Triomphe race, and he used to meet up with Nessim's father at the private sales in Deauville or Chantilly where they would stroke the necks of the same yearlings, the way they would stroke the asses of the same women in Damascus, and don't bother looking at me that way, you tell Thirteen's daughter, what I just said is not particularly sexist: first of all, it's the truth, and then it's from Apollinaire, OK? Both of them dressed in gray flannel, twin images photographed in *Jours de France* to inflame the antiplutocrat imagination of Lucien at the TEE. There were two skyscrapers, two towers actually that faced each other above the ruins of Beirut, on either side of the demarcation line, shattered, burnt cement, blistered and sinister, filled with snipers: on one side the Murr Tower and the other, the Holiday Inn. The sea quite close, a long mauve line, a strange calm. The Murr tower was the rifle range for the "Palestine-Progressives." One day they found Nessim's broken body at the base of the tower. What prompts people to head right for the places where they are going to be killed, toward the ambush, the slaughterhouse prepared for them? Beware the ides of March, yet still go to the senate. Few escape this unconscious fascination; only the most instinctive, the most animal. But Nessim, complicated, refined, torn, was the opposite of an animal. Starting with you, from that day—let's suppose—when along with Thirteen, you announced to him the great destiny prepared for him, he had marched, like a sleep-walker, toward the bottom of the pile of devastated concrete that was the Murr Tower, where these guys, probably bearded (just like him), in combat fatigues (he preferred Prince of Wales suits), probably wasted on heroine (he did cocaine), would help free him of the self-hate that the revolutionary idea had nurtured in him. Beirut, you went back there not long ago. For a lecture at the university. That's your job now: man of letters. You tried to find the places where Nessim had taken you back then, several months before his defenestration. You were a journalist then. You had marched at twilight under the stacks of containers pockmarked with bullet holes, some of them puffed up like popcorn by the explosion of a mortar shell inside them, forming a wall of sheet metal that separated the two parts of the city. And on this wall of containers, rusted from one end to the other, over which Beirut hovered, obstinate in its hatred, buried alive in the hate-filled soil of the Near East, you could see painted the names of seaports from around the world: Singapore, Yokohama, Pusan, Dubai, Buenos Aires, the names of the great open sea, Rimbaud's ocean run off with the sun, and the world's languages, like Baudelaire's invitation to the voyage. This was the only time in your life that you actually heard bullets whistling by just above your head, indeed, whistling by, or buzzing past like mechanical wasps, drills looking for a skull, yours personally, just like the beginning of *Journey to the End of Night*. Not pleasant, but Nessim, so gutless in the past, had become curiously phlegmatic, so you had not dared to rush for shelter while he was walking along calmly, hands in pockets, smoking his Bensons (maybe they were Murattis). That phlegm was the approach of death. Trees had torn up the macadam, the city was returning to the vegetal state. You tried to find these places, but in vain. You saw buildings so gutted, gaping wide and melted down like candle wax that you would have thought they were grottos, with stalactites made from scraps of cement. Fig trees, acacias grew in parts of empty lots, goats munched there as well, in the midst of the din caused by automobiles. Yet all around was the new, the flashy emerging from the ruins. Life, also known as cash, was cleaning house in grand fashion. Here as well you move from the time of History to the reign of Money. Have to admit it's less bloody. Your last walk with Nessim, a few months before his defenestration, had been buried in the foundations of a new city, between marina and shopping mall; the walk was now in the domain of archeology. It was just like the walk you had taken one night, zigzagging somewhat, downhill from the neighborhood called Achrafieh, in the company of an old retired army doctor who had known the lieutenant. This guy had been at Cassino; he had done amputations without anesthesia just below the walls of the Benedictine monastery. He remembered the lieutenant perfectly. Damn! This was the first time you met someone, besides your mother, who could talk to you about your father! You had drunk arak with him by candlelight in a cellar where you wound up after Nessim had left you (you'd never see him again). The retired army doctor was a helluva drunk; lacking any real convictions, he used to kill the boredom and sadness of aging by volunteering his services to a humanitarian organization where some of the section chiefs were former comrades in The Cause. According to the doctor, everyone was dealing, as best he could, with the idea of his own death, if he happened to be in Beirut; it was not so much out of love for suffering humanity, which only got what it was looking for, such was his view after several of shots of arak; as for you, in whom alcohol always provoked an exaggerated sentimentality, sometimes bellicose and sometimes fraternal (but the fact that the retired army doctor was a fellow soldier with the lieutenant encouraged a slobbering indulgence), you shared completely his way of seeing things. *Za zdarovié.* You really liked drinking in Russian. By chance it was in Beirut in 1941 that the army doctor had met the lieutenant just off the boat from equatorial Africa, after having sailed up the Congo and come down the Nile in a dugout canoe, or something like that. According to the doctor, he did not go unnoticed, one day claiming to have entered the casino on a motorcycle, and on another occasion, dumping a bucket of ice water on the head of a Vichy officer in an eatery on the coast road. Quarrelsome, arrogant, the kind of guy who would wear white silk scarfs and flirt openly with the wives of the bourgeois and the well-to-do. You wondered whether you could find the casino now in this pile of rubble that Beirut had become. The city where the lieutenant did his young stud routine and where Nessim was your guide had disappeared in the ruins, which had in turn disappeared today under the cement of reconstruction. The few character traits the retired army officer could dredge out of his memory did not necessarily paint a very appealing portrait; let's say he was a bit of a show-off like Romain Gary, but you liked what you thought you understood about each guy's immodesty: a scorn, certainly born of despair, for the gutlessness of their fellow citizens. In the name of what principle should men who freely risked their hides to cleanse, as much as possible, their country's humiliation have to act like good little boys? Those who made it a duty to die so that, without laughing, people could attach to the noun "French," the adjective "free," had perhaps the right to behave as insolently as those "revolutionary" writers who had never imagined fighting against Nazism, and who had found the Southern Zone or the cocktail parties in New York "free" enough for themselves. I don't know if I can make you understand one or two things about our lives, you tell Thirteen's daughter, but we were full of distrust for intellectuals, for their love of oratory, their penchant for comfortable heroism, with large bathrooms and ocean view . . . with breakfast in bed . . . Rightly or wrongly, this distrust, this conviction that there was no such thing as a courageous intellectual, pushed us to become apprentice barbarians. We were very young, very radical, pretty ignorant also, to tell the truth. But not blasé, not inoculated against disgust, and that's what counts. To tell the truth, as far as humanity goes, the retired army doctor wanted to have nothing to do with it. He found the idea burdensome. That didn't prevent his treating humans as much as he could, because they always found a way of winding up in the emergency ward. Both of you stumbled home, zigzagging through the labyrinth of a city completely black under a sky radiant in the Mediterranean night; the city was an immense, intact form (because the darkness hid the thoroughness of the destruction), yet apparently purged of all human presence, a cityscape by de Chirico of empty streets, moonbeams, a place permeated with the shadow of facades that no light pierces, windows darkened by sandbags, not a street lamp, not a car, no night-crawling drunks except us, a silence you sensed composed of thousands of agonized expectations, insomnia, held breaths, a silence occasionally broken by distant explosions, confirming the existence of hidden lives, since certain people, in this noisy way, were doing their best to eliminate others. Between the blocks of shadows from the mountains and the phosphorescent sea, this desert that you and the retired army doctor were wandering across was so strange (because it was made up of settings accustomed to attracting life, excitement, light) that it invited you, you tell Thirteen's daughter (and even if we had not been in that state of total disconnection from the self that happily accompanies drunkenness), to take leave of yourself and fly away toward the pure, cold stars so as to contemplate from on high this minuscule frenzy, this incongruous residue of humanity in a purely mineral setting: the retired army doctor and you, stumbling, staggering, zigzagging, you, drunk on arak, but also on the idea that you were walking the streets where the lieutenant had been, in the company of a guy who had shared with him the test of ultimate truth that was war. Like in a little while, when I accompany you home, you say to Thirteen's daughter, because I will accompany you, you'll be with a guy who shared picaresque metaphysical adventures with your dead father, my eternal friend. Amidst the shadows of a Paris that no longer exists. You see, the stories are not very numerous; it's inevitable that they repeat themselves.

Anyway, that's what happened to Nessim, you continue after a short silence while you examine deep inside yourself whether the vaguely Borgesian proposition you just floated makes sense or not (decision deferred): a broken body under the Murr Tower's cement scaffolding.

That afternoon, years ago, while Thirteen and you were announcing to him the great destiny reserved for him in the library of his house in the sixteenth arrondissement, his hand was trembling a bit as he raised the bourbon to his lips. Your look (trench coats, etc.), your cold determination, the brutality of the dilemma you placed him in—all that reminded him of scenes from the movies, bad guys or Resistance heroes, somewhere between *Cercle rouge* and *Armée des ombres*; it was all the same in his eyes, the explosion into his pampered life of an outlaw fraternity. For that, he could have kissed you. But at the same time his rich-kid pragmatism suggested to him there was something phony in this scene, that you were perhaps not made of the stuff of either Pierrot le Fou or Jean Moulin, and that as a result it was imprudent in the extreme to link his destiny to yours. His hand was trembling as he dropped ice cubes in the bourbon, but he accepted. He quickly grasped that his forebodings were not misplaced. To stake out Chalais's house with no problems, in order to learn his daily routine, you had decided to disguise yourselves as rich people. But your idea of the rich was about as accurate as the one that prompted the Duponts in *Tintin: Objectif Lune* to deck themselves out in Greek costumes to look like Syldavians. You'd gone to the flea market and bought yourselves a couple of white, double-breasted jackets, yellow actually, under which you slipped false guts made of kapok. With your phony moustaches and dark glasses, you looked like you were playing the role of South American waiters in a musical comedy. The basis for these grotesque disguises was the idea that a rich guy is always fat and old, or at least not young. This blindness was even more ridiculous because you had in front of your eyes a rich guy, a real one: young, thin, and bearded. As for Nessim, who knew what a rich person looked like (himself, for example), he was alarmed to see these clowns with their Cloroxed clothing set out from his house every day to go and post themselves in a stolen car in front of Chalais's door, on the rue des Marronniers (or maybe rue des Belles-Feuilles? In any case there was vegetation in the name). Given such a start, he foresaw the serious screwups to come.

3

Remember is an old Citroën-Goddess, silver-gray, a real beauty with a front that looks like a stingray and headlights that move like eyes. As is often the case, you don't remember where you parked her; you have to hunt around near the Place des Fêtes, up and down Belleville, and gradually, as you turn in circles, the yarn gets more tangled . . . Black towers against a black-eyed sky, antennas with red lights, like a ship's crows' nests. Drizzle under the orange street lamps, sheets of it falling on the city like the waves of defoliants over there, in the delta's jungle. At the top of the rue des Solitaires, you can see the pile of cement that is the Place de Fêtes, BRZAN SPÉCIALITÉS BALKINIQUES RESTAURATION RAPIDE, rue des Annelets, wait a minute, I've got a pal who lives there, rue Arthur-Rozier, trees silhouetted against the mauve sky above the long, low-tiled roof of what used to be a shop, at the corner of the Place, facing the Rainbow Eatery, lunch and dinner sixty-five francs, the gingerbread-brick public baths have a chimney that evokes a crematorium oven. Farther down, the rue de Belleville shines amid the drizzle's vapor, SANDWICHERIE FALAFEL, a pay toilet and a phone booth whose glass windows are in smithereens under a

66

vaguely African umbrella-shaped acacia; the shattered security glass brings back memories of shaved ice in a cocktail, drinking your tenth *mojito* is like racing down a snowy ski slope, but without skis, Papa Hemingway used to say (you think), staggering along in the streets of Havana. Damn, where could you have parked Remember? It seems to you it was on a street with an incline, with the front pointed upward toward the black sky, but obviously around here there's lots of streets like that. BAR LE MISTRAL BOXES AUTO À LOUER ALIMENTATION GÉNÉRALE OPTICIEN LENTILLES DE CONTACT to the right the rue du Télégraphe. Hey, what do you know, over there you had your first bourgeois apartment with Judith, bourgeois in a manner of speaking, that is: it must've had two rooms (indeed, three). It was at the end of The Cause; sick at heart, you had decided to call it curtains, to break up the group. In Germany and Italy, the story of those years ended in blood. You had enough common sense not to want that. For you guys it was just alcohol and drugs, a suicide here and there, just life itself . . . Look, now there's a little park at the corner, with games for kids, wasn't it a cemetery then? The bocci courts of the rue Télégraphe, a sandy area that once again reminds you of an African village, and then a quarry-stone wall; hey, there's the cemetery, with a double water reservoir in cement dwarfing it. On the wall, a plaque: it's here that Claude Chappe, in 1793, performed "the experiment with the aerial telegraph which announced the victory of the armies of the Republic." Oh, soldiers of the Year II . . . The great forge was roaring then. Another small plaque: "This altitude marker situated at 128 meters 508 above average sea level is the highest in Paris." Just imagine the tides coming and going about one hundred and thirty meters below . . . History going and coming too . . . in order to finally withdraw . . . definitive ebb tide . . . Now good-bye to the great waves, it's low tide forever, for us, the dirty pleasures of shell fishing, the dangers of quicksand . . . Have you read *Quatre-vingt-treize*? you ask Thirteen's daughter. You make fast her right arm, and unfurl above her the beat-up vault of an umbrella. No. It would have amazed me if you had. Yet you should.

Victor Hugo, he probably seems like an old fogey to you, but we grew up on his stories. OK, you want to know where Judith and I lived, a hundred and twenty something meters above that damn thing for measuring sea level. The Saint-Fargeau municipal child care, and then suddenly that star of streets, Borrégo-Devéria-Télégraphe, with the La Poste brasserie and the bar-tobacco place, Le Cantal; yeah, suddenly you're sure, it was to the left, in one of those peeling projects with a flight of steps to climb to the lobby and the bull's blood elevator door . . . with drawings of pricks and cunts scratched all over it . . . Right across from the bistro, Le Mercure . . . You used to go bet the tierce at Le Cantal hoping to hit the number . . . and especially it was the idleness, the despair (you have to call things by their name) that brought you there, to knock back glasses of Côtes du Rhône . . . to constantly play pinball . . . all alone. Judith, less worthless than you, or more pragmatic, was working. Where? You don't remember. You had tried the truck-driving business, driving for the sleaziest company at the Tolbiac train station, got fired real fast. These were also the years when Thirteen started to get stoned. You were no longer revolutionaries, but there was no way you would have wanted to quietly become bourgeois. You no longer believed in anything, you no longer had any goals. Suddenly, the lieutenant's story seemed very close to you, his absurd death in a rach in the Mekong Delta, torn to pieces by his own shell, on official duty, duty on behalf of rubber planters, after having been a hero in the antifascist war. Fair is foul, and foul is fair, the witches in *Macbeth* were right. Funny, right now in front of Le Mercure two cars from that era are parked, an AMI 8 and a Simca 1000. The Simca with white sides and a roof rack.

An old silver-gray goddess, that should still stand out at a distance. A historic car . . . The retired general Chalais had one like that, a pearl-gray Pallas . . . When he parked and got out in the rue des Marroniers (others say it was the rue des Belles-Feuilles) you stuck the barrel of the machine gun in his gut, an old Sten gun from the war, with a horizontal cartridge clip, one of the guns that the Allies, toward the end of the war, were parachuting in by the thousands. André had gotten it for you, the Sten, along with a supply of sticks of dynamite that came from the mine, ripped off from the foreman. You were real careful with explosives. You had read somewhere (not in Proust for sure) that dynamite didn't go off on impact. That was nitroglycerin, the wages of fear. So what: it was one thing to have read that, another to be sure. Particularly since you had also read in the same book (a Swiss Army manual, in fact) that dynamite became dangerous, unstable, when it got too old and started to "sweat." Just go see if the stick of dynamite, examined in light of this knowledge, doesn't sweat a little, just a little? It doesn't seem to, but then, looking more closely . . . maybe a slight dew? Shit, who can tell if it's just your own perspiration that . . . ¡Cabrón! For sure, in *For Whom the Bell Tolls* Robert Jordan made less of a fuss. This stock of dynamite, minus several sticks used to blow up an extreme right-wing newspaper, you went to bury it with Thirteen in the Fontainebleau forest, when it was all over, you tell his daughter. That was our farewell to Fontainebleau, sort of. His mother lived around there. Your grandmother, by the way. A head case, as you know. He had thought it would be a good time to go see his "old lady," as he used to say. She was chief of a sect vaguely inspired by Reich, Wilhelm, not the Kaiser. God was sexual energy, the orgon, OK, I forget the doctrine, but obviously, with premises like that, you can imagine how one rose to sainthood; she lived in a stylish bungalow, with a well-tended lawn and garden statuary, on the edge of the forest, in the company of the high priest, a gigantic former cop. The place was not far from Nessim's father's house, but completely different. But you must know that? No, she never went there. The popess of the orgon burnt all her bridges after her son's death. You're now back at the rue du Télégraphe again, where it continues to rain but luckily you have an umbrella with stars on its dark blue dome, Altair, Vega, the Swan's Cross, Cassiopeia, and God knows what else; so you are walking with Thirteen's daughter under a little domestic vault, celestial to boot, you've almost forgotten you're looking for the old goddess, Remember, you're a pre-Copernican sun in the center of the cosmos, although you're staggering a bit, but not too much, on the arm of the daughter of your eternal friend; you feel her breast (and the serpents hissing around your head) against your arm, and since you are a pedant you go for the super-famous phrase about the moral order and the starry sky, but to tell the truth, it isn't the moral order that's on your mind. In the orange glow of the street lamps, the drizzle creates undulating beaded sheets that make you think of Agent Orange raining down on the Mekong Delta, burning the leaves under which are hiding serpents, monkeys, giant butterflies, iridescent birds, and Viet Cong guerrillas. The popess offers you and her son an apéritif, and then the former cop gets it into his head to try your car. It was another Citroën; you really used to like that make, a BX. He was thinking about buying one, and since he had the chance to get behind the wheel and try it . . . You guys were really pissed. You had to give him the keys or it would've seemed fishy. The dynamite was still in the trunk. Apparently it wasn't sweating, but if he had an accident, imagine what could happen? You were the ones sweating. The ex-cop took off for a ride in the neighborhood at the controls of a bomb on wheels; you stayed to drink some Cinzano (maybe it was Campari) in the company of the popess, waiting for an enormous explosion to put an end to this nonsense, and then suddenly Thirteen started laughing like hell, I mean like hell; he had a case of the epileptic giggles, falling off his chair in the process, at once you followed suit, by the time the ex-cop got back, quite happy with the way the car held the road, turning the keys around his index finger, you were both hiccupping on the ground, his mother between you, choking with indignation, her dog — obviously she had a dog — her crummy little poodle (unless it was a boxer) was racing from one of you to the other, frantic, yapping, slobbering; for sure he thought he was dealing with his own kind. And that's how you left, bent over in two, tears streaming down your faces, mumbling excuses that only made you roar all the more with laughter, leaving the mother beside herself and the ex-cop confused. And you were still shaking with laughter when you buried the dynamite in a clearing, noting landmarks for the day when, like Jean Valjean digging up his little box in the clearing at Montfermeil, you would return to get it, because you did not doubt for a minute that "the bad days would end," like it said in the song of the Commune, and that there would be revenge. And now, you say to Thirteen's daughter, your father's dead, and I am an old man of letters, the Revolution is decidedly not on the horizon, and somewhere under the humus in the forest of Fontainebleau (where? Naturally I've completely forgotten, maybe not in the Fontainebleau woods, but at Sénart, for instance), somewhere below the earth in a forest located in Île de France, there are several dozen sticks of dynamite that will explode when a bulldozer unearths them, at the end of the twenty-first century or later, when the trees are cut down to build a new town, an airport or internment camp, or who knows what, I have no idea; and nobody will know what these explosives were doing there, someone will say they come from the Second World War, or the Third, if between now and then there is one. André's the guy who will have given them to us, one day in the second half of the twentieth century, stolen from a foreman at the Houillères du Nord, or Pas du Calais, along with a Sten machine gun, coming from a bunch parachuted by the English in 1944. I was saying to you, you tell Thirteen's daughter, I was saying to you . . . what was I saying to you? You survey yet again the Place des Fêtes, so unworthy of its name as it is, CLINIQUE VÉTÉRINAIRE COLLÈGE GUILLAUME-BUDÉ PRESSING BLAN- CHISSERIE SANTA MONICA PIZZA GRILLADERIE, ESPACE VIDÉO, you cross a sort of forum, extraordinarily seedy, with a sharp pyramid in opalescent plexiglass and a gangway mounted on skinny cast-iron paws in the middle of thick, ugly, disjointed cement blocks scattered randomly around and smelling of piss; some hooded guys are walking a pit bull, what was I saying? you ask Thirteen's daughter between the posts for the outdoor market in the Place des Fêtes, this sinister Place des Fêtes wet and sloping like a beach in Hell. Right. I was saying that

I had stuck the barrel of that Sten in the stomach of the retired general Chalais as he was getting out of his Goddess-Pallas. I had to push him inside the van Fichaoui-called-Julot was driving. And Thirteen, what was he doing? his daughter wants to know. He was covering the general with a U.S. military rifle, a sort of blunderbuss we also got from André (unless it might have been Walter). But earlier, on another occasion, Thirteen had almost screwed up the operation. How? She feared weakness, cowardice . . . No, not at all, don't worry, it was nothing serious. He just had this terrible need to piss while we were waiting in the van, and that had made us laugh so hard that we had to get out of there. We thought that Chalais was going to put up quite a fight, so I pushed him with the Sten as hard as I could toward the open door of the van. Just the opposite happened; he almost fainted, meanwhile, my momentum knocked him down, and we both fell, me on top of him. Just imagine! In the process the Sten's cartridge clip released (this machine gun was an antique) and spurted into the gutter, the spring, the trigger, all that stuff clanging around in the gutter. No bullets, since we did not load our guns to avoid fuckups, "screwups," as one says, exactly in this type of situation. ok, you get the picture. Me and the general stretched out on the pavement, and the weaponry scattered around . . . Fine, we grabbed the hardware and the general, more dead than alive, by the overcoat collar, and all aboard. Fichaoui took off like a shot, a first-class driver was he. It's funny, you tell Thirteen's daughter, but when I think back to burying the dynamite, it was a little like burying our youth. A magic ceremony. All those explosives at the bottom of a hole; it's like images, fetishes of what we had been, but would no longer be. Maybe that's why we were shaken by a nervous laughter, Thirteen and me. Several years later he's dead, in what year? Right, 1980. Six years later he would be the one underground, in that tiny cemetery in that godforsaken place where his mother, the popess of the orgon, lived, on the edge of the Fontainebleau or Sénart forest, not far from the dynamite's long-forgotten tomb. And that day back then, how old were you, six? No, four, of course, four, and anyway you seemed not to understand what was going on; you were doing somersaults on the cemetery grass, laughing your head off, you must have already decided to react happily. Despite her sorrow, your mother was terribly embarrassed, didn't know what to do. I remember the dazzling autumn leaves in the forest, fountains of fire spurting forth in the shade, just like the day when, together with Thirteen, we buried the dynamite.

At present you're leaning against the metro's granular wall, across from the flower shop; the stairs go down between two chrome handrails, between two white ceramic-tiled walls, beyond the station gate, shadows devour everything. Hell's staircase, you think. It's not for nothing that the flower shop up top, across the street, is called "The Garden of Eden." "Birth, marriages, funerals," says the sign. The whole cycle . . . "Eden," that's also the name of the hotel in Berlin where the Freikorps arrested Rosa Luxemburg. They're all down there, you think, at the bottom of the stairs. Rosa Luxemburg and Che, with his bloody face, and the militia man at the gates of Cordova, and the high school kid, Gilles, drifting in the Seine like Rosa in the Landwehrkanal, or like Tamara, known as Tania, in the Rio Grande (or was it the Rio Masicuri?), face turned toward the sky like the king in Apollinaire's poem, the philosopher who strangled his wife, and Nessim, the lieutenant, and Thirteen and Jean d'Audincourt, and all the rest. And like the man who was the hero of your youth (and remains the hero of your old age), Jean Cavaillès. Philosopher, logician, saboteur, arrested, writing a book on epistemology in prison, freed, again the dynamite, again arrested, tortured, executed in 1944. Buried in the Arras citadel under the marker, "Unknown Number Five." A learned, quietly heroic figure who prevented us from believing absolutely what I said a little while ago, you say to Thirteen's daughter, that there weren't any courageous intellectuals. And someone who holds us back from really becoming barbarians. This guy, you have to understand, didn't create a discussion group at Saint Germain des Prés, the way Sartre did, no, he wasn't that sly; he used to blow up bridges, he got into the Kriegsmarine base at Lorient, dressed like a worker. Philosopher, logician, saboteur. A hero, for sure, and this word does not stick in my throat one bit, just the opposite. He comes from the depths of human history, from the moment when man freed himself from the gods. One of the degrading, exasperating things of today is the rejection of heroism. That means we don't believe in humanity. A hero is nothing other than a fully human being, the opposite of mercantile man. And the opposite of the abject creature before God. A humanity without heroism is good for God and the marketplace; certain contemporary little cynics don't seem to get that. Keep talking: I sense Thirteen's daughter wants to dump me. Anyway, that's what I do: I keep chattering. The stairs go down into the darkness between the two chrome railings, across from the Garden of Eden and the sinister chimney on the public baths. There's a bar, over there, and below it, you say to Thirteen's daughter, the bar for the dead. A hundred and twenty something meters below, just above average sea level. They're all there, seated in the darkness, in rattan chairs. The black water slaps on the shore. They don't say anything, or rather, yes, they murmur, some sing very softly. Old songs of war and hope, liberty guides our steps, in the ranks all eyes are fixed on our flag, let Boudienny lead us by the old roads, "El Ejercito del Ebro" at present they sing that like lullabies. Don't you hear them? She doesn't hear anything. Sure you do: just listen. What are you, deaf? You drag her down the stairs, between the white ceramic tiles, right to the gate. Listen. Come up from the mine, come down from the hills, comrades. But us poor silk workers haven't got shirts. Bella ciao. *Dong-fan-ang hong, tai-yan-ang sheng* . . . Oh, no, for pity's sake, not that! Not "The Red East"! André's down there too at the Black Water Bar. The guy who slipped us the dynamite and the Sten. A real prole, rough-cut version, a miner, resistance fighter with a northern accent you could cut with a saw, not a head case like Lucien, nor an informer like Gustave. A comrade of the celebrated Charlie Debarge, a guy whose courage was legendary, the organizer of "Armed Work" in the mines, killed in

1942, gun in hand. Now that, that impressed us, and it still impresses me. Silicosis got André, his enormous body could scarcely breathe; he died asphyxiated like a fish brought up from the depths of the earth. It was really crummy weather when he checked out, the only thing he had in common with Mme Pompadour. The snow was really coming down and melting on the slag heaps, mud all over the place. It was between Roubaix and the Belgian border, the area where *Germinal* takes place; you and Thirteen had fled through those parts after the General Chalais affair, little brick courtyards, beet fields, massive slate bell towers, barges decked out with the owner's laundry, flower beds of cobblestone once graced by bicycle racers, rusted pithead frames whose wheels were still turning, the Flanders of mist and slag that the highways were just beginning to rip apart. André's funeral procession was making its way toward the cemetery under a downpour of melting snow, through a neighborhood of small courtyards that the philanthropic owners of the Houillères plant had decorated, in Zola's time, with exotic names, doubtless assuming it would be nicer to asphyxiate in the rue Panama or be a widow in the rue du Détroit-de-Magellan. Behind André's hearse, fists raised, waving faded red flags that seemed to have been cut out of old curtains, trotted retirees from the mines, former members of the Communist Resistance, bocci players and pigeon fanciers, or lark breeders, and you were of the generation that was beginning to laugh at these symbols, but they could still make you cry. Amédée (pale, ensconced in a long, dark overcoat) was already a famous journalist, Gideon (whose down jacket made him look like a dot on an *i*) was a rabbi at Montluçon, you (duffle coat) a man of letters, Foster (overcoat, woolen gloves) was aspiring to die a prefect. Thirteen had already been pushing up daisies for several years.

Leaning against the wall of the metro Place des Fêtes, between the descent into hell and the Garden of Eden, under the umbrella's starry sky and the rain trickling from the mauve sky, you remember it was in the rue de la Terre-de-Feu (or was it the rue du Rio-de-la-Plata?)

that Roger the Belgian made his theatrical entrance, unshaven, fists dug into the pockets of an old parka stained with grease and fuel oil, barely making out the world through a myopic's thick lenses, one of which was cracked as if it had been hit with a .22 bullet, but to tell the truth, it was simply because one day, in the heat of a political discussion, Rolge (his nickname) had abruptly torn his glasses off (so much had the quibbling of his social-democratic interlocutors pushed him to the limit) and by mistake bashed them against a Pilsen mug. Given his history and bizarre appearance, Rolge was probably the most sought-after guy by all the different political police between Amsterdam and Paris, even farther than that, most likely; all he needed to do was to show up someplace and a flashing light would go on at the local police station, but he never moved about without extraordinary precautions, jumping from moving trams, buying a train ticket for Knokke when he intended to go to Paris, getting settled in a movie house and then leaving fifteen minutes later, going the wrong way through one way streets in his old 4L; and that's how he did it, showing up the day of André's funeral, like a spy in a movie comedy, having crossed the border through workers' gardens, slinking through the muddy snow, winking furiously at everyone through the busted portholes perched on his nose; he was showing he didn't want to be recognized, under no circumstances should anyone shake his hand. You know, that reminds me of a guy, you say to Thirteen's daughter leaning against hell's wall; you have to imagine that he still lives in hiding today, at the beginning of the twenty-first century because he thinks in the past he did some important, extraordinarily illegal things. Denis, that's his name. Denis Masseclous. We explain to him that even if he had killed someone—which is not of course the case, the worst thing he did was to take part in some tract distributions that got a little rough—even in that case the statute of limitations would have gone into effect long ago; and, well, he just shakes his head and looks at us with pity, he knows that what he did was infinitely more serious than that, a simple murder, and besides, bourgeois justice . . . Have we so forgotten our

Marxist principles that we now trust bourgeois justice? No, it's not like that; "they" are always on his traces. Ours as well, and besides "they" are just waiting for the right moment to haul us in. If we are currently so castrated that we are just waiting around to be grabbed, well, that's our business. But as for him, "they" will never get him. He looks at us with commiseration. He lives under false names, changes his address twice a year, gets his mail at friends' places, and survives through translations and shitty little jobs. Damn it, Denis, what in fact did you do that was so serious? was our annoyed response. He looks at us with a knowing air: we are perfectly aware of what he did. Or, even if we don't know, he's not fool enough to tell us. He has apparently dug an immense mine that goes right to the heart of the old world, but if we're not in on it he's not about to draw us a map. Lest we do something with it . . . I think, you say to Thirteen's daughter, he's quite happy like that: he's exchanged a slightly complicated present for a fabulous past that spills over on the present and makes it grandiose. That's how he deals with time. I bumped into him, a month ago, at the bar in a bistro at Odéon, and he pretended not to recognize me. What, you don't recognize me? I shouted. Denis Masseclous! I shouted his name on purpose. The asshole was terrified; he literally ran away.

The first time you met Rolge, he indicated with his chin a building on a broad Brussels avenue. (He was at the wheel of his 4L—unless it was a R6? In any case a mini, no Aston Martin.) Quietly he said, "NATO's going to blow tonight." With the professional tone of a guide indicating to tourists in a bus: "NATO, constructed in 1950 in the pure International Style." With a smug little smile at the corners of his lips, on the order of "you see the incredible sources of information I have?" but nothing more. In an era when nothing seemed impossible, you'd still been a little amazed, but you didn't let on; you neither acted surprised nor asked indiscreet questions. Naturally, nothing happened that night; the Third World War had hung fire. Roger the Belgian was like that: talkative, boastful, dangerous, yet effective all the same for certain things. He liked to help, without worrying too much about the nature of the job. In his soul he was a baggage carrier who didn't ask what was in the bags. Or rather he knew perfectly well, but he left it to others, the recipients, to deal with the consequences. He had begun his prodigious career at fourteen as a Resistance courier. "A ragamuffin," as he used to say, employing an old, almost forgotten word. Arrested, tortured, deported, he had managed, thanks to a bombardment, to escape from the train taking him to Dachau and crossed Germany on foot in the snow and fire of the 1944–45 winter. In Moscow, twenty years old, he was taught to make false papers, and he had shaken Comrade Stalin's hand. He'd preserved a bad photo of this event cut out from *Komsomolskaïa Pravda*, as well as his talent as a forger and a vodka drinker, willingly offering these services to others. This double specialty almost cost him his life one evening in 1960, when, after getting a little loaded, he forged, for an illegal from the National Liberation Front, a technically irreproachable Swedish passport in the name of Sigbjorn Wilderness (or maybe . . . anyway, a name like that), height 1.86 meters, blond hair, blue eyes; the Algerian brothers-in-arms, who were scarcely known for their sense of humor, must have had a hard time holding themselves back from slitting his throat. "They were nice about it," he recalled, "I only had to pay a fine. A big fine." At the time, Rolge was earning a living making handbags in the chic neighborhoods of Brussels, and by painting fake Delvaux and Magrittes, painters who made metaphysics available to the middle class and whose commercial value was climbing as a result. To save his skin he painted and sold, at very high prices, two canvases by Magritte, ironically catalogued under the idiotic titles *A Little of the Soul of Bandits* and *The Memoirs of a Saint*. Rolge also claimed that, while working as a pickpocket, he had by chance, on the Avenue Louise (on other occasions he would say the Place de Brouckère), swiped the wallet of a middle-class woman who was Henri Michaux's mother. You couldn't help liking Roger the Belgian, poetic to the core, an anachronism, an aging player on the margins of history. However, too much exposure to the underside of the world revolution, or whatever was left of it, had made him skeptical, and even a little cynical. Doubtless he was no longer a believer in all the movements, but, over time, they had become his livelihood, or in any case his calling card. The way Bloch made much of his association with the Guermantes, Roger boasted of his relations with the Black Panthers, the IRA, the ETA, the Tupamaros, the Montoneros, the Zengakuren, the Weathermen, and other groups that mingled nicely an aspiration to sanctity with a taste for assassination. He used to speak to you about Eldridge or Ulrike like they were old bar buddies. That annoyed and disturbed you, but it also impressed you. If you believed him, in 1965 he had been Che's driver in the ex–Belgian Congo, and maybe it was true, who knows? Guevara's escapade in Africa had been such a farce . . . "I was his chess partner, he was nuts about chess, all the rage that the amateurism and corruption of the Congolese evoked in him came out in that game. His obsession was to play with his back to the chessboard; he'd announce his move, I would change the piece, would tell him my move, he could visualize in his head all the positions, I'd never seen anything like that. Most of all, I handled his sex life. People offered him women right and left, at the entrance of each village above Lake Tanganyika, he used to tell me, in those smoky bars in Mouscrons or Tournai where we sometimes met to plan dirty deals, "magnificent virgins, dark and shiny like vinyl records, breasts like bomb shells, and not in the least frightened, on the contrary, very happy to be served up to the great, white revolutionary. Except that Ernesto was puritan as hell, and asthmatic to boot, as you know: so I got to screw them in his place, for the future of the African revolution, of course; refusing these girls would have been a grave insult, and the village would have turned against us. We already didn't have much support . . ." But the chiefs, I asked him, weren't they annoyed to see you deflower their Iphigenias instead of Che? "Not at all, because they thought I was the great Cuban leader, not that uptight bearded guy, sweaty and panting, whom they called 'Tatu,' 'Three' in Swahili and who couldn't even speak Belgian." Rolge had also become a little bawdy

79

with the passage of time and the disillusionment; he let it be known that he would easily exchange a delivery of plastic explosives to Athens hidden in the doors of a Volkswagen ("the most bomb-friendly of all cars. You can jam thirty kilos in each door") for a night with a young muse of the resistance to the colonels. But you couldn't help liking a guy who had crossed Nazi Germany on foot, shaken Stalin's hand, and slept with cheerleaders destined for El Commandante. In his way this old dirt bag was History, and History was in your eyes the great book where all was written, past, present and future, the compendium of traditions and prophecies.

It was like Demetrios; he was another one you could not help liking and respecting. As a young guy in occupied Greece, he had been a partisan, a member of a group directed by an Englishman from the SAS. When the Germans caught him, they put a helmet on his head, with screws on each side that the interrogator slowly tightened. He became blind in this vise. Liberated in 1943 by the Communist partisans from the ELAS, he couldn't fight anymore, so he sang for the comrades in the bivouacs. That seems a little too Homeric to be true, but it is true. Sometimes life imitates art. During the first civil war, after the liberation, he was captured and tortured again, this time by the royalists whose instructor was the same SAS officer who commanded his first partisan group; I hope you are following, you say to Thirteen's daughter. Later, Demetrios became a sailor, a radio operator on a cargo ship; he was blind, not deaf. One day in 1947, his boat was underway from Port Said to Marseille, he got a message ordering the ship to reroute for Piraeus. He didn't transmit it to the captain. He knew what was going on. The second civil war had just started, and the crew was a pile of reds, sailors like those on the *Aurore*: the government wanted to throw all of them into a dungeon, if not into a mass grave. At Marseille, the dockers who were members of the Communist union went on strike so he and his comrades could get political asylum. That was a few months before the lieutenant died in a rach on the Mekong Delta, on the other side of the world, torn to pieces by his own mortar shell. Nothing in common, except it was the beginning of the Cold War. The lieutenant and Demetrios, in different parts of the earth, found themselves on opposite sides in this war. They had been on the same side against fascism. A little later a transport would dock in the port of Marseille, carrying along with those of others the lieutenant's coffin, draped with the French flag. You could not have even been a year old. The blind guy couldn't see the shipping office's boat clear the piers, but he probably would have heard the siren. Like all blind people he was sensitive to noises, especially to port sounds since he had passed part of his life among them. Later he would open a restaurant at Estaque. Much later, maybe twenty years later, somebody (you don't remember who) would give you his address, telling you that he could help you. You would eat paella in this restaurant with Thirteen (the cook was a former Spanish Communist, just like Demetrios's wife). The sea was exploding against the walls. On a perch was a parrot whose horrible noises vaguely resembled the hymn of the Spanish Republic's fifth regiment, the right arm of the Stalinists in Madrid: *con Lister y Compesino, no hay miliciano con miedo.* Anyway, all parrots are Stalinists, you tell Thirteen's daughter: Stalinists or fascists, you didn't know that? That beak, those claws, those clippers, that inexpressive eye . . . That pleasure in screaming, that passion for imitation . . . OK, at the time, naturally, I did not think exactly like that. I thought the parrot was right to holler the hymn of the *quinto regimiento*. I fell into a certain complicity with him, as if we were both members of the same secret society. ¡*No pasarán*! Later, when we were paying, we asked to see Demetrios. We're friends of . . . of I no longer know whom. Let's say Comrade Schmoll. But maybe it was Fichaoui, that's what I think now. And that's how we started working together. Demetrios is the gutsiest guy I ever knew. His house was always open to friends wanted by the police; at night he used to cart our stuff through the police roadblocks in his car driven by the Spanish rooster, secure in the respect that the cops were supposed to have for his license plate, wwv, wounded war veteran. Still, if he got caught, it would be extradition, and at the time Greece was under the dictatorship of the colonels. Demetrios used to risk his life hiding our buddies or transporting our junk because he thought we were more truly his sons than his own son. I remember one evening in the upper part of Marseille, you say to Thirteen's daughter, the city below was sliding in shadows and sudden lights toward the sea where cargo ships were drawing their wakes; I don't know where it was exactly, but I remember a mauve wall of ocean streaked with white lines and the landscape framed by a pergola with trellised vines. And I remember thinking with sadness that this beauty was lost forever on Demetrios. This remembrance surprises me because, as I told you, we were not sensitive to beauty. However, I'm sure of this: the serenity emanating from that glowing twilight where the ships' wakes flew about like feathers. Detaching itself from the twilight, Demetrios's face stood out, etched with cares, telling me that his son disappointed him, betrayed him; the idiot was only interested in cars and girls, he was not like us. And it appeared to me that night that to be part of this "us" was at once an honor and an injustice. Demetrios's suffering, which the twilight's glow and his own dead eyes invested with a tragic mask—old Oedipus's mask—I found this suffering both beautiful and crazy. He made me, he decreed me his son—forget the fact that my father "met death," as one says, before he met me, replacing a son who, I sensed this despite my striking narrow-mindedness, was only asking to live his life, with the inalienable right that everyone has to be a fool. That Demetrios, this martyr blinded by the fascists, this poet-partisan who sang in the bivouacs, that this man made me a member of his family filled me with pride, yet also fear (*Domine, non sum dignus* . . .), and finally embarrassment, since it seemed to me it was at the price of a usurpation. I was thinking these things watching the wakes cut through the sea. The cargo and passenger ship from the shipping office that had brought back to France the lieutenant's coffin—I had learned about it many years later when "I was old enough to know these things"—was called the *Galapagos*. Maybe I was old enough to know these things, ten or twelve, you tell Thirteen's daughter, but still, the name made me laugh, "Galapagos"; I was terribly embarrassed and ashamed by this desire to laugh. I used to repeat it in my mind for hours on end, "Galapagos, Galapagos," trying to cry, or at least stay serious; yet a mighty impressive laughter rose up in me, and ended up exploding. Fortunately, my mother did not know the reason for my hilarity; she thought I had fragile nerves, my brain was all screwed up. Maybe she was right.

I was remembering those things as well that night, watching the wakes streak the ocean. *Galapagos* made me recall this incredible story that Jan Valtin tells—he was a German, a Communist sailor, officer in the Comintern. The Comintern? Go look it up in an encyclopedia. You'll find it on the Internet. He ships out on an old steamer from Hamburg (maybe it was Bremen) in the spring of 1919. The Spartacists had been crushed, Rosa Luxemburg killed and her body thrown in the Landwehrkanal. The boat is loaded with revolutionaries, radicals of every stripe, fierce men fleeing the firing squad and the Freikorps. Once at sea, they seize power. The officers barricade themselves on the bridge and in the boiler rooms, a savage freedom reigns over the rest of the ship. Whorehouses, gambling, tattoo artists, meetings, political assassinations. The future put to a vote. Some people imagine becoming pirates in the South Atlantic, but the motion that carries is to establish a Soviet republic in the Galapagos islands, and then ask the Bolsheviks for arms and women. Funny, that makes me think of a wacky idea we had, with Thirteen, when everything was over. I told you, we were in despair. Relieved, but in despair. We had no intention of becoming middle class, but we sensed that was going to be difficult. So, while downing beers in the Belgian bar at Port-Royal—that was our hangout—we got this idea for a burlesque farewell to the Revolution. The whole nine yards once again, from start to finish, but accelerated. A bunch of us would disembark from a motorboat on a little British island, Sark. This island is a toy; ten of us could take it over within an hour, even with plastic pistols. We'd control everything. There's some sort of king we'd depose and imprison. Day One: we'd raise the red flag on the country house like the one Dumas's lady had, proclaim the Soviets were in power, the complete collectivization of the land, whiskey and beer for everyone. On Day Two we'd close the borders, ban the sale of newspapers, decree industrialization to the limit, and economic planning, open up the port (the size of a tennis court) to the Cuban navy (the Russians struck us as too soft, too reasonable, and the Chinese too far away). On Day Three, we'd invent a conspiracy and arrest a couple of us. You could be Trotsky-Lin Piao, I told Thirteen, and would try to escape in a rubber dinghy. He preferred that it be me. We'd see. The trial would begin on Day Four. A farmhouse would be requisitioned for a work camp. We didn't plan any further, because we figured the patience of the British Crown would have its limits, and that our guerilla theater wouldn't last more than four days. We would defend ourselves heroically with cap guns and water pistols. Yet one more time the Revolution would be assassinated. What happened? Thirteen's daughter wants to know. Nothing. We didn't have the balls to do it. Demetrios was wrong to make me his son. We were paper tigers too. The German boat? Ah, that's even more like a novel. In the middle of the Panama Canal, half of the prospective citizens of *Galapagos* wanted to get off. The light, the Americas, nature . . . They were all German proles, don't forget; they were coming from a burned-out, ruined world, a world littered with millions of dead bodies, which stank of death, just imagine . . . the parrots, the butterflies . . . all that virginity. They couldn't resist. They jumped overboard with their clothes in bundles, and swam to the bank of the canal. Then they started marching through the jungle, completely lost and soaking wet. They get to a railway line, undress and put their cloths on the tracks to dry. A locomotive passes by and there they are: one with a pair of shorts, another with pants with one leg, a third guy with a shirt cut in a diagonal, all of them more or less buck naked. They got arrested like that. I thought of this story that evening back then, watching the wakes slice the ocean's blue wall, framed by the trellises, that twilight beauty that could not calm Demetrios's tormented soul. That face of a statue with empty eyes . . . *Galapagos*! *Galapagos*! The name didn't make me laugh any more, but the story of the naked Spartacists in the jungles of Panama sure did. I was afraid of not being a son worthy of him. And that's what's happened, since I became in the end a sort of man of letters, hard to imagine . . . One of the things that made me realize how much time had passed, changed, and me with it, is that when I returned to Marseille, after all was over, I didn't dare go see him. I knew he wouldn't understand, that he would scorn my new scepticism, this man who had never stopped believing in the world revolution. He used to spend his nights, after the restaurant closed, twisting the dial on an ancient radio, listening to the revolutionary stations throughout the whole world. This is Radio Beijing. Then the first notes of "The Red East": *Dong-fan-ang hong, tai-yan-ang sheng.* "The East is red, the sun is rising." One night in Harry's American Bar, Angelo, dead drunk, had begun to intone these sorts of Chinese squeaks; it was the evening of an incredible France-Wales rugby match, the joint was packed with rugby players screaming out manly Celtic chants, and things almost got out of hand. Comrades! Comrades! Compañeros! President Mao is the world's greatest halfback in the scrum. Indeed! The Long March: you retreat to better advance! Just like rugby! Get out of here . . . The musclemen in club ties didn't see things that way. Obviously this is not the sort of reminiscence you could tell Demetrios about. *Zhong-guo chu le yi ge Mao Zedong* . . . The Soviet revisionists tried to raise a big stone, only to have it drop on their feet. The revisionists are paper tigers like the U.S. imperialists. The Political Bureau of the glorious Chinese Communist Party, under the direction of the great Comrade Mao Zedong, exposes the conspiracy of the antiparty clique led by the archtraitor, Lin Piao . . . This is Radio Vietnam coming to you from Hanoi. Arise the wretched of the earth. The heroic members of the Haiphong antiaircraft squads, driven by the desire to defend the Socialist Party against the imperialist aggressors, have shot down . . .

Two divisions of the puppet government annihilated in Quang Tri province . . . This is Radio Havana. A conspiracy of exiled counter-revolutionaries in the pay of . . . This is A Voz da Liberdade. Contra o fascismo. Contra a guerra colonial. Por um Portugal livre e democrático. This is Radio Magallanes. In response to the sabotage perpetrated by the truck drivers' bosses, President Salvador Allende decrees martial law . . . I was thinking of Demetrios's old face, suffering yet radiant, eyelids shut, clenched like fists over dead eyes; I remembered his face strained by the effort to pick up on the radio the floods of revolutionary rhetoric coming from Africa, Asia, or South America, despite the crackle of interference that so deformed and corrupted the messages that they seemed to come from Mars. How could you expect me to see him again? I was sure he would reject me like a bad son, and that I would not be able to make him understand that a bad son is still a son. I didn't want to witness the pain I would cause him, because I knew what it would cost him to disinherit me morally. I felt I had exploited a weakness in this courageous man, as if I had profited from his blindness to steal something from him. And that was not even considering that he would have asked me about Thirteen: and what do you think I could have said to him? That he was dead, sure, but how did he die? Do you think for a minute I could explain your father's death to him? A long time later, several years ago, I went back to Estaque; enough time had passed, I was ready to see Demetrios again, I looked for his restaurant, but where it once was, there was now a branch office of a bank.

Well, there you are, there both of you are, her, tugged along by you under the umbrella's portable celestial vault, once again on the rue des Solitaires, the downward slope this time, toward the west RUE DE PALESTINE CHIRURGIE DENTAIRE AVOCATS À LA COUR ÉCOLE COMMUNALE DE JEUNES FILLES PHARMACIE DU VILLAGE BOUCHERIE BELLEVILLOISE RED PARTRIDGE RESTAURANT, what do you think that is: a meeting place for Communist partridges? Sorry, couldn't help it. The River Jordan church that looks like a little cathedral.

Damn, where's that car? For some reason Nino Ferrer's song, "'Ave ya seen Mirza?" pops into your head. It seemed to me I had parked it over there. OK, between the River Jordan and Télégraphe, let's say . . . in the street on the incline . . . Take a good look, Marie, you've good eyes, you know you really have good eyes . . . A Citroën-Goddess, you know what she's like: weighted toward her backside, ready to surge forward, her shark's mug pushed forward, exactly, a hybrid animal, amphibious, half-sphinx, half-shark, with large turning eyes. Metallic gray, a piece of silverware. You'll recognize her from far away. Also a good car, let's note in passing, for discreetly transporting explosive substances: quite curved those doors, maybe even more than on the Beetle. Rolge used to live in a bungalow in the Brussels' suburbs, in Waterloo. That address pissed me off, because I've always been something of a Bonapartist, even then. I didn't brag about that; it wasn't done in our world. The people of Paris, at the time when they were revolutionaries, had nevertheless bowed their heads from the barricades when the funeral procession of one of the emperor's generals, Lamarque, went by; that's when Gavroche gets killed. But who remembered that? The Bonapartists had filled this area with barricades in 1832, you tell Thirteen's daughter, stretching your arms toward the rue des Pyrénées and the rue des Rigoles, including everything that extends in the direction of Ménilmontant. A dump made of millstone and crammed from top to bottom with old newspapers, such were Rolge's haunts; you used to ease about the place moving your shoulders around carefully like you were in an excavation pit, an ancient tomb whose walls consisted of yellow piles of newsprint and reviews, millions of pages, millions of decaying lead lines, the whole history of Europe and the world since the liberation, Rolge's treasure. And it really was a tomb, an immense common grave that these walls of paper reinforced. In these collections, gnawed by the mice from Waterloo, you saw for the first time briefly mentioned in a 1948 *Le Monde*, the death of the lieutenant in a rach on the Mekong Delta, not far from My Tho, "in the course of an engagement between the expeditionary corps and Viet Minh rebels."

You had, through repeated inquiries, tried to find the year when, only recently born, you had been marked, like a carcass in a butcher shop, by death's violet ink. By death and the irony of fate. Spartacists naked in the jungle, Resistance heroes killed by their own shells on the canals of a river in the Far East . . . thus history shifted its course. That filler in *Le Monde* moved the lieutenant's death from the level of a domestic tragedy to that of a *res gestae*, an event inscribed in *The Great Book of Life*, almost an exploit: so much is the written word (not the image) linked with history. *Galapagos! Galapagos!* A little later, when you were preparing yourself to grab the retired general, Chalais, CEO of Atofram, you would give him the code name "Galapagos," because the first two letters were the abbreviation of his rank, General in the Army, yet also for reasons that came from the past. You had never dared to reveal your discovery to Roger the Belgian, any more than, several months later, chain-smoking with Thirteen in the stolen white Citroën, you would dare to tell him what the name My Tho you heard on the radio awakened in your memory. At the time Rolge was housing a deserter from the American army, a big black guy who had fled Vietnam with the help of a pacifist whore from Frankfurt. Black Jack, that was his name, used to sleep on a pile of *Humanités* from the great years, between *Esprit* and *Temps modernes*. When you arrived at Rolge's place at twilight, you would see in the distance his shack at the end of the road, on the plains of Waterloo, a sort of sorceress's chalet, lit up like a famous Magritte painting, this time a real one.

Once I bombed Vietnam, you tell Thirteen's daughter. No kidding. I remember the blinking lattices of Haiphong coming up on the horizon to meet me; the weed I had smoked and the piercing whistle of the eight jet engines had driven me half-crazy, already five hours of this crap since taking off from Guam, Bob Dylan softly humming in the darkness of the night "I seem to wander, to wander," how does it go, "unhappily, restlessly?" as the instrument lights glimmered sadly in the cockpit of the B-52. The B-52, one of the rare things that hasn't changed since then. I've already said that? So what. I'll say it again. When it's done, it's just begun. We're going around the city, around the past, around the black sun of melancholy. The anemone and the columbine. The city of the Great Gibbet and the Wheel. Just touched up a bit, the B-52, and on we go nonstop from *Dr. Strangelove* to Desert Storm. This plane allows us the illusion that we have not aged; it dates from the time when we drove "two horsepower" cars with antiwar stickers on the windows. A bomber that flatters your ego in all the right ways, so to speak. I was in the cockpit putting away a not-very-cold Budweiser when the Congs turned off their fucking lights, as if we had to see what we were bombing; the Paulina L (I had christened the plane with the name of the woman I was in love with) was still about forty nautical miles from the objective, Haiphong harbor. I remember the bombs making fountains of flames spurt upward in the blue distant night so far below, columns of flame in the sepia night, under wings the color of razor blades, Pauline L's long, flexible wings, so slender, shapely, and troubling, shimmering in the moonlight as at 35,000 feet I began the flawless turn that would take us back, badly shaven and a little stoned, exalted, fatigued, and not very proud of ourselves deep inside, toward dawn over the Indian Ocean, and the beach bars complete with whores. Down there, "the heroic combatants of the Haiphong antiaircraft emplacements" were firing their missiles wildly; you could see their vapor trails twist around each other in pursuit of decoys. Goddamn gooks . . . You'd have thought it was the crummiest Memorial Day fireworks display in the crummiest town in the Midwest. "I'm beginning to doubt, I'm alone and there is no one by my side." It was the Fête des Loges, near Saint Germain, and I was getting myself off on a pinball machine, Bombing Vietnam, which was obviously more appealing, more ironic than The Indianapolis Death Ring, or kayaking down Niagara Falls. Pauline L was still with me at the time, expressions of juvenile enthusiasm and impenetrable bourgeois boredom passed successively across her oval face. Dressed all in black, as she always was. On other occasions I called her Leïla, my little night. She was . . . it's funny, yeah, she was your age, you tell Thirteen's daughter. I loved her and I think she loved me too, yet it was like we were no longer in love. I loved her quite simply because she was beautiful, but also because in my eyes she was the inexperience I was happy to instruct, maybe that was presumptuous, maybe despotic. I loved her because she incarnated the youthfulness that, without realizing it, I was beginning to lose; she was a sort of radiant future that was different from the other, abstract, grandiose one; I could make her in my own image, but I'd lose this radiant future more suddenly than the other one. And finally I loved her because it was destiny, because it was supposed to be that way, it was the fate awaiting me. Irrational? Sure. Why were you no longer in love, Thirteen's daughter wants to know. Well . . . We lived in worlds that were quite different. You see, I was still in this comedy . . . this comedy of shadows . . . this mythology, if you want. I was an aging ghost. Maybe she lived more in the real, I don't know. Somewhere else, in any case, far away. So you see, I'm really not very clever, I didn't always understand.

Now you are going down the rue de Belleville, as if dragged along by the slope in the road ZHEN FA TRAITEUR ASIATIQUE, BOUCHERIE DES BUTTES TRIPERIE CINQ À SEC BIJOUTERIE PLAQUÉ OR ET ARGENT MASSIF FROMAGER, FRUITIER the sky is somewhere between yellow and rose, you'd think it was a slice of foie gras, beads of rain on the cars' windshields, BISTRO BAR À VIN BUFFET FROID LA CAGNOTTE AUX JARDINS DE FRANCE LE DRAGON GOURMAND TRAITEUR ASIATIQUE CARLA CHAUSSURES BOUCHERIE HALLAL, a male torso in plaster with white-and-black striped underpants in a pharmacy reminds you, although quite confusedly, of a distorted passage in Nabokov, isn't it *The Gift*? anyway, you don't remember, and besides you didn't understand much, that you do remember, CONSOMMEZ DE LA TRIPERIE FAITES DES ECONOMIES. Jean d'Audincourt used to live with Clara over there. Over there, but I couldn't say exactly where. Besides, the building's probably been destroyed. It was one of those small, two- or three-storied places with chipped wooden shutters facing the street and sloping zinc roofs, might have already been there at the time of the Commune. You can't imagine how different the city was then, you say to Thirteen's daughter. Especially around here, we were in the middle of the nineteenth century, the proximity of ghosts was almost palpable. Small houses, tiny gardens, workshops, staircases, paved alleys. This old Paris fitted perfectly into our interior landscapes. At the time of President Pomp they began razing the past. President Pomp had edited an anthology of French poetry, but he hated the past. Death to history . . . Get rich, these slogans won out. To tell the truth, Pomp, that fat coal merchant, was quite modern. Man, did we hate him . . . For DeGaulle before him, we tried to feel the same, but for the less stupid among us, it was hard. Still, as for Pomp . . . Jean and Clara lived around here before leaving for Sochaux. I told you that for us Sochaux was like Siberia. The immense factory, Peugeot's own militia, the cold, the middle of nowhere . . . Not a large city in sight. And the nights . . . If they were sent, it was to "reeducate" them, as we used to say. Just imagine . . . They sometimes went to the movies, and they had refused to sell an upright piano on which Clara occasionally played an étude of Chopin; they kept in their pathetic library, in full view, Lacan's *Écrits* (behind which they had a revolver). All that was very heretical. Even Jean's nonchalance was suspicious, his strange appearance like the comic book character, Gaston Lagaffe; in those days even with your body you were supposed to bear witness to the purity of your working-class beliefs. Jean was rather a Girondin, that was obvious just looking at him. He had a camel's placid, disdainful look. So they had been sent there to get recycled. Much later, in fact several years ago, after Jean's death, Clara told me about the "temporary settlement" at Audincourt, you say to Thirteen's daughter. The dishtowels swarming with cockroaches. Returning from work early in the morning, finding the dirty dishes left over from the "comrades'" dinner, the smell of tomato sauce and stale tobacco, cigarette butts stuck in the congealed tomato sauce, ink from the Vietnamese Roneo on the sheets, empty beer cans in the linen chest. Wanting to weep and sleep, but no, no time. There's a "meet" right away, in their joint. The Yugo neighbor that his wife leaves for five minutes, then returns to find hanged in front of the turned-on TV. This total sadness, along with the fog that permeates everything. The severity of those they thought were friends. And me too, I was a bastard to them, you tell Thirteen's daughter. In fact, the most lavish thing Jean d'Audincourt had in his life was his funeral. Because he's dead too. Death is the child of *La Bohème*. The funeral was at Saint-Louis-des-Invalides: worthy of a marshal of France. There were, under flags riddled with bullets and by the winter sun, generals, prefects, priests, former leftists (that had become a calling card). Everyone retired. I was there, a former leftist in retirement, taking part in the religious and military funeral for my friend, Jean d'Audincourt, a former leftist stone cold dead. Makes you want to laugh. Oak leaves, Republican symbols, sabers and aspergilla, Légions d'honneur and red stars, all under the flags of kings and emperors. All this patriotic pomp was because Jean's father had been part of the liberation. Those elderly, decorated gentlemen, those ladies whose furs recalled the age of cave dwellers, some of them must have been in their day young people as courageous as we were, and for better reasons.

Some time ago, on a June 18th, one of these heroic old guys had invited Danton to lay a wreath, alongside him, at the memorial of the Mont-Valérien Resistance. A loud-mouthed Christian leftist, Dedieu was famous for having "liberated Chartres Cathedral." What exactly did that mean "to liberate Chartres Cathedral?" you wondered (even during an era where, in terms of questions, you asked the strict minimum). Had the Germans entrenched themselves in the confessionals? Were they firing v2s from the crypt? Chartres Cathedral was not exactly the Alcazar in Toledo . . . For sure, eggheads are hopeless. Even when they were courageous, there was still a touch of the charlatan. Hemingway "liberating" the Ritz, for example. At the time Danton was wanted by

the cops for encouraging the murder of police officers. This too was
a bit overstated, but the minister of the interior, the infamous Saint-
Marcellin, was no opponent of rhetorical overkill, and it had to be
said that Danton, as the director of your newspaper, had authorized
articles whose delicacy was not immediately apparent. Dedieu, Chartres's
liberator, had only invited Danton to get on President Pomp's nerves,
since he had declared that, as far as he was concerned, the Resistance
fighters were getting on his nerves. His wreath of red roses in his arms,
Danton was representing you, the leftist leftovers, the "rioters," the
so-called new resistance. Because, listen, you tell Thirteen's daughter,
pomposity, and even turgidness, we were also capable of that, sadly.
Everything happened as planned; the cops jumped on Danton at the
moment he was laying the wreath, he struggled a bit, causing scarlet
petals to fly, and flashbulbs to pop, billy clubs, decorations and eye-
glasses flew about, along with truly historic insults; they got him on
the ground and handcuffed him, all to the sound of the "Chant des
partisans," this made for a grand scandal that pleased the old Resistance guys even more than us. Danton was arrested, of course, but in
any case, that would have happened sooner or later, so it was worth it
that it happened like that. At Saint-Louis-des-Invalides, I was looking
at these old Resistance guys. Dedieu was no longer with us; he died
ten years before and I was wondering what would the lieutenant have
looked like. He would have been there, I'm sure. Some people there
certainly would have known him. All the same, these decorated types
were not there to bury the son, rather the father, as a precaution. In fact
he would not last much longer. His son had given him the privilege
of attending his own funeral. And Jean d'Audincourt himself, what
did he have to do with all this? Booming organs, Brahms's *German
Requiem*, the bleating of contemporary Catholic eloquence. Beneath
the fashionable underside of French history, radiant in gilded dust and
beams of blue sun, was our aging little band, Amédée, quite at ease
with these fossils, Angelo, Fichaoui, Judith, Chloe, Foster, and even
Gideon: wrapped up in a Prisunic jacket, goateed, his baldness topped

with a kippa, with that odd Neanderthal way of standing, slightly bent, hands on hips—there was Gideon, hardly prehistoric at all, but rather deeply anchored in history. Distant as always, but affectionate, a clumsy, almost timid affection, which was the mark of the years, the distances that separated us. Gideon was a rabbi at Montluçon; he never had much of a sense of humor and his new career was not about to change that, yet he wanted to show by some friendly gesture that he had not completely forgotten us, that scraps of old ties between us still remained. Only his whole being was so alien to familiarity that all he knew of its manifestations were stereotypes he probably picked up from the *Tintins* of his childhood (because, strange as it seemed, there must have been a period in his distant past when he had read *Tintin*). "How's it going, old man," is how he greeted me, along with an impressive slap between the shoulder blades in the square in front of the church, where we were standing around freezing, after the *Ite missa est* waiting for the coffin: a pure puff pastry, varnished, carved, crested with trimming and pine cones that made it look like a carriage or a birthday cake, and I was ashamed because I felt a little responsible.

Jean d'Audincourt had become a journalist, a great reporter as we say, and then at Sarajevo a shell killed him. You went there to bring his body back, that was the least you could do. You had caught a ride on a plane chartered by a French relief service, an Iliouchine 76 (or maybe an Antonov?), piloted by Ukrainians. This fat Duralumin whale was filled with air freight pallets of sardines in oil that were jammed in the luggage racks, this whole pile of tinned goods slid to the back during takeoff from Ancona. When we were over the Adriatic, the Ukrainians in khaki overalls started strolling around the cabin, a can of beer in hand, studying with a perplexed yet fatalistic eye these shaky piles of sardines; if they fell down they risked not just crushing the benighted Western assholes including yourself (the Ukrainians would have had no problem with that), they could in fact bring down the airplane. *Niévazmojna, niévazmojna,* nothing can be done: your vague memory of

Russian allowed you to catch that. Nevertheless, risk estimations varying enormously in accordance with national traditions, basically, they didn't give a shit. They had been chartered by the French to haul some eats to Muslims; already that did not fill them with much enthusiasm. If they had it their way, they told the Western do-gooders, they would have preferred drinking Slivovitz with the Serbs who, in a few minutes, would be firing wildly at them from the hills around fucking Sarajevo; this would force their cargo plane to attempt a dive that was not suited to the plane's age or girth. The thousands of sardine cans were destined for the enclave at Srebrenica, but by the time they got there, the besieged would no longer have the leisure to lick their lips with the stuff while thanking the European Union and its flag with the Marian stars, they would already have been sleeping in quick lime for a week. The mess in the Iliouchine's cockpit, with light coming in through a latticed glass window, like the ones you see in World War II bombers, seemed more like a student's room than what one would expect in a military plane (even a Slavic one): pinups taped to the walls, guys sprawled left and right, putting out their butts in Coke or beer cans that rolled right under the pilots' feet as the fat flying scrapheap tilted back and forth. A tangle of electric wires snaked along the perforated sheet-metal floor (some of the wires joined together by adhesive), uniting the navigator with the rest of the world by means of an anachronistic Morse ticker. Fine. At least these guys must know their job, despite appearances. This obese flying machine, seemingly suspended in flight by its wing, began its dive toward Sarajevo. Through the windows you could see the tattered clouds speeding by. A siren started to scream, and since you had already clocked thousands of flight hours in the movies or in books (you had also bombed the gas factories at Teruel at the controls of one of the Spanish squadron's Potez's), you knew it was the blackout alert. The Ukrainian in chief hit the flaps and the gas; the jet engines kicked in sharply, this sort of glass-encased veranda that was the Iliouchine raced at excessive speed into the clouds, pushed from behind by the mass of sardines in oil, which, tilted now toward the front, threatened to come down like an avalanche and pitch all of you, Ukrainian mercenaries and Western do-gooders, helter-skelter into the Bosnian sky amidst the splendor of gilded-brown sardine cans. A second siren started to shriek, you'd been awaiting it for awhile, your head sunk into your shoulders, it indicated the proximity of the ground. There was a guy decked out with headphones crouched up front in the bow windows; the angle of the dive inexorably squeezed him up against the glass, he seemed to be there to hit the break at the last moment. While he was waiting he kept making the sign of the cross, backwards, the orthodox way. The gray sky was clearing, exploding, melting around the plane's glass nose, which seemed to be diving almost vertically. Suddenly, in the blink of an eye, the ruins of Dobrinja jumped out at you from the yellowish soup, the landing strip's lights, bathed in fog, toward which the plane, shuddering, righted its course. At the end of the field, feet in the mud, hands in the pockets of his battle dress, sinister, Angelo was waiting for you.

At the time he took himself for Malraux, which really wasn't the worst way to get old. You explain to Thirteen's daughter that this guy, whose lack of common sense was proverbial, who had demolished a car trying to get a driver's license and never tried again, who once had called an electrician to change a light bulb, who confused a beer glass with an ashtray—and almost conversely—who lost his keys and credit cards, forgot the code to his apartment building, put his dirty laundry in a dishwasher—the list goes on forever—anyway, this guy had been capable of starting from bits and pieces a kind of cultural center in Sarajevo; that was enough to make you laugh and in fact it made him laugh. No doubt he was here, in this sinister valley, looking for something that had proven irretrievable: our past. Not an intimate, self-absorbed past, but rather a past that had made him communicate, from time to time, in dreams, with great and violent stories that now are almost forgotten: the Garibaldists, the International Brigades. Yes, that's it, you say to Thirteen's daughter: the heart, the beauty of the Revolution is internationalism, the history of revolutions is filled with horrors and even disgraceful behavior, and they're not the same thing, but this idea, internationalism, there's nothing more grand, more sublime, in the entire history of humanity. You see that I don't mince words. An internationalist, a real one I mean, the pure sort, someone who makes a free choice to risk everything with no ulterior motives, an Orwell in Catalonia or a Malraux at Alcaca de Henares (right, him, no matter what the prissy and the tight-assed say), he represents the portion of humanity that stands up to the gods, which we used to call and what I still call, heroism. And if your past was lost forever, you were thinking as the armored vehicle was taking Angelo and you to the PTT building, the headquarters of the UN, it wasn't just that it was the past, something only literature perhaps (even then, you weren't so sure) could allow you to visit on the sly; it was because at the time when it was the present, it was essentially a pipe dream. Already for some time we'd given up measuring ourselves against the gods. What sometimes made Angelo appear ridiculous in the eyes of the world was that he was less trivial, less cynical, than the others. He was "out of fashion," because he didn't think that History, in other words, the chronicle of ghosts, the lesson of phantoms, was out of fashion. Or believing it was, recognizing this truth, he "didn't want to accept it," as they say. In the armored vehicle, painted the UN's virginal white, and lumbering on enormous tires toward the PTT building, Angelo was devotedly contemplating a famous photo of his hero, a cigarette dangling from his lips, lock of hair falling over his forehead, a print of the Gisele Freund photo for which he had paid a fortune, had framed on the quays, and which he had you bring to him to decorate his cultural center. He was holding this icon on his knees, one hand grasping it securely (the other clamped to the handle hanging from the roof of the armored tin can), the cigarette stuck to the corner of the lips (his, not the ones in the photo), his eyes brimming with emotion; you sensed transubstantiation in the air, and that pissed you off a little. That pissed me off a little, you tell Thirteen's daughter. I have nothing against Malraux, just the opposite, I was a student and already a leftist when he gave the funeral oration for Jean Moulin, he was De Gaulle's minister, but I still went to hear him in the rue Soufflot, in the freezing wind; it doesn't embarrass me one bit to say that I wept listening to him that evening, in fact, I want you to know that I choke up again every time that I hear that speech or even read it. I'm happy as hell to have gone to hear Malraux that night and not François Mite at the Bastille in May '81. So you get it. Still, the way Angelo imitated the essence of his hero, right up to the misty eyes, that pissed me off a little. Ever since he had fainted in Mao's presence, he never lost his inclination toward adulation. To piss him off a little in his turn, I tell him that he could just as well take a photo of Che Guevara, the famous one where he's lying dead, eyes wide open, like the Christ of Mantegna, surrounded by military assassins, on the hospital gurney (or maybe it was in a school?) at Vallegrande; couldn't he? Don't shit me, he hollers over the roar of the motor; you know it amounts to the same thing. Except that Guevara didn't leave behind any literary works. Not easy to discuss in these contraptions where soundproofing isn't exactly one of their selling points. And since you can't see the road, the sharp turns and the speed changes take you by surprise. At certain moments, imprisoned in this blind casing, you have the impression that the guy driving, who vaguely sees something, has decided to scale the ruins of a building; at other moments and for unknown reasons, he stops and all you hear is the gasping of the powerful engine, or the crackling of the radio. Of course, it's against the rules to smoke, but Angelo has become so popular with the French soldiers, a real mascot, that he's allowed to break all the security rules; he fills up the overheated air in the armored vehicle with smoke, shakes his ashes on bandoleers of bullets, then he opens a hatchway and exposes his racoonish puss (he's got dark circles under his eyes and protruding ears) to potential snipers.

When I went to Sarajevo to recover Jean d'Audincourt's body, Thirteen had been dead for a long time, you say to his daughter, believe me, I know that; but I tell you all the same because your father was part of us, part of this multiple being, somewhere between a hero and a clown, that's called "us." I'm aware of that, she responds, you've already told me. Yeah, but wait a minute: since part of this sort of sponge called "us" is still alive, your father is still partly alive through us, ok? And the opposite as well: we're a little dead through him, Jean d'Audincourt, and Nessim. It's a kind of fraternal and romantic insurance company, in life and in death, you get it? We lump everything together and share what we have. Some help us die—a tough training, but a necessary one—others help the dead survive. This is real communism: each according to his needs. No kidding. In fact your father, you know where he got his nickname, don't you? No? Really? Your mother never . . .? ok, she detests that era, but . . . all the same, I thought . . . Alright, it comes from a photo, one of the very rare pictures from those days. To tell the truth, I don't have any others. The photo was taken during the summer of 1969; just think, seven years before you were born, even then we were no longer taking pictures, it reminded us too much of bourgeois vacations, cute cousins at the beach . . . Rohmer's films . . . most of all, it wasn't worth making the police's work easier. I really don't know why, the summer, the enthusiasm, a couple of drinks at the bar in the train station . . . we took a picture of the group getting off the train from Paris to Guingamp. Guingamp or Saint-Brieuc, but I'm pretty sure it was Guingamp. We were going to work with the peasants, toughen ourselves up, learn to stick our hands in shit while at the same time winning the countryside over to the Revolution; we called that "long marches," in reference, of course, to the Chinese Long March, we were making a big deal out of nothing, it was at once ridiculous and beautiful, or at least that's how it seems to me today. In this photo, taken in front of the station, you'd think we were a football team, there was Jean who was not yet d'Audincourt, with his look of a slightly disgusted camel, or maybe a llama, dark glasses, tweed jacket with the lapels turned up to his ears; Clara, short, frizzy hair, turned-up nose, Indian dress; Angelo, curly hair, stocky, protruding ears, leopard-skin vest; Fichaoui-called-Julot, small, hands in pockets, just turning gray; Judith in frayed jeans, wide mouth, hair pulled back behind her neck. Pompabière, ruddy complexion, drooping moustache, looking in a surprising way like Flaubert; Momo Lock-Eater, shaven head, looking like a cunning convict; as for me, I looked a little like a musketeer, with a large schnoz and shoulder-length hair; Victoire and Laurent were hanging on one another's neck (I wasn't even next to Judith), both of them sporting dazzling smiles; Danton is already a little chubby, he's laughing and you can see his upper incisors are separated, I believe that's called "teeth of happiness?" That makes eleven. Delacroix's the twelfth. Good-looking kid, show-off, black leather jacket, white scarf around the neck, a certain swagger . . . Delacroix had it good from the beginning, like Nessim he was born into a family of industrial barons, and that was a bit too obvious. Yet strangely enough, when it was all over he didn't go back to the rich, he remained something of a rogue, a gossip columnist for a scandal sheet, moving back and forth between cops and thugs, a friend of both, a little anyway, I don't really know, but if that was the case, I'm sure it was for the sport of it, the excitement of being a double agent, just for fun, nothing else. A lover of half-ass schemes and bungled con games, a dispenser of incredible tips. There was a time when I saw him again for a little while, I needed his connections to get a gun because bizarrely, stupidly, I hadn't kept a single piece from those days. What did I want it for? Nothing special. But the time will come when I'll have to make an end of it, Marie. Before cancer or cirrhosis takes over. Or mad cow disease (the human form, as they say) . . . I felt very distant from him, the pimps, the dealers, the drugs, the slot machines, their bloody little wars among themselves, their secret pacts; this is not my world, not even my imaginary one, I don't read whodunits, and yet I saw him in all his squalor, stinking Nikes and a backpack, fifty years old, still with a hint of beauty, but worn out, puffy, not stylish at all, writing his gloomy stories for a rag that no bourgeois, no egghead would read; rightly or wrongly he imagined he was threatened by a gang, his phone tapped by a branch of the police, speaking in a coded language on the phone, paranoid and a pathological liar for sure; I told myself there was something in his absurd existence—and notably just that, perhaps: the fact of being absurd—which was linked to our earlier lives, at the time of The Cause. Yet the fact remains it was Delacroix in a black leather jacket, white scarf around the neck, number twelve in the photo. The number of apostles, I'll have you note (assuming that means something to you, the twelve apostles, you say to Thirteen's daughter, and once again a little pink triangle shoots out of her mouth) that inspired Alexander Blok's famous poem. "The snow flies about, the wind wanders around / Twelve men set out on patrol / Black rifle slings / In the city lights," you know it? No. Me neither at your age; Blok, "The Twelve," that wouldn't have meant a thing to me, absolutely nothing. Sorry, I'm a pain in the ass from time to time. Often, even: ok. Of course, it was pure chance we were twelve that day, getting off the train at Guingamp (or Saint-Brieuc) to go preach in the countryside. The same Paris-Brest train that long black locomotives with red-sun wheels pulled toward the Emerald Coast when I was a boy. We were twelve, or rather thirteen. Twelve posing and Chris, the thirteenth, taking the picture. He was excluded from the snapshot in order to "immortalize" the others, so to speak; yet also excluded as if a superstition had forbidden us to appear as thirteen in a group photo, the only picture that attests, as far as I know, to the fact that all these people, living and dead, did indeed meet up together one day. A July day in 1969, at the Guingamp or Saint-Brieuc station, on the Côtes du Nord, now called the Côtes d'Armor. Thus your father's nickname, which he never got rid of: Number Thirteen, then simply, Thirteen, because otherwise it was too long. The invisible one, the guy not in the photo. I'm telling you this, the story of the origin of your father's name, but I had completely forgotten it. I no longer recall if I got a print, most likely, but I destroyed it quickly. We distrusted pictures, like I told you. So I really no longer knew why he was called that. At Sarajevo, I remembered. In Jean d'Audincourt's wallet, which was given to me, was this photo. Yellowed by age and blackened by blood. The photographic salts had turned; on the darkened photo we looked like a group of gold-plated ghosts.

OK, Che wasn't a writer, you scream at Angelo over the groaning of the motor, but all the same, the last sentence in his notebook, "seventeen of us set out under a very small moon," was as perfectly beautiful as Rimbaud's last sentence, "tell me at what time I am to be transported on board," don't you think so? This sentence, addressed to the director at Marseilles of the shipping line, the company, let it be said in passing, that would repatriate the lieutenant's body sixty years later. In the end, isn't literature a pile of variations, more or less profound, more or less truthful, on the theme of the last sentence, a way of beating about the bush, around the point where words stop? Angelo let loose a shower of sparks into the snowy air, pulled down the hatch, cleared his throat, and shot back at you, sarcastic in his turn, OK, tell me, this sort of vast reflection . . . you're the one playing Malraux now. . . . At the PTT building, a palace of drafts that was the terminus for the military lines, everybody, right up to the high-ranking officers, raised their hands to their temples to salute Angelo. The general, a show-off hussar who prided himself on being an intellectual, bolted down the stairs four at a time to shake his hand politely. Gigantic guys with shaven heads and childlike demeanors came to tell him about exploits that their modesty did not prevent from being half-imaginary. With a twenty-millimeter cannon they'd demolished the bathroom where a sniper was holed up, stuff like that. Erect in the oily snow that had been soiled by the exhausts and churned up by the tracked vehicles, Angelo accepted their compliments with affability, swapping a cigarette here, exchanging a witticism there. He was flattered by the friendliness offered by these minor officials whom, in spite of everything, he forced himself to see as soldiers of Year II of the French Revolution. This friendship freed him (as earlier the camaraderie of the proles had) from the shame of being an egghead, he also accepted their boasting without comment. As for them, when they saw he swallowed their stories whole, they wound up believing them a little, and considered themselves vaguely heroic. Everybody was happy. You, stamping around in the snow, embarrassed by the portrait of Malraux he had saddled you with again, you wanted to hit him over the head with it, you found this jerk reviewing his troops laughable. But you tell Thirteen's daughter that, at the same time, the dream this nut was pursuing was perhaps the one that the most troubled, the most demanding of our generation, born right after the war, had sought after without realizing it (or rather knowing it, but refusing to admit it) in the bizarre figures of the Revolution: the dream that June 1940 and all that came after, never took place, that all the filthy crap we're ashamed of without being responsible for, the stuff that was like a pus, a gangrene in the body of France, never happened. With all his credulity, his martial fantasies, Angelo was trying to convince himself that he had rediscovered, beyond the infamy of the century, a strong and generous country, where "La Marseillaise" was once again a war cry for liberty. Me too, I would have liked to believe that, you say to Thirteen's daughter, but you feel quite removed from that nostalgia (she probably finds it "uncool"). That would have been easier to take. You know, life and all that.

And suddenly, almost at the angle of the rue des Pyrénées in front of a fence marking off a construction site that an Arab walks along with a plastic sack on his head for protection against the rain — there it is: shining, dilapidated, beaded with water, seated like a big dog on its hindquarters, the Goddess Remember. Wow . . . Finally, there you are, Thirteen's daughter and you, seated on the old black leather. Can you smell it?, you ask Thirteen's daughter. The scent of time. Scent of time, spray of heather. We'll never see each other again on earth. Apollinaire once again. Maybe the most beautiful poem in French. That makes me think . . . it's odd, but it wasn't too long ago that I ran into Pauline L in a train. She was seventy years old and seated on the other side of the corridor. It was her for sure, with the little turned-up nose, the deep-set eyes, the beautiful cheekbones, such delicate wrinkled features. Pauline had exquisitely fine and fragile skin; it was already that way when she was twenty-five and left me, a fold on each side of her mouth, like two parentheses; I think she made an effort not to laugh too much because it accentuated them (she managed that quite well). Over there, on the other side of the corridor, against the countryside rolling by in reverse, was this elderly lady with a white beret on gray wavy hair, a maroon sweater and beige plaid skirt, unbelievably, Pauline L, quite creased by time, yet still pretty, but creased by time. I asked myself how old she must be? Seventy, seventy-five without a doubt. So it must be . . . somewhere beyond 2030. How long have I been dead? Does she still sometimes think of me? Does she regret not having made a life with me? And the guy facing her, the old fellow asleep and dribbling on his tie, is he the bastard she left me for? At one point she got up to go to the bar car, I'm not sure you'll be able to understand, you tell Thirteen's daughter, but I followed her and it so happened that the train began to sway and she almost fell, I caught her, I'm not sure you will be able to understand, but I was on the verge of tears, just holding in my arms the woman I had loved so deeply, the woman on whose account I had suffered so much, just from not holding her in my arms, fifty years after she left me, and a very long time after my death . . . She said to me, thank you, sir, with a lovely, weary smile, she didn't seem to recognize me, but that's normal since I've been dead for a long time. You see, my little night, I wanted to say to her, you waited too long, now I'm dead, it's cruel . . . We'll never see each other again on earth. And remember I'm waiting for you. Turn the key. The majestic noise of the Goddess's motor, the suspension that rises with the clicking sounds, the steering wheel attached to a cylinder that trembles with little sighs, all that voluptuous . . . the headlight eyes that turn and spin . . . The white streetlights against the mauve sky, Simon Bolivar takes off on a plunging angle toward the Buttes Chaumont. MEGA KEBAB SPÉCIALITÉS TURQUES, a McDonald's on the corner with a big black guy in a track suit sweeping the white tiles, what time is it, two in the morning, the rue de Belleville descends sharply between the water flowing from the gutters toward the dark lake of Paris FRAICHEUR DE VIE COSMÉTIQUES PARFUMS, creamy facades rush by under a blue-green slate sky studded with pink lamp-posts; over there, the Eiffel Tower's great rusted crest with the beam of blue light coming from afar, from my childhood, illuminating the nether regions, the petticoats of the clouds, a burst of thirty seconds, the sky seemed like marble. Jean d'Audincourt's coffin awaited you, lying on a trestle in the PTT building courtyard. Wrapped in a large jute bag, and given how the fabric stood strangely on end, appearing to cover not a coffin, but a carriage, you had begun to suspect that the fucking undertakers had stuck Jean in the most expensive model, the most grotesquely ornate one, a piece of kitsch that must have been in the showroom since the Austro-Hungarian empire and that not even the most nouveau riche apparatchiks of the former Yugoslavia had wanted. War's always good for something. You had to move fast, the Ukrainians from the Iliouchine (or the Antonov) were in a hurry to leave. Some sort of agent from the consulate in a Prince of Wales suit and a bow tie was crouching between two armored transports; he had had someone boil a pot of wax on a camping stove in order to seal the packages with the arms of the Republic. A little snow was falling. Malraux in a trench coat, butt hanging from the lips, was leaning against an enormous tire from an armored vehicle. Malraux, the real one, not the portrait, the commander of the Alsace-Lorraine Brigade, the tall, skinny guy with all those tics, sheepskin jacket and beret, machine gun in a shoulder strap—it seems that the lieutenant had met him during the terrible winter of '44–45 while their forces occupied neighboring positions around Strasbourg, the city that the German counteroffensive was once again threatening. This legend, fueled by your mother, was that together they had organized a rabbit hunt to improve the troops' ordinary fare. Obviously, this was less prestigious than discussing Martin du Gard or *The Ramayana*, but as recollections go it was still pretty good. Hunting rabbits with a machine gun in the thickets around Erstein sparkling with frost. Your mother told that story for the millionth time in the Frégate Renault (or maybe an Onze Citroën?) driving toward the Emerald Coast. Runstedt's Tiger tanks surrounding Strasbourg. Your uncle nervously tapping his fingers on the plastic, cream-colored steering wheel. Malraux, Colonel Berger, that meant nothing to you, but you understood he was an important guy, even though a lousy rabbit hunter. Shaking too much with tics to shoot straight, according to her. You were thinking about that hunting party in the Alsatian hills while you were looking at Malraux's portrait leaning against the enormous tire of the armored transport in front of the jute sack that covered the coffin, or carriage, of Jean d'Audincourt. The consular agent was trying not to burn his long, well-cared-for fingers with the wax. Angelo was standing at attention, more or less. Later, you would be seated in the empty hold of the Iliouchine, deafened, exhausted by the jet engines' howling. Sunk down next to you on a canvas berth, burping, was a drunk Ukrainian nursing a can of beer. In front of you Jean d'Audincourt's coffin, sticking up under the jute like a cathedral wrapped by Christo, strapped in at the place where the packs of sardine tins had been piled up. In this strange funerary chapel, the name of a book that had once got the Goncourt Prize would come back to you: *The Funeral of a Sardine*. And once again, coming back to you from afar, laughter would rumble inside you, laughter in the face of death, laughter against death. *Galapagos! Galapagos!* It was, you would think, as if you were in the hold of the cargo ship that had brought back the lieutenant's body forty-seven years ago.

4

So the lieutenant's dead in a rach on the Mekong several months after your birth; that was why you knew that word, *rac* or *rach*, well before reading *The Sea World*. The word's disappeared today; no doubt it entered the language with the conquest of Cochin-China and tiptoed out after Dien Bien Phu. It left the French language quietly, the way the French left Vietnam, reduced henceforth to traces that are rarer, deader than Latin in our own country, a "veston" advertised in a tailor's window, a "Villa Les Roses" long buried under a mauve festoon of bougainvillea, a logo, "RF," barely attached to the pediment of a post office. Your lifetime was also the time necessary for your language to become an archeological rarity in this part of the world, and certainly, that was well deserved. Killed in the rac or rach Kim Son "at mile 64 of the Mekong" is what the military documents said. Yellowed sheets of paper, brittle, dog-eared, scarred by tiny tears, replete with stamps, printed in violet ink like the menus in workers' restaurants used to be or like the carcasses of animals in the butcher shop, and you were rereading them in room 501 at the Hotel Huong Duong at My Tho, forty-five years after his death. Huong Duong, you had learned, meant sunflower, heliotrope, so your return to the source was taking place under the eye of the red sun. Peeling, humid walls, a little mossy. Three beds with mosquito nets, but, having shelled out seven dollars, you get the room to yourself. At the bottom of the gangway that the rooms front, at the entrance to the canal, there were bunches of fishing boats perched, in a lopsided way, one on the other, red flags with a golden star clacking at the mast, lighted by green and white neon tubes, the boats crackling with electricity. The tiled pagoda roofs of a large colonial building stood out against the Mekong's black sky. "Amphibious Flotilla, South Indochina. Madame. I have the privilege of acquainting you with the circumstances surrounding the death of your spouse, Lieutenant R. In the morning of March 14 he had left on a mission down the river as he often did, on the PL 42 heading toward Vinh Long." What does that mean, PL? Patrol Launch, I guess. "Around nine in the morning the PL 42 had to take up a position against a large rebel force that was surrounding one of the posts held by the army. In the course of this engagement your spouse was struck in the heart by fragments of a shell that exploded on the bridge of the launch. He died instantly . . ." "Amphibious Flotilla South Indochina. Subject: loss of personnel, an officer. Dear Minister: I have the privilege of acquainting you with the circumstances surrounding the death of Lieutenant R. on March 14, 1948 at 8:15 the PL 42 leaves My Tho in the direction of Vinh Long and then Cai Be. Lieutenant R. travels with the PL 42 in order to settle some details concerning a future mission with the squadron chief in charge of the sub-sector of Cai Be. At 9:00, at mile 64 of the Mekong an intense firefight attracts the attention of the PL's commander, junior lieutenant D. He moves in the direction of the outpost in the rach Kim Son, which is being attacked by a large rebel force. He enters the rach and opens fire with the two 20 millimeter fore and aft cannons, as well as the port side 12.7 machine gun. The rebels abandon their position. To put them completely to flight and free up the parameters of the outpost, the PL 42 goes up the rach and starts firing again. In the course of the shooting a shell from the 20 millimeter aft cannon that was firing from the front of the beam explodes on the port rigging of the mast. A shower of fragments falls on the bridge, mortally wounding Lieutenant R., and the second in command, Lieutenant G. R. died instantly. The PL immediately turns back and regains My Tho in order to disembark the wounded. The second in command, G., died in the hospital at 13:45. I am including a copy of the letter that I am sending to the wife . . ." A certain sense of storytelling. Efficient. The narrative present. Some corrections (letters, numbers) in red and blue pencil on this document. A rusty vestige of a paper clip. And also this, in the left margin in black ink, circled: "filed." What's filed? The circumstances of the death? The death itself?

Things were swarming on the canals, going down toward the Mekong, sampans with prows decorated with a large vermilion eye to ward off demons, filled with portholes choked with the heads of children, laughing, toothless, skulls shaven to avoid lice, barges slapping the water with long propeller shafts, sinking under the load of unknown vegetables, and then some sort of gondolas stuffed with the same vegetables that were almost phosphorescent in the twilight; what makes them glide silently along is the movement of women standing on the poop deck wearing conical hats made of palm leaves, tossing the oar out far in front, drawing it back in a bending-arm motion right until it floats in the wake, a little like it was a net, constantly repeating this slow gesture, perfectly identical each time (oh, the brooding eternity of Asia! Such a cliché!). Petrol lanterns were lighting up with the evening, on the banks, on the boats, giving everything the faraway air of a Venetian festival. A real skinny guy in shorts and yellowish green shirt had come to talk to you, on the sampan; he remembered a couple of words in Phap, in French. He was the mayor of the delta village. I'm a poor old man, is how he introduced himself. The communists are all rich, sir, the country people are poor. He latched on to you, this skeletonlike guy, confident that, except for you and him, nobody on this tub understood Phap. My father communist, in the Resistance with the French since

1938, sir. The people from Tonkin control everything. They don't like us. The Tonkin . . . He was using the old colonial word to designate the North. "In the Tonkin men are in cages"; this refrain came back to you there, on the bridge of the sampan, in the humid wind; an old servant woman used to sing this sad song, when you were a baby, in the house on the Emerald Coast, she was born at the end of the nineteenth century, at the time of the conquest. You look deep in your memory to find other bits of this song, but no luck. A smell of earth, of rot, of wood smoke was floating in the air. Where was it, the Kim Son rach? Maybe we were just passing it? You had no idea where you were; you were now sailing in a night studded with little glimmers of light, you scrutinized the darkness, or rather the darknesses, because there was a confusion of shadows, some truly black, others the color of coffee grinds, still others ever so slightly gilded, or even velvety, like the skin of mushrooms; certain were liquidy, others dull and earthy, veils of soot, pavilions of ash, you could sense murky forms moving about—like when the scenery is changed on a stage, you went by sampans that were dark and massive like coffins. Amphibious Flotilla, South Indochina. All this business was quite Shakespearean, right up to the witches of sorts who were busy in the stern castle preparing a disgusting swill, illuminated from below by the glow of embers, enveloped by swirling smoke. You must have stuffed yourself with the greasy tripe washed down with rotgut kept in a plastic bucket, as peasants watched from the corners of their eyes, and it had seemed to you that all of it, the movement of the night, the witches' slop, were part of an initiation, a descent into hell.

"The French Republic. Official report. Lieutenant R., South Amphibious Force. Dead as a result of wounds received by accident while on a mission. Serious wounds in the left scapular—vertebral region from shell fragments. Signed: Medical Captain N., Medical Head of the Hospital, crossed out, the My Tho Infirmary." "The French Republic, Overseas Ministry. Infirmary of the My Tho garrison. Death certificate. We, the undersigned, N., medical captain for colonial troops, certify having examined the man named R., lieutenant, commander in the amphibious flotilla. This man received serious wounds in the left scapular-vertebral region from shell fragments. In witness thereof we have issued the present certificate attesting to the truth of these events." The manuscript parts of this certificate are filled out in blue ink, handsome and rapid handwriting, you could say modern; one can date handwriting the way one can date faces. Printed in the upper-left corner of the form were the specifics of the lieutenant's wound, demonstrating that the bureaucracy leaves nothing to chance. Length: 0.360 meters. Width: 0.230 meters. Clearly, this is the sort of attention to detail that allows an empire to endure and prevail against all comers. You will not be able to sleep that night in the Hotel Huong Duong. Too excited by the proximity of the places where the event occurred that made you who you are, even despite yourself. The obscure center of your life, hollowed out here, on the banks of the Mekong, even though you were not yet born. It's from here that flow the waves of melancholy that washed over your childhood, this black water forms their concentric circles. The fall of a body here, or not far from here, at mile 64 of the Mekong, the neck and left shoulder gashed as if by the blade of the Grim Reaper. "This man received serious wounds in the left scapular-vertebral region from shell fragments. In witness thereof we have issued the present certificate attesting to the truth of these events." It serves this evening, along with other yellowing, brittle papers, printed in violet ink, as part of the wake that has been delayed half a century. Here's where it all finished for him, where it all began for you, this place that the vagaries of toponymy have given the name of My Tho, the vagaries of a forgotten war have made My Tho the origin of your personal mythology. You didn't always know it; it took you a long time to understand that. Those stories used to get on your nerves, your mother engulfed in her grief. *Galapagos! Galapagos!* You wanted to laugh. But no, you would not get off that easily. The certainty there was no victory, that courage always finished badly,

Trintignant cut down in the snow at the end by a bunch of bastards, that the important thing was to hold your head high, to go down with the flag flying, like that ship, the *Avenger of the People*, whose heroic demise was reproduced in the Mallet-Isaac schoolbooks, the flag nailed to what was left of the mast, during the wars of Revolution: that was the lesson you absorbed imperceptibly without it even being taught, rather, you took it in through a sort of moral capillary movement. Try to be "modern" with that kind of baggage . . . The examples you learned, you retained, concerned beautiful defeats. Father, look out on the left. Father, look out on the right. All's lost, save honor. The Guard dies, but does not surrender. Winning was a rather vulgar ambition, and irrelevant besides. The genius of your country didn't excel in victory (people still used to say that, "my country," and even "my homeland"). Other countries knew how to win, but yours, from Agincourt to June 1940, no way. You had to be Charles d'Orléans, or Charles de Gaulle, or Cambronne, men capable of extracting some harsh beauty from defeat, artists of collapse. The Revolution, its procession of the murdered, "struck, beaten, enchained in prison," according to the words of the *Call of the Comintern*, deep down it must have been this tragic side that seduced you. Rosa, Che. When, quite by chance, the Revolution triumphed, obviously the perspective changed. But, thank God, most often it was crushed. In room 501 of the Huong Duong Hotel, you were still going through the little pile of papers from a half-century before; you had brought them with you here in your bags, even though you had known them by heart for a long time. In any case, the prattling on the fishing boats and the humid heat would have prevented your sleeping. "Amphibious Flotilla South Indochina. Saigon, April 7, 1948. Inventory of Lieutenant R.'s effects: 1 wooden trunk, 2 bath towels, 16 formal white shirts, 3 white jackets, 2 pairs of black socks, 6 pairs of khaki pants, 2 khaki shorts, 1 bow tie, 1 leather expanding valise, 1 cloth officer's jacket, 1 pair of Turkish slippers, 2 talcum containers, 4 pairs of white pants, 5 pairs of white socks, 1 set of epaulettes." You knew the list by heart, you would later tell Thirteen's daughter; it wasn't any harder than learning *Le Cimetière marin* or *Le Bateau ivre*, was it, and in the end it amounted to the same thing. The lieutenant was one of those figures in that immense procession. Not a revolutionary, no way, but a man of courage, an antifascist. A patriot, as people still said back then. Someone who believed in things that came from the depth of time, from the Roman republic that we used to learn about in school. Someone who believed there were elements in Titus Livius and Plutarch that defined what made humanity human. He had been a member of the Free French Forces, fighting from Libya to Alsace, and right into the heart of Germany, and then a volunteer in the Expeditionary Corps. Leclerc was the commander, one of the few indisputable leaders. Many Resistance members, even reds from the Communist Resistance, had joined up for the Far East. Raymond's brother from the Paris Public Transportation Service, for instance. You think that there was without a doubt a desire to prolong this ascetic life, dangerous yet fraternal, the life they had shared during the tragic years, also, a fear of falling into the cesspool of petty interests, that is to say a life without any interest. And probably as well the false idea, yet one widely shared at the time, of "France's civilizing mission," etc. After all, it had been the creator of the public school system, Jules Ferry, who had also been the instigator of the conquest of Indochina. And then quite simply, the fascination that those words evoked, "the Far East." A sentiment they still evoke, despite the trivialization of the world. *Far East . . . Extrême-Orient* . . . The Russians say *Dalnyi Vostok* . . . You're no longer Christopher Columbus when you set out for America, but you're still a little bit of a Marco Polo when you head for the Far East. So he had gone there, to Cochin-China, to die there, at nine in the morning, at mile 64 of the Mekong, killed in an unjust war, as they said later. A colonial war. An imperialist war. Killed by the explosion of a twenty-millimeter shell, fired by the launch he was on. All imperialists are paper tigers. They pick up a large stone, only to let it fall on their feet. You could say that Mao had created some of his most famous images just to evoke the lieutenant's death. ". . . 8 boxer shorts, 1 black tie, 1 civilian tie, 1 pair of leather gloves, 1 pair of white shoes, 1 pair of yellow shoes, 1 shaving brush, 1 razor, 1 toothbrush, 1 Croix de Guerre medal dated 1939, 1 Medal of the Resistance, 1 Colt revolver with cartridge clip, 1 automatic." "He had set out on the morning of March 14 in the PL 42 heading toward Vinh Long"; it's really stupid, but you find something Racinian in this administrative phrase. "Scarcely had we departed the gates of Trézène." The death of Hippolytus.

Around midnight, the canal where the sampan was sailing had emptied into the northern arm of the Mekong. Above the river, a vague light was radiating. In the steerage, the mayor was sleeping, all curled up, looking like an old baby. A petrol lamp made the feet, the uncovered legs, the faces with mouths open under their hats, gleam. Just below your buttocks (you were in some sort of chaise longue) something was moving. Something in a bag under your cheeks, not a noisy creature, just a little fidgety. A chicken? A demon? Afraid the thing would bite your ass, but no. A sour smell was floating about, but of what? Dried fish, bird droppings, rotted fruit? Sweat too. The smell of the Far East. You had seen in front of you this weak luminous halo on which palm leaves, dazzling at the end of long, slender stalks, made designs like black stars. You had gone up on the deck. On the right the city lights were shining: My Tho. There it was, at the bottom of that pit with the clammy shadows. The sampan was going by bungalows with verandas, from what you can tell from the little black-and-white photo with the serrated edges, one of them could have been the lieutenant's house: a raised veranda under a tile roof where strange indentations carved out crevices like you find on a pagoda's roof, a staircase at the bottom of which six sailors were carrying on their shoulders the coffin draped with the French flag. "He died instantly. The launch immediately turns back and regains My Tho. All of us here mourn this officer so filled with energy and cool determination." A very small, yellowed photo with serrated edges: the coffin is at the bottom of the stairs, under the veranda, carried by six sailors in dress uniform. Forming a row, a squad presents arms. You can make out a white uniform in the middle, and on the left two specters that appear to be two white robes. Tall, slender trees against the white sky. Distance and the night made it impossible to discern, from the bridge, when the bungalows with verandas were built. Do they date from the French war? The American one? This incredible thing, unacceptable, yet incredible also because so far away, at the other end of the world, death, the death of a thirty-year-old man, incredible, unverifiable because it took place at a time when Southeast Asia was still an infinitely distant universe, a time when distance had not been overcome by air transport, telecommunications, television, etc.; how could they have believed it, you ask yourself on the sampan's bridge in the middle of the sticky night, what did they do to accept, to absorb that claim, your mother and his mother, how could they have believed this incredible thing, the death of a thirty-year-old man, their husband, their son, in a place in the world about which they hadn't the slightest idea, the slightest sense of what it even looked like? "It's not possible," people often say; but at present in the era of "real time," a thousand pieces of evidence instantaneously prove to us, practically at the moment of death, that it is only too true. But back then? This crummy little picture, these letters in violet ink emanating from the "Amphibious Flotilla South Indochina," that arrived how much time, how many days, how many weeks, after the Grim Reaper had practically detached his head from his left shoulder? "We, the undersigned, N., medical captain for colonial troops, certify having examined the man named R., lieutenant, commander in the amphibious flotilla. This man received serious wounds in the left scapular-vertebral region from shell fragments. In witness thereof we issue the present certificate attesting to the truth of these events." This unacceptable thing, unbelievable, but which they had to believe. These papers you know by heart, but that you still brought with you as if they represented a free pass to the distant regions of memory where you are venturing, this antipodes of the mind where you risk going, contain a letter from the lieutenant to his wife, to your mother; on the blackish-brown thirty-seven-centime stamps, marked "Indochina-Air Mail," where you can see, quite poorly drawn, a single-engine plane at fixed speed, a little like the *Spirit of St. Louis*, you can read very easily the postmarks of the mail service: My Tho, Cochin-China, 10:30, 3/14/48. If the republic has a special genius, it's surely not for war, nor for commerce, once it might have been — but it's no longer the case — for education, but it has to be for the post office (besides, there is nothing more beautiful at Saigon-Ho Chi Minh than the main post office, apparently the work of Eiffel). So on the postmark from Cochin-China you can read quite clearly, a half-century later, the time and the date the lieutenant's last letter was franked: 10:30, March 14, 1948, that would be an hour and ten minutes after his death on the rach Kim Son, at mile 64 of the Mekong. His head was dangling half-separated from his shoulder on the launch that was going back down the Mekong at full speed, at the base of his neck was a large gaping gill, foaming like the gills of the fish you would see unloaded, fifty years later, in front of the Hotel Huong Duong — this unacceptable, unbelievable thing, they had believed it — while on the telegram-blue envelope the unrelenting postal administration was stamping the first hour of his eternal life.

From the sampan's deck you couldn't take your eyes off those fires sparkling in the shadows; it was the primal scene from whence you issued. One was quite close to the big bang here. "In the course of the shooting, a shell from the 20 millimeter aft canon which was firing from the front of the beam, explodes on the port rigging of the mast. A shower of fragments . . ." It was here on this river, where, barely born, you had been decapitated, your father torn from you, like his head from his shoulders, and all the rest that followed. And among the things that followed, you say to Thirteen's daughter while, having just arrived on the Boulevard de Belleville, you turn the Goddess Remember around, you have just realized you're going in the wrong direction and that you are bearing down on Paris like a giant butterfly fascinated by the Eiffel Tower's lights, instead of aiming at orbiting on

116

the beltway, which is what you really wanted, among the things that followed was the certainty that History was an ironic killer, that you could and should dream of making History your mistress, but that she would always skin you alive, with a smile on her lips. One of the sailors on the sampan wanted to absolutely force you to go down into the steerage, you could not understand why since he was urging you along in Vietnamese; why he was gently pestering you, taking your hand, then your arm, trying to pull you toward the ladder, then he would leave you alone, only to return a minute later to start up again, obstinate, stubborn, humble, tireless, this whole business would have been in any circumstances exasperating, but here, it distracted you from the fascinated contemplation of the nocturnal glow where you saw the true beginning of your life, and made you want to just throw the guy overboard. Imagine, you tell Thirteen's daughter (as the Goddess Remember goes along the rue de Belleville, the right way this time, with its nose pointed toward the sky and the direction of the rising sun), imagine a servant who, in the Prince de Guermantes's library would be constantly disturbing Marcel with a tray of petits fours, a cup of tea, a tiresome phone call, Marcel, absorbed in the discovery of Art, the true life, the past regained. To tell the truth, she can't imagine anything, Thirteen's daughter. OK, not that in any case. Doesn't matter. She has time to look it up. To improve her mind, as we used to say. As for that sailor, you made it clear as hell to him that you didn't want to be disturbed, that your entire life, for all you knew, had been spent in the anticipation of this moment, that somewhere in the night was a ghost whose uneasy existence your presence on the deck, above the black swirling water, could comfort. You were, you tried to make this sailor understand, like Ulysses descending into hell to meet the shades of Tiresias and his mother, Anticleia. Go fuck yourself. He was getting nothing out of what you were saying. Finally, despairing of ever convincing you, he went and woke up the mayor. The skeletal old guy explained to you that the sampan was not stopping at My Tho. It was going more deeply into the night and the Mekong, pushing farther into the delta of the night toward Vinh Long and Cai Bei, which were the destinations of the PL 42 as well. In the steerage a porthole was open right on the level of the black water, lacquered by light. A dugout was moving along right next to it. Damn, it must be Charon's boat! "He died instantly. The launch immediately regained . . ." Fires from the riverbank filing by quite close just now, gas lamps, fluorescent tubes before which you can make out the hulls of fishing boats, clumps of palm branches, forests of pilings, sheet-metal roofs. The dugout was right up against the hull; the sailor threw your bag into it and gestured for you to get in, you jumped onto the dugout; for a split second the dugout remained glued to the sampan, sucked into it by the wake, the little boat sped up without moving, the outboard at full throttle on a black, shimmering wave, movement seemed paralyzed as in a nightmare, then slowly you separated from the sampan, which was disappearing into the night, going up the Mekong toward Vinh Long and Cai Be, toward the rach Kim Son, the sailor and the mayor waving good-bye from the porthole. The violent current plowed through the waves where the light sparkled, the sampan's anachronistic silhouette, with its curved bowsprit and stern castle, faded into the night, a ghost ship whose lines brought to mind the galleon on which Camões, the poet and soldier, had been shipwrecked near the mouths of the Mekong, not far from here, almost five centuries before.

The dugout passed by clusters of fishing boats moored together, listing one against the other, garishly lighted, all their generators chattering away; each flew on the mast the red flag with the gold star, you remembered seeing one in calico, along with a scarlet flag transversed by a swastika, in the house on the Emerald Coast; they were, you mother had told you, the lieutenant's spoils of war. That's how you formed your first idea of war: a game that consisted of capturing the enemy's flags. At Saint-Louis-des-Invalides, above Jean d'Audincourt's kitschy coffin were hanging Russian flags from Austerlitz, chewed up by moths and grapeshot, pierced by rays of light in which dust was dancing. They had seen Napoleon's sun and Prince André's great blue sky, you tell Thirteen's daughter. Just to make things clear. Does that mean anything to you, the great blue sky, Prince André at Austerlitz? you risk asking, but this time not sarcastically not at all, more like just trying to be helpful. Prince André? Well, to tell the truth . . . not really. So you come up with your little explanation, because you have the soul of a pedagogue, of a Pygmalion, because you're overflowing with stories, with History, and you no longer know to whom you should offer them, so you proceed slowly, carefully, because, to be frank, it's been awhile since . . . OK, you mix together a little Kant and Tolstoy, the moral law, the great blue sky, the dizzying depths of the soul, the pettiness of power and glory . . . That could have come from Bossuet as well; you're jumbling up the sources. In a word, all those red flags were flapping in the night, glowing in the halos from the neon and the acetylene, and under one of them was a guy entirely naked, seated on the gunwale of a fishing boat, calmly taking a shit, he was pushing his cheeks apart with two hands, but he let one go to wave hello, then he got back to work. Asia's not prudish. And that red flag with the gold star, you were thinking as you responded to the shitter's salute, that flag that the lieutenant had taken from some "rebel band," according to the official terminology of the era, and which was now the flag of crab fishermen and nocturnal shitters, was also the one you'd brandished in the demonstrations, for example, the day you got your face busted up, but also met Chloe. It was all that, the flag: a "spoil of war," a manifesto, a rag. The lieutenant had seen in it a bloody old rag, worth ripping off like the flag from the Third Reich. As for you and those of your generation, you had thought you found in that cloth the symbol of the world's poor standing up against the world's rich. The fishermen from the delta considered it a pennant like the ones that mark the placement of their crabbing cages. The dugout shot into a canal bordered with high pilings made from palm tree trunks, blue crabs and rats were crawling about on the bottom, a ladder stretched down into the water; that was where you were getting off.

Remember was on the rise, going back over the road it had just nose dived down: the McDonald's where the black guy in the track suit was still sweeping the white tiles, MEGA KEBAB SIMON-BOLIVAR, the wall around the work area, the Arab with the bag was gone, still a little rain, the windshield wipers (in the Traction there was a knob to turn them on manually, but it wasn't a Traction, it was a Frégate Renault, wasn't it, on the road to the Emerald Coast?) ATOUT COEUR CADEAUX GADGETS BOUCHERIE HALLAL CONSOMMEZ DE LA TRIPERIE CARLA CHAUSSURES LE DRAGON GOURMAND TRAITEUR ASIATIQUE AUX JARDINS DE FRANCE SERGEANT MAJOR BISTRO BAR À VINS BUFFET FROID "LA CAGNOTTE" BIJOUTERIE PLAQUÉ OR ET ARGENT MASSIF 5 À SEC FRENCH CHOCOLATES FROM NEUVILLE. Why "French," maybe chocolate is the last outpost of patriotism, we're not quite Swiss, but hardly any better, BOUCHERIE DES BUTTES SHEN FA TRAITEUR ASI-ATIQUE. The next day you had first of all gone up and down the rows in the market, along the canal, amid bowls teeming with the pearly flesh of frogs skinned alive; ducks and young pigs were splashing around in the mud, stalls of quivering catfish displayed on banana leaves. A shimmering mist covered the Mekong, ghost ships, just like the one that had dropped you off, glided through the blood-red water. There you were, sunk into a half-stupor, which the high-pitched jabbering, the exotic stench, the Far East's kaleidoscope inevitably communicate to the West's simple souls (so inevitably that you wondered whether the intoxication you were experiencing didn't come from the simple recognition of this enormous cliché for what it was, at the very moment you were yielding to it); you had begun hunting about in the piles of old papers on sale at your feet for a thousand dongs a kilo: hoping to uncover something, a letter, a photo, a page from a newspaper, an administrative document—anything at all dating from the time when the lieutenant had left here one morning. "He had set out on a mission down the river as he often did. He had shipped out on the morning of March 14th on a PL 42 heading toward Vinh Long." In fact, amidst the piles of onion paper covered with violet type in Vietnamese (it amused you to imagine, for no conceivable reason, they were police reports), you had stumbled on a French edition of the Great Helmsman's *Four Philosophical Essays*. Foreign language edition, Peking 1966. Did that bring back memories! Boy, could you spit them out, all that crap. "Where do good ideas come from? From the sky? No. From within? No. They come from social practice." Now that's well put. "Generally speaking, if it works, it's good, if it fails, it's bad." You leafed through the little book written with such pomposity, yet a book in which the best philosophical minds of your generation had claimed to find the summit of thought. What were you thinking? "When the real facts have been sufficiently accumulated, a leap occurs through which they are transformed into rational cognition, that is, ideas." What could be simpler? You saw it clearly, the leap . . . the great leap forward, the facts of experience jumping into an idea. Wow! Feet first. Like kangaroos! Unbeatable, that Mao! You were laughing reading that stuff on the side of the canal; people began looking with amusement at the Phap chuckling all by himself reading Mao (they knew it was him because his name and picture dominated the cover). They'd never seen anyone discover humorous qualities in the Great Helmsman's prose. Sometimes the style, while remaining pompous, shaded a bit toward the eighteenth century, most likely because of the translator's classical background: "Now if the proletariat wants to know the world, it is in order to transform it. He has absolutely no other aim." This "absolutely no other" was admirable. You remembered having taken notes on these platitudes as, some years before, you had done with Kant and Hegel. And yet you . . . you were not really a philosopher. But Gideon! Right now it seemed that what fascinated you in those texts was precisely their rustic character. The charm of ugliness, the seduction of the nonthought, the desire to be weak and stupid. In brooding over the Great Helmsman's obtuse utterances, you doubtless had the vague sense that you were sacrificing your intelligence. That was good, since your so-called intelligence made you bourgeois intellectual: first fold.

Yet on the other hand, if it were really necessary to sacrifice your own intelligence to get something out of Mao's works, it was because they were . . . : second fold. They were what? asks Thirteen's daughter who's having a problem making her way through the maze of this Maoist thinking. They were a jumble of commonplaces, alright. Suspicion, unmentionable doubt. I was telling you: second fold. Fanatical thinking, contrary to what one thinks, to what one would like to think, is never of one piece, the product of a single movement. Listen! It's important what I'm telling you, you explain to Thirteen's daughter who, jammed up against the car door, looks at you ironically from the corner of her eye. OK, a polite irony. To better make your point, you double-park the Goddess Remember in front of the Church of the River Jordan. Fanatical thinking is thinking that folds back upon itself, like a zigzag or an accordion (you mime the movement with your hands), its violence comes from there, from the fact that the last fold tries to cover all the others, tight, piled up, crushed under it. I hate Jews, or the West, or women, because I admire them, or fear them, or envy them, because I have contempt for myself, etc. Inadmissible things. Let's pull the spring taut. The brutality of the invective is in proportion to the effort to crush the twists and turns of inadmissible thoughts. You mime all that as best you can. Listen! These are good ideas, you tell Thirteen's daughter, but in a clowning way so as to diminish the solemnity of your previous outburst. Besides, ideas don't fall from the sky, they come to me from social practice. Yeah, right . . . They come leaping toward me from the social practice of fanatics and fools. And you mime that as well, however, while squeezed up against the door she is looking at you with an edge of sympathetic irony, your eyes slide along her legs stretched out toward the center of the car (the Goddess, allow me to inform those who might be unaware of it, has front-wheel drive, and as a result the floor is flat and unobstructed between the seats), her legs, which . . . indeed, well, which shine in the night. Quite a bit really. "Innumerable phenomena of the objective world are reflected in the brain through the canal of the five sense organs." Of course. "The organs of sight, hearing, smell, taste, and touch." My God! Inadmissible thoughts. Sade's philosophy in the bedroom.

The allegedly philosophical essays by Mao (who, besides, personally practiced philosophy in the bedroom, having had delivered to himself, the old warty bastard, cargoes of pretty, young Red Guards; if someone had argued that to you at the time, you would have been capable of killing him), the allegedly philosophical essays and all that Chinese crap—it was in the name of that stuff, in harping on it, numbing yourselves with it, drugging yourselves with it—that you came to respect the proles who were psychopaths, pimps, informers, or just pathological liars. TEE, Juju, or Gustave, for example. Wrongly, to be sure. We respected them wrongly. Don't forget what I told you, you say to Thirteen's daughter: twisted, turning thinking. Basically we respected them, because we scorned them, because we scorned them for respecting us, because we scorned ourselves for respecting them, and so forth. This Gustave was a disgusting old guy, a former miner like André, but not at all of the same stripe. What interested him were his own little peep shows. That was how the cops got him, really pathetic morals charges, some exhibitionism caught red-handed (an exhibitionist caught with his pants down, so to speak). Of course, we didn't know that, we found out later, after it was all over and Foster had access to records in the Ministry of the Interior. The dirty ole son of a bitch had been blithely informing on us; it was to him, for instance, that Foster owed his stay in the Santé Prison. Personally, you tell Thirteen's daughter, that's not what I blame him most for, but Foster, obviously enough, was really upset with him. That fat Foster, he was real proud to show us that he now had access to several state secrets, category four, some minor cop stuff. He had called us together—Gideon, Amédée, Danton, and me, Thirteen, no it couldn't have been, he had been dead for several years, it was in '81, let me remind you—the famous May 10, 1981, President Mite's glorious dawn! He was running off at the mouth, that squealing Foster, about his little discoveries.

He'd gone over to the other side, the side of the powers that be. Somewhere in the antechamber of power, but so what. It was like he had taken it over, power, I mean. He just stroked his beard with satisfaction. He was in charge of some files; the cleaning ladies in this immense edifice of power where he occupied an attic room, reported to him. Now listen! you tell Thirteen's daughter: what I'm going to tell you is a good idea, the product of social practice; there are no worse suckers for power than certain former revolutionaries. You remember Victor Serge's phrase that I just quoted to you—an eternity ago: "How happy they are to finally watch the parades from the official tribunal." So there we were, in this brasserie at the Bastille (or maybe Place de la République), to learn from Foster's mouth that Gustave had informed on us as best he could. I was not really astonished by that, but there were some colorful details; you could even say like something out of a novel. For instance, when the superintendent from the Intelligence Service went to pick up this big mole at the Gare du Nord, he took him at once to a club on the Champs (he knew, he was paid to know, that the ladies turned Gustave on), where he offered him some champagne. The guy refused, said he preferred a beer. Now that's great! It was The People! Something out of Zola! The cop knocking back his Mercier champagne, the other guy his Kronenbourg, the cop wearing a tie with the knot loosened to conform to the stereotype, most likely a brown jacket; Gustave sweating in his bulky zippered sweater, dark red velour curtains, the girl in a G-string, big tits swaying around Gustave's crimson snout, the cop struggling to catch the denunciations reeled off in an awful northern French accent; Gustave scratching his head to see if he could find something else to betray . . . scraping about as best he could . . . Once you get going, so it seems, it's easier to keep going . . . like puking . . . but of course Gustave would like another Kro . . . and maybe another quick feel . . . of course, my friend, of course. Don't hesitate. And the cop pays and puts the bill in his wallet and Gustave stifles a burp and is suddenly melancholy; he knows that now he is going to have to meet up with us . . . the meeting of the

Political Bureau where for sure there'll be no striptease . . . probably not even a Kronenbourg . . . and frankly it bothers him a bit to be an informer . . . at the same time he's going to have to force himself to remember stuff that will interest the police superintendent the next time. Because the cops are not like those assholes from the prestigious schools, the jerks who make up the core of the political bureau of The Cause; they don't just admire everything he says, to the contrary, they raise questions, they grill him and insist on proof; that's why he, Gustave, feels compelled to respect the cops who despise him, and to despise the eggheads who respect him. And so forth: I hope, Marie, you've kept in your head the notion of spiral thinking, you say to Thirteen's daughter. So the police superintendent notes all that, all the facts, in his report, and ten years later Foster is proud as can be to put us in the loop. And us, naturally enough, you tell Thirteen's daughter, we're plenty pissed off. What to do? Bust up the bar the old bastard had taken over at Lens (or at Douai, who knows) to pay him back for the spying? Since he had become a kabbalist, Gideon didn't feel particularly concerned about stuff that happened in his youth. For his part, Amédée was now involved in serious politics, communication strategies, issue focusing, electoral marketing, program costs, popularity ratings, mainstream matters. He dined with the important; they were the ones who wanted him, who requested he dine with them, he did not see himself participating in some third-rate revenge drama. Danton had always been a nice guy, and he was not about to change. For yourself, you could imagine, if Thirteen were still there, going to Lens (or Douai) and doing a little damage. You pictured yourself in a Western movie (for this kind of stuff it was the only option); you would have arrived, hands in pockets, at the Expectorate Café (because in addition to informing, Gustave used to spit all over), Howdy, Gus, remember us? You could have easily seen Trintignant in your role playing you. You would have drawn out the scene for fun, ordering a couple of beers, toasting the good old days, letting the prick simmer in his own juices, and then suddenly a sweeping motion with the forearm and all the glassware bites the dust, it really would have been a lot of fun. You see, you tell Thirteen's daughter, your father, he was the type of guy I would have done that with, extracted a vengeance that would have been at the same time a little childish, playful, anachronistic, and still quite justified; your father was just that kind of man, I can't say anything more truthful about him. Do you understand? A nod of assent, no need to draw a picture. What did we finally do? Nothing. We were wrong. We could have at least sent him a dead fish in the mail, something like that. Nothing more, of course, and nothing worse, but at least that. Doing nothing was a way of saying that our whole history together had been a fantasy, a dream, if betraying us was not at least worth a kick in the ass. Doing nothing meant accepting that we close the door on a part of our lives. That day, we really became ghosts. A rotten fish in the mail would have been enough . . . So why didn't you do it? Because there was no longer a "we," an "us," a "you guys." Just some "me"s. What can you do with that? And in the name of what? With Thirteen, we would have done something; with Thirteen, we were part of a group, capable of losing ourselves in it, we had the courage one draws from the presence of others. Maybe we were nothing more than an old couple, but earlier, in another era, we had been thousands, millions . . . Our friendship was all that remained of that grand, universal brotherhood. We were survivors; we had survived the massacre of the brotherhood. So with him, we would have done something, for sure. But alone . . .

As for Gustave, what fascinated him about the bourgeoisie was their supposed depravity. TEE believed that every bourgeois was just another Baron de Rothschild, devoted to debauchery, to nonstop orgies. The bourgeoisie inflamed his imagination; the class struggle was for him an immense X-rated film. So when a miner's daughter was found raped and murdered in an empty lot, and when a slightly nutty judge, egged on by the scandal sheets, had the most important pharmacist in the region charged with the crime, Gustave believed his moment had come. This sordid news item was going to become the symbol of the struggle between oppressor and oppressed. This incident had multiplied in him the resources of that "proletarian intelligence," at whose school there was so much to learn. He sputtered with ideas, his eyes glistened, saliva bubbled between his blackened teeth, as he shared with you, the political bureau, his theories. The pharmacist lived with a woman without being married to her, that was certainly proof of something. The bitch was a dyke, he had heard that in a bistro, that makes you think . . . He had also heard in the bistro that she wore red silk panties, and sometimes, you won't believe this . . . sometimes no panties at all! He had learned from the butcher's helper that the pharmacist sometimes ordered 800-gram steaks. 800 grams! Did he have to draw us a picture, or what? Gideon, who had been the most brilliant of the young philosophers at that prestigious school, the disciple of the old professor whose name would only become known to the general public when he strangled his wife, Gideon was gravely nodding his head. Sometimes he would ask Gustave to repeat something, as if his thinking was too complex for him: no panties at all? 800 grams! Did he have to draw us a picture? Gideon, stroking his goatee, would observe a long silence, in order to allow us to contemplate the information just thrown our way, like a steak on a counter. To learn from the school of the proletariat was to understand *concretely*, the way Gustave did, what the class enemy was. Theory, the extortion of surplus value, all that was fine, but what really mattered was *life*, and *life* meant that the bourgeoisie didn't wear underwear and wolfed down a kilo of meat for dinner. Gideon turned toward Danton, who did not really dare show his dismay. We need an article on that in the paper, OK? In the language of the French masses (like for Vietnam and everything else). Danton mumbled a Yes, right. It'll be done. All that in a *lively* language, of course. This sort of death.

You know . . . you're going to see just how old-fashioned I am, you say to Thirteen's daughter. Remember is on the move again, on a cushion of air, a silver-gray flying saucer, a silver ghost on automatic pilot, searching the night with her intelligent eyes, left and right, going up Belleville, the Arab butcher shops, fish markets, French chocolate, Asian caterers, tobacco shop, "La Gitane," poultry, regional products, ADEAUX TORTOLA SERRURERIE CHEZ PETIT LOUIS CAFÉ-BAR a black girl caged in a glass telephone booth, you'd think she was taking a shower in light, we're flying silently (not you), hydropneumatically. Across the city in the depth of the night. Silently, not you, to the contrary a flood of words, stories, slapdash reflections, rash judgments, half-ass pronouncements. Listen, you say to Thirteen's daughter: you see just how old-fashioned I am. What I think is that we were the last generation to dream of heroism. That seems silly now, probably seems to you only good for fools; to tell the truth, you don't even get what that means, I know. But the world hasn't always been such an enemy of the romantic. The world hasn't always been so cynical, so sneaky. So cautious, so sniggering, "it won't happen to me." Back then, young people were happy to have a romantic imagination. Life had to be an epic, otherwise, what was the point? You had to live on the edge, confront the mysterious. It's an old human desire; there's a ton of myths and poems that talk about it, stand up to gods, to monsters, discover undreamed-of lands, explore the unknown region that is oneself in the face of death. *The Iliad*, *The Odyssey*, so to speak. For two thousand years, lots of young people have dreamed of being Achilles, or Hector, or Ulysses. And despite what people think nowadays, this desire fits in perfectly with wanting to write and think. As it happens, they work very well together. The common root is the rejection of monotony. There've been poets, novelists, soldier philosophers, secret agents like that, and you know they were far from being the worst. No need to go back to Cervantes and Camões; take Faulkner who, among the writers of this century, was hardly the nerdiest, the most superficial. Faulkner was terribly disappointed the 1918 armistice prevented him from playing the modern knight in the skies of Europe. That's how it is. Hemingway, quicker, had set out at once for the battlefields. Cendrars is not very fashionable these days, but that doesn't change the fact that, along with Apollinaire, he invented modern French poetry, and that he had volunteered for the Foreign Legion. And Apollinaire, we could talk about him as well. I know you're all pacifists now. Me too, if you want me to admit to you it's nicer to live in peace. Those guys too, the ones who were in the war, and survived it, they say the same thing. Still, you don't write with what's nice, you don't think that way either. You write, you think, with what hurts, what kills. In fact, it's with that you really live. Not with the "precaution principle." Writing (or painting, etc.) is not intrinsically philanthropic. Even less progressive. A great writer in the Green Party, yeah, I'd like to see that. Or even a great painter. OK, so the Revolution was the last epic in the West after which everyone just lay down and went to sleep. Currently, the Revolution, it's a gadget, middle-class junk. Frills and flounces. Marie, look at, listen to, read, what's all around you. Our elites all claim to be "revolutionaries" right now. I'm talking, of course, about the modern bourgeoisie, the one that fabricates images, stories; I don't mean the old-fashioned ones who persist in making train tracks or sheet metal. I'm speaking of the real mentors, the ones that my generation invented. Alas. The Revolution has become their decor, their lovely finery. The modern bourgeoisie is "revolutionary"; it invented this impressive smokescreen to hide its privileges. But before it became a pose esteemed in the "Lifestyle" pages of trendy magazines, the Revolution was the last gasp of the old dream of heroism; I'm speaking on behalf of a young intellectual in the sixties, someone who didn't have to worry about money, I'm talking about what I know. We felt this need for heroism all the more because in general, it was so conspicuously lacking in the France of our fathers . . . You know, to be born just after Vichy, that really creates a need for an epic . . . So, selling coffee and guns in Abyssinia, leading an army of camel drivers along the Red Sea, a squadron above the Tereul Sierra, an assault team in Havana, dying next to a Berlin canal—these were the confused horizons of our ambitions. Confused, arty, but not paltry. Romantic, sure, I think you can say that. Was it a bit of a hoax, since we did not know what economic exploitation was? Of course. Also because our determination to lose ourselves in a collective identity originated in the classic, individualist desire to have a destiny. It must have been because of that, to expiate this literary sin, this "middle-class" foible, that later we were so trusting, so ridiculously humble around types like Gustave or Juju. It must have been because we sensed that deep inside us was something akin to a lie, and we were so appallingly obsessed by this flaw that we were maniacs of guilt. Which is also why the instrument of our punishment has been irony: we wanted so much to have destinies, and we wound up with the destinies of the Three Stooges. Tragedy repeats itself as comedy, and having wished too much for drama, we ended up with farce. The irony of fate.

GÉNÉRALE CASHER SURGELÉS SPÉCIALITÉS TURQUES ET GRECQUES, at least eating ignores war, white washing machines with opened doors illuminated in the night, BEL AIR LAVERIE DÉPOT TROC BIBELOTS BRONZES HORLOGES OBJETS DÉCO ENLÈVEMENT GRATUIT, blue fluorescent rods, exactly the color of those fly-repellent devices you see in the Third World, VIDÉO FUTUR #1 DES VIDÉOCLUBS EN FRANCE, ALIABED SUPERBAZAR, FRANPRIX, you move into fifth gear after Pixérécourt, gearshift attached to the steering wheel, you don't find that anymore; Remember's silver stingray head takes off with a sound like a vacuum cleaner, but almost at once you have to downshift because the street suddenly is climbing steeply toward Télégraphe at 128 meters, 508 meters above sea level, a marble cliff on top of which you lived with Judith when her silky hair slid down between her small breasts, those breasts you loved to caress, very blue neon lights, still very blinking, TRECA EPÉDA DUNLOPILLO SIMMONS SOMMIERS MATELAS MEUBLES SALONS DE CUIR CANAPÉS CONVERTIBLES MOBÉCO GROS DÉTAIL LES GRANDES MARQUES AUX MEILLEURS PRIX, still very blue and very blinking. SANDWICHS GRECS FRITES FALAFEL, her little breasts you used to love to touch and nibble as well, yes indeed. Where were we? Oh yeah, the proles. Juju was a ferocious guy, at least that was his reputation. He claimed it, you bought it. A prole from Sochaux, that meant he wasn't a choir boy. The Peugeot factories at that time, so far away in eastern France and so cold, so harsh, for the petits bourgeois that you were, it was a little like what the German forests must have been for a Roman of the decadent period: a terrible future was in the making amid barbaric dancing and human sacrifices. Even the mines of Nord Pas de Calais—too close to Paris, too unionized and politicized, too civilized—even the mines did not possess this frightening prestige. Renault-Billancourt, let's not even bother talking about it. To go to Sochaux was to plunge into a space-time warp. The absolute sticks, no major city, employers vested by divine right, Siberian climate. The Jura Mountains: even the name has something savage about it, something between a roar and a rale. Who would risk going into the Jura? The Alps, the Pyrenees—they evoked winter sports, the Vosges, vineyards, and cutesy prints, but the Jura . . . You felt the Urals were not far away. Among the militants of the "working-class base" was a guy named Walter, big, ruddy complexioned, a rather calm guy with sideburns and a harelip who liked to tease the catfish in the Doubs River. Silurid fish, to be exact. Jean d'Audincourt once had gone on an outing in the icy mists with him. They came back empty-handed, but he had told you, you explain to Thirteen's daughter, that Walter used twenty-liter jerrycans for floaters on his lines, that gave an idea of the monsters he was hoping to catch: viscous, pustular crap, with moustaches and bulging eyes, a type of giant slug from the lower depths, black as atomic submarines, but nervous and mean like crocodiles; they would climb on the riverbanks and crawl on their clawlike fins after ducks, piglets, dogs . . . small children, so people said. Walter, a sort of Ahab from Franche-Comté, had arranged to meet Jean d'Audincourt while he was watching his cans dance in the fog. According to him, the business about the little children was an exaggeration. So that's what it was like, the Jura: the heart of darkness, prehistory, a land of metaphysical monsters, where was constantly building, or so one thought, the catastrophic energy needed to fire up revolutions. Juju was the leader of the "working-class base." A sturdy little guy, quite muscular with a husky voice, the type of little sailor that Genet would have liked. Several years later, he would kill himself magnificently on one of the roads of this region called "little Siberia" because of its terrible winters; his car would plow through a grove of fir trees before coming to a halt, impaled through the roof on a broken tree trunk. In his automobile armor, Juju was totally squashed. The death of a bargain-basement knight, a third-rate Don Quixote, but still, it was something special, a nod toward the epic, like the quest for the great catfish. It contained sadness and beauty: the jalopy lovingly prepared in the citadel's courtyard, pumped up, customized, decorated with a flaming mane, painted, decked out, dolled up for the ultimate tournament, the vast sun above the snow, the blue sky, the black trees, and then, nothing. An enormous crash, then nothing, all silent again under the branches of the trees. Curtains. You know, you tell Thirteen's daughter, I guess I often seem to be mocking them, still . . . there were a lot of them I didn't like much, that's true, Juju, for example, but yet, they were all looking for something greater than themselves. Fraternity, the Revolution, adventure, something. Otherwise, why bother. This Juju had thought he had found in us, thanks to us, from the scraps of History he learned from us, from his own boasting, from our naiveté, the means to be greater than he was. Then it all disappeared, so his limited imagination turned to his Ford Escort. For that brief moment when he was roaring down the road, pedal to the metal, or taking a curve in a controlled skid, he thought he was Jo Schlesser, Jean-Pierre Beltoise . . . the big racecar drivers at the time. It's not just silly. All of us were piecing together destinies as best we could, that's what united us. OK. "Rest in peace." It didn't take much to get Juju to tell, as if in confidence, that he had been part of a group of hotheads who, defending the "liberated" factories in June '68, had thrown some of the riot police, the CRS, into vats of acid. This fabricated incident was one of the legends that hung around after May (like the supposed mutiny on the aircraft carrier *Clemenceau*). Maybe it was us at The Cause, you tell

Thirteen's daughter, who invented the story. We certainly could have. Maybe it was Thirteen. Or perhaps Angelo, some drunken night at Harry's, or even Danton, to get Gideon to leave us alone. Most likely, it was just one of those rumors born from nothing, that nothing that's called the mood of the moment; and Juju, having heard the rumor, discovered in it a role that suited him, that exhilarated him. Since others, us for example, were stupid enough to find that exhilarating . . . Anyway, he was going to bask in the dubious glory of having dissolved some CRS in H_2SO_4.

The memory that stays with you of the formidable Juju is really far removed from this mythology. One summer, you had organized a "worker study group," a sort of school where the proletariat "could share their experiences," as we said at the time. What was amusing about this, you explain to Thirteen's daughter, the incongruous thing was that the meeting place we had been lent was a chateau near Illiers, in the Beauce, which had been the model of the Guermantes' chateau in *Remembrance*. Alright, the model, I'm not really sure what that means, since, unless I'm mistaken, you don't ever see the Guermantes' chateau in Proust: people walk toward it when they go for a stroll along the Vivonne, beside the water lilies, but I don't remember their ever going up to the chateau, do you remember? you ask Thirteen's daughter. And since she remembers nothing, nothing at all, you continue: in fact, Guermantes' way has no end, no boundary stone; it's the current, the mirror of the water, the mirage of the name, of History. Right, all this seems pretty far removed from Juju from Sochaux, but not really, just wait and see. The proprietor of the chateau, the modern-day Duchess of Guermantes so to speak, was a middle-class hippie, a winsome, funny redhead, wearing, it seems to me, swirling Indian dresses. Alright, I'm no longer sure about the dresses, you say to Thirteen's daughter, but I am sure she was separated from her husband who maybe was a count, something like that, but maybe not, in any case I had been quite tempted to betray The Cause and try to become lord of the manor at

Illiers, but as usual I didn't have the nerve. This Countess Nicole (or maybe Juliette? No, I think it was Nicole) was actually more of a Verdurin, when you come right down to it. Of the count, or the husband, the most obvious vestige was an Oldsmobile convertible, stored away in a barn. An Oldsmobile, a Buick, a Roadmaster, yeah, it's possible. Doesn't change anything. Blue in any case. All my repressed desires for debauchery and class betrayal, I had projected them on that car's long, sparkling thighs. Asshole, I would have loved tooling around the park behind the wheel of that voluptuous vehicle. Get the V12 engine purring. *V* for Vietnam. *V* like a woman's sex and the fold of a book. Maybe I already said that? Unfortunately, the car was equipped with power steering and a load of other electrical devices; at that time it was called "servo-command," I think, and it wasn't yet found on the little European crates, and since the damn count had left, the battery had gone dead. The tires too. The Oldsmobile or the Buick was lying on the hay where I would have liked to roll with the Countess Nicole or Juliette without daring to say it to her, or even to myself, do you understand? you say to Thirteen's daughter. Now that, she understood right away. What a jerk . . . So the worker study group had set up its tents under the trees in the park. Since both Thirteen and you were specialists in matters that required a certain degree of professionalism (sophisticated mugging, kidnapping, false papers, transport of dangerous materials, revolutionary picnics), you were put in charge of logistics for the event. You had spent night after night studying the Chaix timetable in order to work out train routes to throw off the police thugs from the Quai des Orfèves; it was crucial that they could not follow some careless or inattentive person to Guermantes' way. For example, Juju, you had sent him off to Dijon, then from there to Lyons where, if he ran real fast he could catch the Paris train going in the opposite direction; he would get off at Laroche-Migennes where a car would be waiting. At that time, the trains used to stop at Laroche-Migennes. Laroche-Migennes in Yonne. You used to spend an incredible amount of time at these cat-and-mouse games, Thirteen and you, and Fichaoui, and Judith, and all those at The Cause who were involved with dirty tricks, zigzagging across Paris like frightened sparrows, keeping current your listings of buildings with two entrances, going in by one door and leaving by another, jumping off the metro at the moment when the doors were closing, elbowing through department stores or train stations during the rush hour; to go from one point to another in a straight line was strictly forbidden, the labyrinth was your specialty, moving about was an activity that required quite a bit of patience and imagination. OK, nobody missed a connection, nobody had, to employ a delicate expression, his head up his ass. Everybody made it to the chateau. Hairy Reureu who had boar bristles growing even from the bends in his knees and elbows (he was happy to show this marvel to Nicole), Pompabière, Momo the Lock-Eater, and a guy whose intestinal upheavals caused by cheap red wine had earned him the unfortunate nickname of "the Shitter," in fact, the whole crowd from Issy-les-Moulineaux, Gustave the Spitter, that old piece of crap, André from the mines whom the silicosis would choke to death, and whose coffin we would one day follow in the rue de la Terre-de-Feu, TEE with his sinister clown face, Juju H2SO4, and still more, there were not that many proles in The Cause, but they did all show up; Simon (or maybe Gérard was his name?), a young unskilled worker, melancholic and sickly, he used to hide, like it was some shameful vice, the fact that he played the violin, twenty years later he ended up in the National Front; Saïd was a fanatic about horses, he could forget for a moment about the enslavement of the salaried worker by conjuring up in his head childhood memories of the fracas of hooves on the beach at Rabat. And then there was Raymond, a retired public transportation worker, one of the rare guys I still remember warmly, you tell Thirteen's daughter. He had a brother who, after having been in the Communist Resistance, joined the Expeditionary Corps in Indochina, he might have known the lieutenant, and then he had ended up by deserting; he just disappeared and when we heard about him again, he had become some sort of king in New Guinea, all this according to Raymond, but, to tell the truth, he wasn't really sure, the last letters were over ten years old. This fabulous destiny, to be swallowed up in the jungle, made him dream, but without the slightest hint of jealousy tarnishing the mention of the king of the Papua. Raymond was a very generous guy. Doubtless he would have preferred that we introduce him to Conrad rather than Mao. In his watery blue eyes, his extremely gentle, modest smile, you could see the regret he felt for an education he had not had, and that he admired in us, the young intellects of The Cause—he used to say "intellectual" with a stress on the "u," and he was the only one who did not use this word as an insult; on the contrary, he savored it like an exquisite jam. As for us, we were embarrassed and a little angry since our education was precisely what we wanted to free ourselves from and redeem ourselves at the feet of the proletariat, as we used to say. Between Raymond and us the misunderstanding was total. His passion for literature led him to write short compositions in the style of Sully-Prudhomme, which drove Gideon, who was requested to read them, crazy. Raymond did everything backwards; he respected the learning we were ashamed of, when we had to act, he was always inclined toward the most peaceful solution, while we were expecting workers to instruct us in violence. In that respect, Juju was decidedly reassuring. With him, the world was as it should be. It's a done deal, as he used to like to say.

RESTAURANT ASIATIQUE LE MAOFA MIAMI CAFÉ RESTAURANT FRANCO-LIBANAIS green turquoise washing machines, lighted up in their store window like Hamburg whores, SOLEIL DES DRAGONS DÉGUSTATION RAPIDE PLATS À EMPORTER the rue de Belleville descends toward the rue Haxo, and then rises in the direction of the Porte des Lilas, SANDHU BRENDA PRÊT À PORTER FÉMININ FLEURS TEINTURERIE PRESSING BOUCHERIE MUSULMANE LES TROIS FRÈRES FLEUR DE LYS DEUILS MARIAGES BAR RESTAURANT DES MOULINS LE ZODIAQUE BAR PMU PARISTAMBUL SANDWICHES PIZZAS TURQUES. All the same, some things we just didn't buy, Thirteen and me, you tell his daughter. We didn't swallow everything, don't think that for a moment, but it's true we shut up about it. The two of us would talk about stuff, yet of course not everything. Study at the feet of the proletariat, sometimes that was real hard. The pharmacist's 800-gram steaks, his bitch's red silk panties, to tell the truth, we didn't give a shit about them. We didn't just not give a shit, it disgusted us to act like they interested us. I remember one time when Thirteen and me had talked about this business. We had gone into the little city in the north where the incident had taken place. Gustave and Gideon had asked us to prepare the "arrest," as we used to say, of the pharmacist. So we had gone there, depressed, we saw the house, near a massive brick church, an empty lot, and the national highway that cut between slag heaps in a straight line; we came up with a good reason to call the whole thing off: the police station 500 meters away directly in front of us, no curves in the road, no hill, no red light between the cops and the crime scene, gendarmes with a straight shot, and us in the line of fire, so to speak. Too risky: we had invented this bad excuse to get out of there. Gideon, he told me this years later, had been really relieved by our bailing out, he had not even insisted. I remember talking about it several days later with your father, you say to Thirteen's daughter; I feel funny referring to him like that — "your father." I remember we were crossing the Pont Mirabeau, and there was a mist on the Seine. Or maybe it was the Pont de Grenelle or Garigliano. Strange, I'm sure of that, the mist on the Seine. Thirteen was asking me why we had lied, why we hadn't been courageous enough, simply honest enough, to say that we refused this mission because it was stupid, dishonorable. Instead of inventing excuses? Annoyed, I responded that I hadn't the slightest idea, but that anyway, we'd accomplished the essential: we'd refused the mission. He insisted we had not refused it, we'd sabotaged it, and that wasn't the same morally. Morally! You're making me laugh, I said to him. Morally! And him, the bastard, your father, you tell Thirteen's daughter, he begins to spar with me, right there, in the middle of the bridge. Sparring as a joke, but not completely. And then . . . what was I saying to you? Oh yeah, got it: studying at the feet of the proletariat. We really wanted to do it, but still, there were limits. Times when it was tough. The gang from Issy, for instance, when they were really loaded with Kiravi (or maybe Préfontaines wine), they would sometimes go hunting for faggots in the public urinals at the Porte de Versailles. Because they existed then, at that time: public urinals. *Pissateria*, street urinals, the word comes back to me; I had forgotten it. Sort of little dungeons made of sheet metal with openings, black, inside water flowed on slate slats. Oddly enough, the liberalization of moral standards, or liberation, I don't know anymore what people say, sounded the death knell for those useful public conveniences. One more thing gone, like Gillette blades, the studs in the studded crosswalks, and History. But not the B-52s. Anyway, Hairy Reureu, Pompabière, Lock-Eater, and Shitter used to set out on an expedition, completely plowed, shitfaced, tight — only the brand of booze ever changed — to the public urinals at the Porte de Versailles. The faggots, the queers, as we used to call them (it can't be said that our tolerance was any better than the average for that era, but, all the same, organizing ambushes . . .); Thirteen and I failed to see why we had to study at the feet of . . . for that. Still, we wanted to make an effort, to try, but we found it hard to believe that even Gideon would say nothing in front of these yokels. Instead, he would act as if he was learning from them. Our consciously chosen humility was at least supposed to be redeemed by Gideon's glory. He was sort of our delegate to the absolute. As for us, it was already decided, we were bourgeois or petit-bourgeois intellectuals (although . . . to tell the truth, you say to Thirteen's daughter, it seemed to me a little pretentious to take myself for an intellectual, as for a bourgeois . . . Nessim to be sure, but me?). Gideon had raised himself above this miserable condition right up to the level of leader. Now a leader, for as long as he remained a leader, was free of class determinations. Lenin, Mao were not little noblemen, average peasants from a higher stratum; they were leaders, "Great Leaders," even, in capital letters. The miraculous incarnation of the New Man. The perfection of leaders was, for the corrupt and fallen average man, a reason to hope. Those of us who were willing to risk our lives in attacking convoys of CRS, in kidnapping bosses, Gideon would brush off like a bunch of dunces, but that was how it was supposed to be, the rule of self-dislike, we had chosen it. Yet it was not in the order of things that he, whose infallibility was like the transmutation of our imbecility, would deign to think about 800 grams of cow . . . panties in red silk . . . This, we were at a loss to understand. Especially Thirteen. I think he was more of a rebel than me, you say to his daughter.

In a word, all the comrade workers arrived safe and sound under the tents. Buses filled with educated Japanese tourists whipped up dust along the paths, and astonished the proles who wondered what could bring Japs to a chateau owned by a crazy liberal. Gustave the informer, along with Gideon, controlled the direction of the discussions. "The PhD in strikes" is how the big piece of crap nicely called himself. Hairy Reureu, Momo Lock-Eater, Pompabière, Shitter, Simon, Juju, Saïd, Raymond, TEE, Walter, and others, about twenty in all, seated under a large military tent, were listening. When the gang from Issy would hit the bottle a little hard, they would heckle the speaker pretty crudely. Gideon labored to discover in this abuse some sensible element from which he could try to piece together a reconciliation; that was called in franco-Maoist parlance, "resolve the contradictions within the people." Tom, the secretary for the discussions, was also a student at the prestigious school, by nature moderate and courteous, qualities that did not serve him well with this crowd. When the thinking of one person or another became difficult to follow, he would cough, timidly raise his hand, and request a little clarification: Comrade, what do you mean, *concretely*? In a bedlam often worthy of the Cordelier Club such as Chateaubriand describes it in his *Memoirs*, you would have thought he was in the House of Lords. Twenty years later, Tom would make a reputation for himself in a limited circle through learned studies of the role of the infinite in the kabbala. People talked, insulted each other, "exchanging experiences," "systematizing," "drawing lessons." It's amazing what lessons you can draw from everything. Some played volleyball, the young ones, not the ones with silicosis. We ate the eternal rice with tomato sauce that Roselyn and Karin, enveloped in starchy vapor, had lovingly prepared in the chateau's large cast-iron pots. Roselyn made her living playing the violin in a circus, standing on a horse's croup. Her father had been one of the heroes of the Warsaw ghetto. When the job was to go to the rue des Rosiers in the Jewish quarter to put up posters exalting "the just struggle of the Palestinian people," she took it upon herself. Later, years later, she would confess to me that she would be scared out of her mind, all the more because she was not sure she agreed with the simplistic texts on the posters. But also she had learned that great, perverse lesson, namely, that what should be done is precisely what one has not been prepared to do, what one is not expecting to have to do. She would tell me that years later, you say to Thirteen's daughter; after it was all over she had an accident, the horse bolted because of one of the big cats, and she busted up her spinal column. She can't walk anymore, so she gets around in a wheelchair, scraping together a living giving violin lessons. Roselyn has very beautiful blue eyes. Karin has black eyes. Her father was a diplomat for the Reich; he disappeared during a bombardment at the end of the war in East Prussia, at Königsberg. A civil servant in the Reich, but not a Nazi, or so it seems. Loyal servant of the German state. Why not? More or less a Christian Democrat, or so it seems. It's easy to take the word of diplomats whose elegant uselessness distances them from real crimes. Right? The missing father was Karin's hope and shame. A highly placed civil servant in the Reich, but not a Nazi, is what she wanted to believe. Dead, to be sure, in a Russian bombardment, but his body was never found, and with the Russians, you never know, anything could be possible, even that he's alive in a Siberian gulag; that's happened before. Karin's father was a non-Nazi Nazi, a dead or maybe living person. Totally disappeared, more radically erased than the lieutenant or Thirteen, you say to his daughter. Disintegrated. And therefore completely explosive. Karin was older than us, but still she was not that old, yet in her short life she had really kicked around a bit, she was a worker in a factory in Chemnitz in the German Democratic Republic, the place that made those funny little moped-motorcars, the tin cans on wheels, the famous Trabant that became trendy after the fall of the Berlin Wall, then she succeeded in getting to the West where she became a hostess in a Munich bar (or maybe Hamburg, but I think it was Munich, you tell Thirteen's daughter), later she continued her trek westward and eventually arrived in France where she did a little theater. Her accent prevented her forever from playing Célimène, but on the other hand she was enthusiastically sought after for Marlene or Mata Hari. Someone offered her a tremendous contract to play Eva Braun, but she refused. She was lucky that Brecht's theater was quite the rage during those years. All of that helped her become the mistress of an industrialist, an attractive guy, a little old, a little bit of a patron of the arts, a little groping, and finally, to nobody's surprise, an enthusiast for May '68. At The Cause she atoned for her sins. She wanted to convert to Judaism, something from which Roselyn, all the while stirring the bowls of rice in the kitchens of the Guermantes' chateau, tried to dissuade her. Currently, Karin is a trainer in a gym that's part of a club. She helps the old limousine-liberals keep a little muscle tone. She's sixty, thin as a rake, short hair, muscular, only drinks mineral water, doesn't smoke, voted pink then green; she'll bury us all. Not you, of course, you say to Thirteen's daughter. Just me, Judith, Roselyn, Fichaoui, the others.

PÈRE-LACHAISE on the right AUBERGE DE PÉKIN PLATS À EMPORTER LE CLAIRON LE BISTRO DES MOTOS QUI ONT DE LA BOUTEILLE AU MÉTRO DES LILAS CAFÉ GLACES BRASSERIE MAC DO TRAITEUR ASIATIQUE BANG PHANG AUX DÉLICES DES LILAS PATISSERIE SANDWICHES BOULANGERIE, Remember eats that all up, the red lights are green. PÉRIPH INTÉRIEUR FLUIDE PÉRIPH EXTÉRIEUR FLUIDE, emerald green in the blue night. So, we used to eat their damn rice with tomato sauce. The Issy gang would fall asleep in the middle of their empty bottles, their ruddy faces nodding like a stunned Hydra. Soon they would wake up, and with them the contradictions within the people. Fortunately for Thirteen and me, you say to his daughter, it wasn't our job to participate in these jousts. Our business was logistics, protection, administration, exact sciences. In this respect we were responsible for sleeping arrangements. As it happened, there was a problem: not enough beds. Even counting the ones Nicole let us use in the chateau, plus the cots under the tents, it wasn't working out. We were going to have to share. As for me, you tell Thirteen's daughter, I know quite well with whom I would have liked to share, but it didn't happen that way; in the evening I found myself in the sack with Juju, the terror of the Peugeot factory. I don't know if you can imagine how funny this was, my head and the head of the old cop killer side by side on the bolster, under the wine-colored canopy, the inevitable licentious print, along the lines of Fragonard's *The Bolt*, and the no less inevitable portrait of the ancestor with the starched collar . . . OK, in the middle of the night, I suddenly awaken . . . No, it's not possible! This hand groping around my balls . . . No, I must have fallen asleep again; it's a nightmare . . . Not at all, no doubt about it. It's the other guy, the famous gladiator from Montbéliard who must be sleeping. Easy does it, let's push away his hand gently, without awakening him, without his dying of shame when he wakes up to discover what the night demons, abominable succubi, profiting from his fading consciousness, pushed him to commit . . . But it comes right back, the hand of the red proletariat! Cunning, groping, yet quite insistent, knowing what it's doing. Shit! The leader of the workers' base number one is a faggot! A queen! A revelation so astonishing and for which I was so little prepared that for a long moment, immobile as a dead person, paralyzed, I let this Jean Genet imitation play with my balls! You know, you say to Thirteen's daughter, you got it, we were extremely puritan and conventional. And macho, to be sure. A worker, and what's more a revolutionary worker, can't be a queer. Of course, theoretically, it's possible, but practically speaking . . . It's a done deal, according to Juju's expression. So his hand there . . . What to do? Grab the creep, throw him out of the bed, the chateau, History? But then the scandal, the comrades demoralized by the terrible news . . . The new Spartacus a faggot! But to let this sodomite continue to dishonor the Revolution? OK, calm. "A lift of the eyebrow," according to a brilliant thought of the Great Helmsman, "and a plan will come to mind." Finally, I just told Juju (whose ridiculous nickname I then decided must come from Proust's Jupien) in no uncertain terms to let me sleep. I imagined, pitied even the confusion he would feel in the morning, his terror at being exposed, stigmatized; nothing of the sort, he was a lot less embarrassed than I was, brazenly he moped around the chateau's kitchens, mug of coffee in hand, talking to Nicole about ferocious ambushes in the mechanical jungles of Sochaux-Montbéliard. And me, for whom sex was the region of the secret, of the secret and of fear, me who would not dare put his hand on the Countess Nicole's hand as she was swirling around in her large Indian skirt, laughing, pushing back here and there a lock of her russet hair, I was in deep thought, drinking my mug of dishwater, watching this fag bullshit, thinking that he didn't lack nerve—not the nerve of the assassin he boasted he was, and whose imagination impressed us, but nerve all the same, nerve I did not possess. So in the midst of my scorn, there was a sort of admiration. In the end it was true that we learned something at the feet of the proletariat.

5

Five in the morning. How long have we been driving around? Two, three hours? How many circumnavigations have we made, Thirteen's daughter and me, at the controls of Remember? Don't know. Around this large dark ball pockmarked with electric lights, blue, red, green, blue, red, red, white, green, blue, red. A free-floating rainbow. Stroboscopic trails of light. Seven, eight. Watch the gas. Not too tired? No, fine. They're just getting up, over there on the right. Windows lighting up, the night's blinking. Arise the pyjamaed of the earth! And in the sky over there, it's coming up, isn't it? Yeah, probably a little, think so. It's moving. Greenish glows. Pretty soon the awful moment when workers set off to work, in the windy dawn, bags under the eyes, nausea, sour stomachs . . . Exhaust of the semis heading for Rungis. Exhaust of the semis orbiting toward Garonor. What nerve. I'm not getting on your nerves? No? Not too tired? No, fine, I told you. So we continue, CASINO CASTORAMA PORTE D'IVRY NANTES BORDEAUX ORLY RUNGIS ÉVRY LYON PORTE D'ITALIE CHAMPION IBIS, emerald green in the blue night, PÉRIPHÉRIQUE INTÉRIEUR FLUIDE PÉRIPHÉRIQUE FLUIDE blue, red, white, green, aurora borealis, the black steeple of Montrouge towering against the red sky, a rocket on its trajectory. v2-Chartres Cathedral. The retired general Chalais, the CEO of Atofram, a company that had fired strikers while also producing certain basic electrical components for the construction of bombs that the U.S. Air Force was dropping on Vietnam—this Chalais then—you had managed to load him into the van, and Fichaoui had taken off like a Formula 1 driver, a jolt that sent you all flying around. That became a leitmotif, you tell Thirteen's daughter. The rest of the operation was extremely delicate; it consisted of injecting Chalais with a muscle relaxer. You had no intention of holding him, just stuff him in a trunk, then drop him off at the Gare Saint-Lazare, and call the journalists. To do that we needed to stun him a bit, thus the shot. Klammer had procured the drug. Klammer was truly a character out of Dostoevsky; sorry for the stereotype, you apologize to Thirteen's daughter, but really it was as if Dostoevsky had been invented to create Klammer, not Klammer to incarnate a Dostoevskian character. He was the son in a family of Jewish diamond merchants from Antwerp who had been able to escape to America during the war thanks to a Resistance network for which Rolge was the "go-between." Klammer despised his wealth. Without him, the war chest of The Cause would have been empty, in spite of all the "democrats" or "progressives" or "sympathizers" (these words were synonyms, slightly pejorative in our mouths) whom we invited to cough up some money. But just imagine, Marguerite Duras, for instance. We had a terrible time just getting enough from her to run off a tract. Others were not so cheap; from time to time a painter would sell a picture, I would work on Nessim, but all the same, when it came to money, on the whole they did not like to part with it. Not necessarily because of stinginess, but rather because it humiliated them that nothing about them interested us but their wallets. Anyway, Klammer was the only one—the only person I ever met in fact—who wanted to get rid of his money as if it was something immoral. He must have told himself that his family had been saved because it was rich, and he couldn't stand that. I think our hitting him up gave him some comfort.

Really. I never knew anyone as negative — now wait a minute, don't get me wrong, you tell Thirteen's daughter. I'm using this word in an extremely positive way, if I can say that. Anxiety, dissatisfaction, insubordination. Doubt, intelligence, actually everything that is really human. Klammer was rich and wanted to destroy the injustice of his inheritance. In my opinion he was rather good-looking: a long face, hollowed out, high cheekbones; there was something Russian about him, not a lifeguard's or a playboy's beauty, to be sure, in fact I never knew anyone who looked so much like what people call an intellectual. Or an artist, or in that case a musician. Not a painter, no, he wasn't much interested in things, in my opinion. He was good-looking, but he thought he was frightfully ugly, obviously, I learned that later; at the time we didn't discuss stuff like that. Klammer was a young head of a clinic, the white hope of cardiac surgery, but he had sent that all packing to devote himself entirely to abortion by the Karman method; I'm not saying that wasn't useful, that he shouldn't have done it, but in fact to play with a fetus pump in the dispensary run by the Movement for the Liberalization of Abortion and Contraception, when one had been a great surgeon, that seems to me to suggest a desire to humiliate, to mortify oneself. At the same time the irony in the whole business is that by giving himself over wholly to inglorious, even a little disgusting tasks, Klammer was perhaps the only one of us who was in the sense of History, as we used to say, the only one to participate in History's invisible, unpredictable movement. He was pushing with all the obscure, unknown of the earth, and the enormous social machine was imperceptibly moving. When you look at these things thirty years later, you say to Thirteen's daughter, there's plenty to laugh at. The rest of us, with our Robin Hood act, we were completely out of it, even going against history's tide, in the wrong sense, full speed into the past, into the depths of fantasy. While Klammer, working the piston of his fetus pump in the bathroom of a bourgeois apartment in the fourteenth arrondissement, was participating, without making a big deal of it (and without realizing it himself), in the movement of the world.

I kept some newspapers from those days, you say to Thirteen's daughter. Some no longer exist, like *L'Aurore*, an incredibly reactionary rag, but one we liked because if we busted some windows somewhere we get a whole page in *L'Aurore*; it was a paper that helped us feel important, it gave us the impression we were doing something right. When you think it was the name of Clemenceau's paper . . . of the paper that published Zola's *J'accuse* . . . In the 1970s, *L'Aurore* was really Vichy repapered. I kept the issue of *L'Aurore* from the day when we grabbed this Chalais. In fact, I didn't keep it, obviously, that would have been too dangerous, we were not all idiots to that extent. No, Rolge gave it to me, years later, along with *Le Monde* and some others. I saw him for the last time after André's funeral; he had me meet him at the bar in a big Brussels' hotel, what was it called, the Metropole, maybe? With breathtaking ceilings, frescos, chandeliers as tall as church spires, acres of ironwork and elevators with gilded gates run by bellboys who looked like comic book characters. I think it was the Place de Brouckère (or maybe the Place de l'Albertine). Anyway, that's where I was going to meet Rolge, for the last time. After that, I don't know what happened to him. People told me he had dabbled in the arms trade with "progressive" African countries, Angola and others, but that might just be idle talk. He had put on a lot of weight. Still quite grungy, even though he had eventually changed glasses, and developed a taste for luxury items; he smoked Partagas cigars, supposedly because of Che, and drank Knockando, maybe because of Brel's song "Knokke-le-Zoute." Rolge claimed that it was in this bar—but he had told me so many stories since that long-ago evening when he had announced that the UN headquarters would be blown up that very night—OK, in this very bar, and probably sitting around the little table on which the waiter put his pure malt (and mine too, at the same time), that the liquidation of Patrice Lumumba had been decided; Lumumba was one of the few real African revolutionaries from the decolonization period, one of the few honest people, he was tortured to death, then cut up into pieces and dissolved in acid at Elisabethville in 1961, six months after independence. Well, according to Roger the Belgian, the crime had been decided here, at the bar in the Metropole, maybe right where we were sitting, decided between an old Nazi who served as an instructor for Moise Tschombe's mercenaries, a representative of the Miners' Association of Upper-Katanga, another one from the Chase Manhattan Bank, and a CIA agent who was also, so said Rolge, a Roman Catholic bishop *in partibus*, but Rolge used to tell so many unverifiable stories . . . The fact remains that he was evicted from his villa at Waterloo to make room for a highway; the modern, prosaic age was upon us, so he had to get rid of his files, and he gave me as a gift some newspapers that might interest me. Unfortunately, in the pile there wasn't that 1948 *Monde* where a brief article noted the death of the lieutenant "in the course of an engagement with Viet Minh rebels." I never had spoken to Rolge about this; anyway, he wouldn't have found it interesting. The Great Helmsman has said that some deaths weigh less than a feather. On the other hand, there were the papers from the day we kidnapped Chalais. Yellowed paper, deteriorated, brittle, torn at the folds, it seems today to have emerged from a space-time zone as distant as that of the letters, reports, death certificate, and inventories certifying the lieutenant's demise. You see, it's curious, you tell Thirteen's daughter: human skin, when it's young, yours for example, is pure and smooth like beautiful paper, like vellum. You would like to (but you're also afraid to) write on it. And paper, as it gets older, starts looking like leathered skin, like parchment. A paper used to cost less than a franc at the time. *L'Aurore*, seventy centimes. On the front page, under the headline denouncing "Maoist terrorism," and next to an editorial making Sartre responsible for "morals worthy of a small tribe of primitives" (how that must have delighted Sartre, reading that . . .), there's a marriage photo of Franco's daughter with I no longer know which Bourbon asshole. All these crazies decked out to the nines, "the caudillo and his spouse," says the caption surrounding the two turtle doves, with military braids, embroidery, swords, and feathered hats all over the place. That "Latin bastard," with Sartre on the same front page. I'm a contemporary of the caudillo, more or less. And of Eddy Merckx and also Nixon. Merckx was in the middle of the Paris-Nice race, and Nixon in I don't know what primary race at the time. Merckx was a guy who didn't hesitate to push himself to the front. But, listen, his opponent at the time, Ocaña, a Spaniard in fact, wasn't legless either. Luis Ocaña, the name doesn't mean a thing to you, does it? I bet neither does Franco, you ask Thirteen's daughter. Still, you remember his death, already half-decomposed, limbs falling off, the old swine, rotting, bristling with catheters, tubes wound all around him. You can say he got the death he deserved. According to the *Le Monde* headline, President Pomp also believed that the kidnapping of Chalais was "an act worthy of a country of savages." But what was almost as surprising on this page, what confirms that we are in the presence of a document issuing from the night of time are two items — the newspaper's phone number on the masthead: PRO 91 29, Provence 91 29. Three letters, four numbers, that was a telephone number at the time. The Doppler effect, indeed! The proof that everything is separating from everything else, the wake of the expanding universe. Isn't it? And the second item from before the flood is a little article on a just promulgated decree authorizing the use of an IUD under certain conditions. Just imagine! Back then contraception didn't exist. It was before the Veil Law, and the enlightened era of Giscard . . . So Klammer with his fetus pump was contributing to the writing of History. He was pushing society's great sunken wreck in the right direction, the one where it wanted to go, where in any case it would go; meantime, us with our Sten submachine guns and our false beards, we were trying desperately to turn History back, we were products of the time of the caudillo, of the Spanish anarchist, Durruti, and even of Don Quixote.

And besides that, you explain to Thirteen's daughter, in that edition of *Le Monde* there was some news that had devastated you when you read it the day after your citizen's arrest of the retired general Chalais. Roger the Belgian has met you on the other side of the border, at

Estaimpuis for sure (or maybe Néchin?), an enormous red sun was sweeping over the roofs while you were crossing the border, you and Thirteen, even though it had made you laugh and you had begun singing the East is red, the sun rises, tra lala lalere; it was cold and your breath was blowing smoke into the Belgian dawn, an enormous grenadine sun was blazing forth into the winter mist. It was over there that you would bury André at least a dozen years later (you, not Thirteen, you remind his daughter: he had already been pushing up daisies for sometime already when you would bury André, not far from, really quite close, to the place where you crossed the border). Rolge had housed each of you in the homes of "progressive" Belgians in wealthy neighborhoods at Ixelles, where you were; the owners lived in a dark brick Flemish house with high jagged gables, you particularly recall that the young lady of the house was a nice bit of stuff, and under her fur coats she wore quite revealing dresses. But in the end it seemed to you not to be the moment to do something stupid. On the Belgian TV that you were watching with your hosts (and thus Mrs. Mechlin Lace, whom you checked out from the corner of your eye), you saw on the Royal Belgian Television News General Chalais's face with, to tell the truth, two very black eyes, that had provided you with a rather unpleasant surprise, then the prune-faced interior minister, Saint-Marcellin. "A Resistance hero," is what Saint-Marcellin called Chalais. What was that all about? Saint-Marcellin (as for him, he was the type who would have stood at attention in short pants every morning to sing "Marshal, here we are"), Saint-Marcellin was known to be a shameless liar, an expert in low blows, but still . . . In any case, the effect had been immediate on Mechlin Lace and her husband (he was a lawyer), who both opined that it must have been fascists who had done this. The very idea of blackening the eyes of a Resistance hero before locking him in a trunk! Sure, presented like that . . . the whole business was basically indefensible. Your hosts did not know the reason that brought you to them; Rolge had made up an edifying tale about the defense of deported immigrants, this was the kind of tall story that automatically calmed the suspicions of middle-class leftists, you say to Thirteen's daughter at the same time as you give her a sarcastic look, a look asking for a fight. The reaction didn't take long. What are you, a racist?, she asks you. Repeat that, and you get out here, on the beltway, right now, is your gracious response. Still, you add: Excuse me. I hate racists, believe it or not. But politically correct sentiments disgust me, progressive conformism is no less stupid, no less blind than the reactionary sort, and these days, since the progressive version is culturally on top, it's more aggravating, not to mention potentially harmful; you know what the road to hell is paved with. OK. I'll continue. A fire was burning in the chimney, whiskey on a low table, good whiskey smelling of peat, copies of *Le Nouvel Observateur*, reproductions of Magritte on the walls, Mao's complete works in the library between Mallarmé and Marcuse, a truly p.c. house. There was also a dog, I forget what model, but top of the line. Lace, graciously curled up on the Persian rug, at the foot of her lawyer's armchair, legs pulled up under her, leaning on an arm, of the two she was the more convinced, the more virulent, she would have executed on the spot those who had pulled this stunt. The lawyer, because of his profession more inclined toward relativism, was less adamant. As for you, fearing you might give yourself away (and besides hoping to please her), you agreed completely with Lace. Caught between frustrated lust and abjuration, it wasn't a good evening. So the next day at dawn you ran all the way to the Midi Station to buy *Le Monde*. There it was! The disaster confirmed. Mother of God! "A soldier in the Free French Army." *Le Monde* said it, not Saint-Marcellin. Prisoner in 1940, he escapes, makes it to London then from there to the Levant where he rejoins the First French Free Division. Wounded at Garigliano . . . Wounded again before Strasbourg . . . Shit . . . This guy, maybe he was a boss, but before that an antifascist soldier (it ran through your mind he might have served with your father) who you beat up in a van . . . Because it was just bound to happen like that, it wasn't your intention for sure, but nobody gave a damn about your intentions, and people were right not to give a damn. It wasn't our intention, you say to Thirteen's daughter, we just wanted to put him in a trunk and leave him at the Gare Saint-Lazare, because lots of people went by there, because it was from Saint-Lazare the trains departed for the Atofram factory where the strikers had been fired. The place that produced the basic electrical components for the construction of certain bombs the U.S. Air Force dropped on Vietnam. Klammer had gotten us a tranquilizer. A light tranquilizer, it's important to be clear about that, you tell Thirteen's daughter: Klammer had explained that with a stronger substance there was a slight risk, but a risk all the same, of cardiac problems, so we had chosen the weaker one, bottom of the line, a sort of enhanced chamomile. I'm not trying to suggest it was a question of politeness, not at all, but all the same for outlaws we did prefer the kid-glove approach. But was it because you were afraid? she replies. Afraid for yourselves. No, Marie, if we had been afraid, quite simply we wouldn't have done that sort of thing. When you get to that point, you no longer fear for yourself. Or in any case it has no effect. On the contrary the fear is part of it, part of the drug. Anyway, this chamomile, was not at all like the "soporifics" in Tintin, that type of drug where a badly shaven guy pours three drops in a glass and bingo, that's it. No, we had to inject him in the butt to be sure to get the right result, and all that in a moving van. Judith was in charge of the procedure. Strange how we relied on clichés: a good injection required feminine delicacy, etc. For a job having nothing delicate about it. OK, it was still necessary to get this Chalais to drop his pants. There, he refused. We explained matters to him, really, we tried to be persuasive, to play down the situation, but no, nothing could be done. And besides, he was right. There is an ancient and barbarous relation between nudity and torture. The Roman legionnaires threw dice for the clothing of the crucified. The Nazis loved to hang their victims nude. The Chetniks, in the caves where they went to shoot their prisoners, stripped them first. So just imagine how grotesque the situation was. Some of us grabbing on his belt, so was he, Judith brandishing the syringe, trying to keep her balance in the careening van. In the struggle I lost my blond wig. Finally, Momo Lock-Eater, I think it was him, got fed up. Maybe it was Thirteen, but I think it was Lock-Eater. He was a good little boxer, was he, and he gave him a quick punch in the nose. Look, I'm not throwing stones at Lock-Eater, you say to Thirteen's daughter, given the mess we were in, it was the only thing to do. Chalais suddenly calmed down, so Judith was able to give him the needle. We felt relieved, but not really proud of ourselves. And not in much better shape than he was. Damn it! Had I known that this guy had been a comrade-in-arms with the lieutenant . . . maybe a friend . . . When we discovered his service record, in our *Galapagos*, that gave us a terrible depression. That was when for the first time the idea of giving it all up passed through our heads (the second time was the business with the pharmacist). Should we be risking our lives to take part in such screwups? . . . Thirteen and I met in a café, an attractive café in a covered arcade near the Grand-Place. I gave him the news. What will people think of us, what will people think of us, he kept repeating, as if that were the problem. We entered the Grand-Place to see the "House of the Painters," where Victor Hugo lived in 1852. We had to admit that, next to him, as exiles we didn't amount to much. Then to calm our nerves we went for a walk in a wood on the edge of the city. I forgot the name, maybe the Soignes Forest? Or the Cambre Woods? A tramline went there. It was either that or get loaded on beer, and that would not have been a good idea. We even saw a deer. That really impressed Thirteen, he had never seen a deer, nor a fox, nor any animal except the ones in the zoo when he was a kid; of course, he had seen rats down in the metro, he was truly the total city dweller, in spite of his "old lady" who lived in the forest of Fontainebleau or around there, but he never went to see her except when we were burying dynamite. Hey, look, it's Bambi! He kept repeating that, all excited, pronouncing the *bi* like *bay*! He couldn't get over it. As for me, by dint of telling him again and again that it was a simple deer, and not "Bambi" or "Bambay," I wound up getting him annoyed and he started sparring with me like he did later on the Pont Mirabeau.

You know, you say to Thirteen's daughter, something you have to understand was that we were kids. We were your age then, can you imagine? I'm not a kid, is her chilly reply. Yes, of course, that wasn't what I meant, of course, but still, just a little? Yes? No? At the same time you glance at her from the corner of your eye, her back up against Remember's door, taking a drag, a leg folded under her butt, knee glistening in the shadows, the other leg stretched toward the center of the car. Not a little girl, not a little girl . . . You try again: OK, what I meant was that we were extremely young, we did some serious things, but we still had very childish sides. For example, I remember that while we were planning Chalais's kidnapping at the house in Normandy Blitz had lent us, we almost killed one another at the end of a round of Monopoly. What a bullshit game that is, when you think about it for a minute. It was the era people had the nerve to call, "The Thirty Glorious Years," in celebration of France's postwar economic boom: a time when children were taught to become landowners . . . real estate agents. The so-called glory was money. You know, you say to Thirteen's daughter, I don't like the year 2000 very much, but frankly I detested the 1970s. The fact remains that Lock-Eater had patiently built a real estate empire, and then suddenly the sneaky deal between Thirteen and Fichaoui made him lose everything, the rue de la Paix, the Avenue Mozart, the Avenue Henri-Martin, all the places where we used to prowl around, where we used to pull jobs, where in fact we were in the process of plotting a job — all these places detested yet desired by the young pimp from Issy-les-Moulineaux, he had been gotten rid of like a piece of dirt with a few throws of the dice; he'd been imagining himself a mogul and suddenly he found himself naked, cleaned out, ripped off, because of a treacherous alliance of two intellectuals against him, the prole! Lock-Eater couldn't take that, he threw over the table and jumped on Thirteen, who held his own, I must say. We had a little trouble preventing them from really busting one another up. Just imagine: there we were, at Blitz's place, preparing a job where in fact we could get killed, an action that President Pomp would find "worthy of a country of savages," and we were acting like kids in the playground.

KOREAN AIR red blue PANASONIC blue SANYO red SAMSUNG blue AI–AI04 FLUIDE a bridge crosses the tracks of the Gare du Nord, sprays of shiny steel, bordered by electric violets, that's how Thirteen and me escaped, in the postal train, on the right Apollinaire's anemone and ancholy, Cendrars's city of the Great Gibbet and the Wheel, the past continues to haunt us, ST-DENIS, CH. DE GAULLE LILLE BRUXELLES PORTE DE LA CHAPELLE AI, hold on, there's something else over there, you say to Thirteen's daughter, shaking your arm out Remember's lowered window, next to the black towers of the Porte de la Chapelle; in front of them you can see the diadems of AGFA and TDK, diamonds and rubies, and just beyond the wheat fields, the beet fields, and the killing fields, the fields that extend toward the sea under the dark rain. Once I was a real bastard with your father. It feels funny calling him "your father," but why not. It only happened once, but it did happen. I'd rather you know. One day, a little after Chalais's kidnapping, there was an incident with Beatrice, the lawyer. At the time he wasn't your father, since you weren't born. He had not even met your mother, so you see . . . Thirteen, he's the one not in the photo, so my memory of his face fades in my mind, for a long time he's been just an image that weakens and dies in the very effort to reappear, that dissolves once I try to fix it in my head, still, it seems to me all the same that he was quite good-looking. Gray eyes, hooked nose, broken actually, the bone was on an angle, short, dirty-blond hair. A dimple in the middle of the chin. And especially something fiery about him, that we all had more or less, but with us it was a few sparks, with him it was a forest fire. Now Beatrice, I've told you this, we were all in love with her, piercing green eyes, almost yellow, high cheek bones, dark hair pulled back, knotted over the nape, cascading down her throat . . . Always dressed in black. Half-Indian, half-wolf. Scared the hell out of the judges. Some of us, I told you this too, were suspected of getting arrested just to talk to her.

Otherwise they wouldn't have dared speak to her. Thirteen, he had this daring. He easily affected cynicism, especially with women — excuse me, at the time we still said "girls" — but that was the posturing of a shy kid. In fact, he was like most of us, a proud, insecure young man. In a word, one day they took off together, without telling anyone. In that direction, toward the north, around Somme Bay. To Saint-Valéry, or maybe Crotoy. But I don't like that name, so let's say Saint-Valéry. At the time, as I've already told you, we used to spend our lives in "meets," so their disappearance was quickly noticed. Right away we got worried, fearing that they were prisoners somewhere, in some secret place, at the bottom of some dungeon. After two or three days, Thirteen contacted me. Now, Marie, you say to Thirteen's daughter, you have to try and imagine this: back then there were no mobile phones or answering machines. OK? And then of course no fixed abodes for us. Get it? So, wherever we happen to be staying, supposing it did have a phone, we avoid using it because we're afraid of wiretaps, and also, possibly, if we were feeling particularly noble — but that's rare — we avoid the phone out of respect for the "prog" who is putting us up, or loaning us a room. We live in a world that, in terms of communication, is closer to that of the soldier at Marathon or the carrier pigeon than the Internet. Everything depends on a system of pre-established drop-off places with the possibility of alternatives (you realize that although these notions are quite obvious to anyone who has ever read a book or seen a movie about the Resistance or espionage, they are beyond the ken of Thirteen's daughter, whose eyes widen in wonder. Have you read *The Red Orchestra*? you ask for the hell of it, her head shakes vigorously from left to right. We've passed from one imaginary universe to another. Serial killers, who occupy the place in contemporary mythology that guerillas and members of the underground did in the past, don't have alternative drops, passwords, etc. They act alone. Progress of individualism, regression of the spirit of organization. Leopold Trepper, the real-life hero of *The Red Orchest . . .* you don't know who . . . ? NO! Fine, too bad. You ought to. You still have the impression you're giving her an

156

exam, excuse me, sorry. OK, he was one of our heroes. He still is, as far as I'm concerned.). Anyway, here's how it worked: if someone was not at the agreed meeting place, or the fallback one, we would wait for him to contact us through a "prog," who played the role for us of liaison agent. Ours, between Thirteen (and Fichaoui, and Lock-Eater, etc.) and me, is Laura, a Franco-Argentine psychiatrist — she has double nationality — and lives in the Boulevard Edgar Quinet, not far from Sartre (several years later, she goes back to Buenos Aires. She becomes a sympathizer with l'Ejercito revolucionario del pueblo, the People's Revolutionary Army, more or less Trotskyist. A few years later, not too many, she will be abducted in her office, which is also her home, in calle Maipú, not far from where Borges lived, by a group of soldiers dressed in jogging outfits and driving a Ford Falcon without license plates. We know she was imprisoned, tortured, and raped, of course, at the NMS, the Naval Mechanical School, on the banks of the Rio de la Plata. Afterwards, what seems most plausible is that her body was burned in an incinerator used for dead animals in the section called Mataderos, on the edge of Buenos Aires. I get this information, you say to Thirteen's daughter, from my friend Horacio, a human rights lawyer over there, also a great admirer of Napoleon, collects his signed letters and lead soldiers of Bonaparte's Grand Army, a magnificent guy who fought a duel with sabers against an officer from one of the torture squads, turned him into a nicely trimmed piece of meat.

So, after two or three nervous days, Laura has me informed that Thirteen called her, that everything is fine, and that he will call me tomorrow at her house. I go there at the agreed-upon time. I wait, and wait. One of the fundamental rules in our lives is punctuality. Without that, everything goes to pieces. Finally the phone rings. It's him. You'll never guess what I'm looking at, he tells me. A great start. He has a curious voice, a little cracked. No, I won't guess, so tell me. The sea. That's just great! The sea . . . I must tell you, you explain to Thirteen's daughter, it had been a long time for all of us between vacations — except the kinds of "vacations" immortalized in the photo where Thirteen does not appear, the photo where he gets his nickname, those vacations where we were setting out to preach to the peasants. So imagine him at the seaside. What are you doing? Nothing. I'm looking at the ocean. Beautiful, extremely beautiful. I'd forgotten that water could be so beautiful. It sparkles, it dazzles, shadows sail just above, under the clouds . . . The color of oysters and then suddenly the color of aluminum wrap. How could we have lived without that? It makes me want to sing, he says. Me, I can't believe it. I didn't recognize in his words the language of the "broad masses." The broad masses don't give a damn (so we thought) about the beauty of the sea. Don't forget to bring back photos, I said to him sarcastically. Send Gideon some postcards, he'll like that. But he kept going on in his visionary tone. It calms him, supposedly. He likes to look at the clouds, the seabirds, so elegant and gracious. Bullshit like that. Elegance! Grace! I must be dreaming. These are words we had forgotten, if we ever knew them. Did the strikers at the Atofram factory worry about elegance? Elegance is a typically bourgeois, decadent notion. Listen, I say to him: the sea is a worker's tool for sailors and fisherman, and an area of strategic rivalry for imperialists. That's it, and that's all! Come back to earth. I'm on earth, he responds. On the shore, at Saint-Valéry-sur-Somme exactly (or maybe Crotoy), looking at the sea. The estuary, more precisely. You're the one not on the earth. We no longer know how to feel. We're becoming violent and idiotic. We no longer love. We no longer love . . . this is unbelievable, I think he's been drugged. Or frankly that he took drugs. What're you on, I ask. Two bottles of Sancerre, and lots of joints. With Beatrice. Because I'm with her, you get it? She's beautiful too. She calms me down too. OK, calm me down, may not be the right expression. Listen, I'm not asking you to draw me a picture. I want you to come back. They came back. I had referred the matter to Gideon. It was the rule, but still, shitty. I was angry at myself for a long time about that. Gideon hadn't taken it well. You have to struggle against a lax lifestyle, etc. The cleverness of any moron is enough to start a political trial, and Gideon was anything but that, a moron. There were plenty of charges. In a world where a beard is required, the clean-shaven go to the gallows. We merely had to bend over to find rocks for the stoning. There was a trial, they were separated. Winter's story all over again. It was claimed that since she had to defend all of us, she couldn't be involved with any one of us. Of course, the truth was that we all wanted to keep her as the imaginary object of our desire. She had to remain in joint ownership. The queen bee. And then, Beatrice and Thirteen were providing the bad example of joyful liberty, carefree, careless about others, we would say. I was part of this crap. One day or another we're all Judas.

About the sea, the last time Thirteen saw it, he had all the time in the world to contemplate it. At Deauville, the summer after the photo, the summer of 1970. Just after the Cambodian invasion and before Black September, I'm telling you this so you'll get the picture, you say to Thirteen's daughter. The Americans had invaded Cambodia, and then pulled out. Leaving from My Tho, Vinh Long, and Cai Be, they had gone up the Mekong as far as Phnom Penh and Tonlé Sap in order to destroy the Communist "sanctuaries." While the armed flotillas were going up the river, the B-52s were raining torrents of Agent Orange and other defoliants on the neighboring jungles. Hundreds of thousands of young people across the United States had demonstrated against the war. Four students had been killed by the National Guard on the Kent State campus. An armada of barges and patrol boats had gone up the Mekong; many of them had cast off from the piers made from coconut trees sunk into the river under the veranda of the lieutenant's house . . . the house such as you found it the day after the night spent twenty-five years later in room 501 of the Huong Duong Hotel, leafing through yellowed documents, torn at the folds, printed with violet ink like the menus in workers' restaurants used to be, or like what was on the carcasses of animals in the butcher shop, documents adorned with faded stamps, soon to be a half a century old, where death appeared in the category "object": "Amphibious Flotilla South Indochina. Object: personnel officer's death."

The major part of the city had been destroyed and then reconstructed haphazardly during the American war; flaking concrete sprouted like fungus in the center of town, with suburbs of sheet iron and wood all around it, the ochre colonial constructions, with verandas and balusters under tile roofs, were no longer the common sights they used to be. You had feared that the lieutenant's house might have disappeared in the landslide of time, carried off like those tree trunks, those dead buffalo, the rafts of weeds turning in the current of the Mekong; rather the house of the coffin since the only trace you had of it was the little yellowed snapshot with the serrated edges, six sailors in dress whites carrying on their shoulders his coffin covered with the flag, standing at the foot of the staircase leading to the veranda capped by a tile roof oddly carved and tiered, a sort of geometrical variation on the theme of the pagoda. You had gone out of the Huong Duong Hotel early, determined to explore My Tho methodically, street by street. You loved the streets in Vietnam, the intense humid heat, the swarms of bikes, mopeds, scooters, rickshaws, the grace of the girls dressed in ao dai, that tunic delightfully half-opened at the side, exposing a flash of olive skin . . . silken cyclists wearing wide-brimmed hats and long gloves to protect their frail arms from the sun, gloves going right up to the elbow like you used to see in your mother's fashion magazines when you were a kid, gloves worn with the evening gowns of Jacques Fath, Balenciaga . . . necks like young bamboo trees, darting glances from black eyes . . . the fireflies also, the butterflies with their languorous flights, the glossy vigor of the leaves, the chattering in tonal sounds, the colorful stench — dried fish, chicken droppings, car exhaust, rotted fruit? As soon as you left the hotel, you plunged into the semi-stupor that the kaleidoscope of Asia invariably communicates to simple Western minds (so invariably that you wondered whether the intoxication experienced was not due, in part, to the recognition of the stereotype amid the stupor, a stereotype to which you succumbed all the same). You had wandered through the rows in a market along the canal, among the bowls piled high with the pearly flesh of skinned-alive frogs, the ducks and piglets splashing about in the mud, the catfish aligned in rows on banana leaves. In the middle of a stall where old papers were sold by their weight, you had stumbled upon a French edition of *Four Philosophical Essays* by the Great Helmsman. You remained for some time fascinated in front of an aquarium where two long fish were turning around in opposite directions, sorts of eel-herrings armored with wide copper-colored scales, jaws like a bulldog's, closing toward the top, monstrously simple, rough, prehistoric fuselages that seemed part of an evolution from stone to life. You even found some charm in the giant signboards at the street corners exalting the Seventh Congress of the Communist Party: hammers and sickles, golden stars on a purple background (like the rustic calico banner, which, your mother had explained to you when you were young, was, along with a large bloody flag from the Third Reich, the lieutenant's "war prizes"), images of the proletariat with impressive fists, joyous soldiers brandishing their AK-47s, robust peasant women in their Tonkinese hats, fighter planes, factory chimneys, very florid and expressionist, intense; in the past you'd struggled to see in these kinds of works a new art in the service of the people (such gross naiveté astonishes you now).

If the house still existed, you were sure to find it on the banks of the Mekong, a normal place for a guy whose job was to command an amphibious flotilla. And in fact, going along 30 Street, which bordered the river, you ran into it quite quickly. In the back of what must have been a garden shaded by a large banyan tree, its tiled roofs, spiked like dragon scales, rose up in tiers. The gate at the street was open, so you went into the garden expecting some serious aggravation (you had already been stopped when you were taking pictures of the hospital where the medical captain N. had confirmed the cause of death as "grievous wounds in the left scapular-vertebral region due to shell fragments," the unfriendly soldier who had nabbed you only decided to release you, relieved of your disposable camera, because he couldn't find anyone to interrogate you who spoke English or French). In front of the steps leading to the veranda was an obviously very old flagpole. You stood before the staircase at the spot where the coffin was in the snapshot with serrated edges. Nobody asked you anything. A woman shuffled across the veranda, her flip-flops clacking. She gave you a gloomy look. You were standing there, at the exact spot where the father you never knew was lying dead forty-eight years ago; from a rational viewpoint, it was necessary to admit this had no particular significance, yet it seemed to you, from another point of view, and not only the superstitious one, it was significant. It seemed to you that you were honoring a meeting that had been put off for a long time; it seemed to you, like to a Greek out of Homer, that your presence here, after half a century, was going to appease a wandering soul (before you would leave My Tho, in the pagoda of Longevity, someone would show you a sort of Christmas fir with seven times seven branches; someone told you it was "the tree of the wandering souls"). You had come to accomplish something like that, a very ancient rite, which, however incomprehensible, unexplainable it seemed, nevertheless appeared a necessity. You had come to speak, to introduce yourself to the spirits. You had tried to explain that to the sailor on the sampan the night before (and he, had he spoken your language, would have had no trouble understanding). Emboldened, playing for all you could get, you went up the stairs. Beyond the interior darkness, framed by three bay windows looking out on the opposing veranda where the light from the river was sparkling, some guys in short-sleeved shirts were drinking beer and smoking. The lieutenant's house had become a bistro (belonging, you later learned, to the Vietnamese navy, who had appointed a manager for it, in order to "do business," the dominant passion of the last few Communist regimes). Alright, this was probably good news. The place where the lieutenant had lived the final days of his life, where he had marked you, scarcely born, with the violet seal of death, was a bistro on the Mekong. Here's looking at you, lieutenant! Getting together at the bar, nothing like it for breaking the ice between the living and the dead. You didn't know his tastes in this respect; your mother didn't fill you in on this side of your father, but certain stories that the retired military doctor in Beirut had told made you think that he didn't just jiggle the ice cubes. Not to mention his engendering a drunk like you . . . On the right and left walls of the vast central room monumental pictures were hanging, one of snow-capped peaks, the other of horses galloping through rushing water. At Saint-Flour or Quimper they would just have been banally hideous, but here, pockmarked with light from the reflections of the Mekong, they achieved an almost moving level of ridiculousness. A moon-faced waitress was behind the bar, and there were also in this room, which opened on four smaller ones, imitation leather armchairs covered with cigarette burns, and a television. It had to be here that the funeral procession began. Over there, in front of the bar, must have been the trestle with the coffin lying on top. His head almost severed from his shoulders. "Wounds in the left scapular-vertebral region from shell fragments. In witness whereof we provide this certificate . . ." Was he disfigured as well? Who came to honor him, and for what reasons? Military duty, friendship, love? Maybe even assuaged hatred. Every life, no matter how young, creates hatreds. Especially in an uptight milieu like the army. A subordinate he was short with, unjust (some of the retired military doctor's stories, told to you in a Beirut cellar where you were getting loaded on arak, indicated he was quite capable of that), a superior officer to whom he had shown his contempt, a Vichy type, for example, an anti-Gaullist officer suddenly and clumsily recycled into a "Free France" soldier. Or maybe somebody whose wife he chatted up? Just came to be sure the lieutenant would be out of the picture for good. And then perhaps also the woman, leaning over toward his face (more or less put back together), but with completely different feelings. Maybe one of the white dresses you could barely see, on the left of the little photo with the serrated edges, under the tall, slender trunks of the areca trees? You went out on the veranda built on stilts over the river. Moored to piers made from coconut trees were bunches of illuminated fishing boats with vermilion prows, nestled one next to the other, with rain awnings and flags snapping on top of long bamboo poles, gold stars on a purple background that the lieutenant had considered his duty to tear away from the "rebels," that you would nail on pickaxe handles when you faced off against the cops, back then — for instance the day you'd met Chloe after getting your jaw busted up. The symbol of the world's poor resisting the world's powerful, is what you used to think. All around the fishing boats unloading baskets of blue and gold crabs, around hampers of fish with bleeding gills, gaping like open wounds, a swarm of launches was circulating.

You had gotten a table on the corner of the veranda, above the water's glitter, and ordered a Tiger beer. Right away an old, very wrinkled guy, with large almost transparent protruding ears, which made him look like a friendly bat, came over and asked if he could join you at the table. He spoke a somewhat old-fashioned, but quite understandable French. He informed you he had been a pianist in the hotel bars at Vientiane and Luang Prabang, in Laos, then at Saigon, and that he had fought the French with the Viet Minh. We didn't have any choice, he tells you by way of excuse, and you agree completely: they didn't have any choice. He assured you that even during the war at the bivouac in the middle of the jungle, he had managed to play on pianos found here and there, and carted around for several days on the backs of mules: tunes by Fréhal, Damia, Maurice Chevalier, Trenet. And even a composer whose name the man's pronunciation initially made it impossible to understand, and that you took to be a Vietnamese musician, Nal Do Anh, or something like that, to your amazement, it turned out to be Proust's friend, Reynaldo Hahn. Reynaldo Hahn in the jungle! In the middle of a war! You really would have loved to have been there for that. Why not Vinteuil's sonata? According to him, those tunes were very different from today's French songs, except that what he called today's music was revolting treacle, dating, it seemed to you, from the pre–rock-and-roll days of your adolescence, stuff that at that very moment was oozing from the cassette-radio on the bar:

"Blue, blue, blue the sky of Provence / White, white, white, the gulls."
As for him, the old bat was intoning "I siing from morning to evening,"
while tapping on the table with his bony fingers. A real enthusiast. Ah,
Trenet! A great poet. "I liiee in the grassy woods, the fliiees don't sting
me . . ." The former soldier in the Viet Minh was wide-eyed with joy
to have stumbled on a Phap, a Frenchman. To tell the truth, since de
Gaulle he had more or less given up on French politics. But de Gaulle
. . . Great leader! according to him (to listen to this guy, you thought
with amusement, was to realize his idea of France was barely more
out of date than yours). When you explained to him the reason for
your trip to My Tho, he seemed truly sorry that Indochina had not
made a better impression on your father, the lieutenant. This guy was
really charming. You ordered another Tiger and some crabs. The fat
moon-faced waitress tossed them alive, blue and gold, gesticulating
with their big claws, on a bed of coals glowing in a cut-down metal
drum; you couldn't help feeling some sympathy for the crabs; there
was something painful in this sight. As for the old pianist, his toothless
mouth was agape with laughter.

Doubtless the rumor of a foreigner's presence had spread along 30
Street and beyond, because at that very moment a guy carrying a python around his neck showed up on the veranda, the thing was about
three-and-a-half meters long, and its diameter measured more than
one of your thighs. Naturally he came right at you, the attraction was
destined for you. Serpents (as opposed to spiders) don't scare you to
death, but that's not to say that you wanted to try on that cold musty
scarf, capable, all things considered, of turning your neck into sausage
meat . . . And what especially got to you was that all eyes were fixed on
you. OK, you had to put up with it, stand up with this soft barbell on
your shoulders (the damn thing must have weighed over fifty kilos), get
a Polaroid taken, acknowledge the applause. Afterward, the python's
owner kindly took it off you, the animal coiled up at his feet like a big
dog gone through a meat grinder, and you bought him a Tiger (the

guy). He plunged into an extremely animated conversation with the old pianist who translated the essential parts. It came out that he (the python's owner) had been part of a tank crew in the North Vietnam Army during the war against the Americans. He had witnessed such horrible things that after the war he slid into a depression and alcoholism. About the final offensive against Saigon, in the spring of '75, which ought to have been his hour of glory as a soldier, he had particularly atrocious memories. The soldiers from the South, the "puppets," in Communist terminology, were scattering en masse, pursued by the tanks. On the delta road his T-54 had crushed an old Renault Dauphine with half a dozen fugitives in it. He said that human flesh was literally sprouting out of the metal. It was . . . according to him it was like stepping by mistake on a tube of toothpaste. Later they had to go clean the tank's tracks in a river. The old pianist translated all that for you. From the python, calmly coiled on the floor, only the little black tongue was moving, but very quickly, and all the time. The former tank crew member ordered another Tiger and so did you. He had sunk into alcoholism and been thrown into prison as an antisocial element. He was freed because of his service record. Presently, he made his living with the python and the Polaroid and he was also a gardener. When there were no tourists, he sold no photos, or maybe one from time to time to a bourgeois communist, but bourgeois communists paid peanuts, and the python had to eat its three ducks a week, otherwise, he got hungry and then . . . and then it really wasn't a good idea to wrap him around your neck. Emerald isles, dead buffalos, hooves pointing toward the sky like the horses Isaak Babel had seen, one winter's night, on the Nevsky Prospect, were swirling downstream with the current toward the China Sea. Shiny clouds, as if made of mercury, drifted over the river. "Life very difficult," the old pianist sadly commented.

Where was I? you ask Thirteen's daughter. Before telling you about the lieutenant's house, I mean. Oh, right, that's it, I was telling you about what was happening in the summer of 1970. You weren't even born then . . . so, I'll have to draw you a picture. An armada of barges, American launches, and puppet soldiers had gone up the Mekong and invaded Cambodia to destroy the Communist "sanctuaries." The Palestinians were getting ready to blow up three planes in the Jordanian desert, while King Hussein's Bedouins were getting ready to drive the Palestinians out of Amman with rifle butts and knives. The world was at war, while we, listen, it's pretty funny, you say to Thirteen's daughter, we had decided to spoil the vacations of the rich. We smeared paint on their villas, their yachts, their cars; we poured liquid manure on their hotel carpets. Let's admit it, it was pretty childish. Certainly not up to the level of what was happening around us. Thirteen led an excellent team whose mission it was to mess up various places at Deauville, the casino, the racetrack, the marina, etc. OK, I am saying "marina," but the marinas you see everywhere today are like the highways, the supermarkets, all the stuff that's now part of the landscape, the center of the landscape, they give the impression of having been there as long as the hills, or in any case, the cathedrals; that wasn't the case then, it had barely begun. A "marina" was a fishing port where there were some yachts. The majority of the troops consisted of the seven Knock-off brothers, a variety of very muscular young guys, not overly given to intellectual speculation, the diverse offspring of a swashbuckling sleeparound who made so many enemies that he wound up getting knocked off, thus the tots' name. To tell the truth the seven Knock-offs were semiretarded, but it wasn't for their intelligence people sought them out (or, more frequently, fled from them). Each one alone was scary enough, but formed into a family phalanx they represented an almost unstoppable capacity for devastation. Their father's death, which they attributed quite confusedly to the plotting of the well-off (a category where judges, garage mechanics, police, and reporters were all mixed together), made this gang of tough guys subversives without their knowing it, but Thirteen knew it for them. He initially put them to use busting up a few Porsches and Jaguars, then he had them smear tar on the hulls of about twenty yachts. This almost turned out to be a disaster. One of the little brothers got his foot caught in some boat cordage and fell into the water; obviously he couldn't swim. It's not that the Knock-offs disliked these excursions, just that they would have preferred a little more rough stuff. A dash of rape as well, if possible. No, really? Why? As for them, they saw no reason to hold back, but Thirteen, as you probably suspect, you say to his daughter, was intransigent on the subject. On the other hand, he thought it would be smart to set them loose on a feline festival organized by the Opal Coast Cat Club held at the Normandy Hotel (or maybe the Grand Hôtel de Cabourg?). The invasion of a bunch of sinister guys in the palace's meeting rooms caused a sensation, not only with the waiters and the dowagers, but the pussies as well. One of the cat contestants, back arched, hair like sizzling sparks, emitted a demonic growl, and looked like it was about to jump on Eddy, the oldest and the largest of the Knock-offs. This blowhard with fragile nerves, I'm talking about the cat, you tell Thirteen's daughter, was named Casanova von Amorsbrunn, a Short-Hair Silver Shaded, and he belonged to the Comtesse du Paty de Clam (Thirteen learned these details the next day reading *Paris-Normandie*). That little snob, I'm still talking about Casanova, nibbled at what passed for cat food, maybe foie gras, in the house of the descendants of Dreyfus's accuser. So this tiger from an anti-Semitic drawing room seemed ready to fly at the gigantic Eddy. Now physical force in no way serves as protection against the fear of tiny critters; La Fontaine has a fable about that, "The Elephant and the Mouse," or maybe "The Lion and the Rat," who knows. There's something in Mao too, in a different style, a different register, but in the end, it's the same encouraging lesson: the small can triumph over the large. American imperialism is a paper tiger, the people's war is unstoppable, etc. Eddy Knock-off, with his brothers, could have driven off a squad of CRS with no trouble, but here, before the simple semblance of an attack from a society cat, he covers his face with his hands and takes off screaming like a baby giant. In this instance, Eddy Knock-off is a paper tiger. The brothers, disconcerted, yet used to following their elder blindly, fall over themselves in their haste behind him. Getting through the revolving doors was like Napoleon getting the Grand Army across the Berezina; the vestibule doors, that Proust had so often pushed with an ivory hand, suddenly invaded by half a rugby team at full speed, jam and then explode, the frame breaks, glass shatters, blood flows, three of the brothers fall into the hands of the waiters. You have to note — you have Thirteen's daughter note — that the abovementioned waiters prudently took cover when the Knock-offs burst in, thirty seconds before. But the disarray provoked by Casanova von Amorsbrunn alone (unless it was Valmont von Thurn und Taxis, or Bazin de Guermantes, I've somewhat forgotten the name today, anyway, it wasn't me who read it in *Paris-Normandie* ou *Ouest Éclair*, who knows, it was Thirteen), this rout, then, rekindled in an instant the natural ferocity of the servants of power. And now, lying in the broken glass, the three fallen Knock-offs are going through hell. And then things just kept getting worse, you point out to Thirteen's daughter; the speed of the collapse had completely sapped the moral wellspring of this formidable fraternity: some of them, screaming and twisting convulsively in the shattered glass, accept without dignity or resistance the blows coming from the waiters, the others run like hell through the streets of Cabourg (or Deauville, I can't remember), haggard, out of breath, losing here and there an accessory — a shoe, a cap, keys, their papers. That's what will allow the cops to pick them up easily, where they are lying still stunned at their campsite on the banks of the Touques, or the Dives, in any case, in their trailers, the dilapidated trailers of the Knock-off tribe. While this is going on, Thirteen who, seeing the disaster, took refuge in the john (like Angelo at Argenteuil), he comes out looking perfectly innocent and tiptoes out of the hotel. Look, I hope you understand, you say to Thirteen's daughter, that this dumbass story of a cat show in Deauville or Cabourg contains enough lessons (the difference between ferocity and courage, the dialectical effect of surprise, the superiority of ruse over force, etc.) to grace a strategy treatise by Sun Tzu — or Mao Zedong. That's what he did best. His

Strategic Problems of the Partisans' War was our bedside reading. And not just ours. The bourgeois used to read that. Along with Lacan. OK, the leftist bourgeois, not the ones who read *L'Aurore*. As you can imagine, the Knock-offs made a full confession in no time. Those guys, who vaguely used to dream of murders, were terrified by the consequences of their actions, which were really not that serious. In fact, it was the modest nature of the crimes they got themselves involved in that made their actions incomprehensible to them, and thus terrifying. In a word, they charged Thirteen with everything, attributing to him the responsibility not only for the damage they did cause, but also for various thefts committed by the criminals in their entourage: stolen cars, minor holdups, etc. They went as far as to invent other, more violent stuff: arson, rape, blowtorching feet, things they doubtless had hoped to do under his leadership. Having become a veritable demon, a Stavrogin arrived from Paris to put the lower part of Normandy to fire and sword, Thirteen did not dare to stick his nose out the door of the room where the "progs" were hiding him — in the former Roches-Noires townhouse I'm pretty sure, where Marguerite Duras also used to stay, so maybe it was in Trouville and not Cabourg or Deauville. His photo had been published on the front page of the regional dailies; a sort of hysteria reigned in the seaside resort. During the day, he would have been immediately recognized by the locals. At night, the cops were setting up more and more checkpoints. That's how he spent the end of the summer, looking at the ocean from the window, watching the tides come and go, spying on the bathing beauties (there were binoculars in the place), eating the spaghetti with jars of Bolognese sauce his hosts had the kindness to go and buy for him. He stayed there until the cops got tired and the good citizens had enough time to forget what he looked like, a month at least. He escaped, I remember (not that there's any relationship between the two things), the day Salvador Allende won the election in Chile.

In fact, during all those years, you explain to Thirteen's daughter, the only vacation we took, it's strange, even nasty, is also the only time we set out to kill a guy. I've told you that usually we didn't even load our old guns so as not to risk killing or wounding someone by mistake, or through panic or clumsiness. But this guy was a former head of the Vichy militia; he had organized roundups, the shooting of hostages, people said President Pomp was protecting the son of a bitch; that had been an enormous scandal. Dedieu, the liberator of Chartres Cathedral, was in a paroxysm of indignation. That's why he had invited Danton to lay a wreath at Mont-Valérien. As for me, he had set me up to meet a cardinal, I swear that's the truth. A cardinal who was a former member of the Resistance; there are some. Not loads of them, to be sure, but this guy anyway. The meeting was very sophisticated, in the restaurant car of the Paris-Rome train. At the time there were restaurant cars with white tablecloths and silverware, tureens filled with steaming consommé; all these railway flounces and frills must have had an easier life than the B-52s. I decked myself out as best I could, and I think I was a little less ridiculous than when I was staking out Chalais's place. Dedieu had explained to me there was no need for a signal because it was rare, not to say really rare, that several cardinals wind up at the same time in a restaurant car; still, in a train for Rome, you never knew, so, should the improbable happen, I would recognize mine because he looked like a rugby player. That was true; he was a very well-built eminence, stone-faced, a native of the southwest. In fact he looked like René Char. All the while eating his pigeon with green peas (or his veal cutlets, maybe), he rapidly confided to me in a low voice that the old bastard had hid in a convent whose name he could not give me, but that he knew from an impeccable source that sooner or later the guy would go back to his house when the public outcry (we didn't say, "media frenzy," I think) had died down. He wanted to pick up some documents in a hiding place that only he knew about. That was it, but it was a lot. A member of the Roman Curia was giving us absolution in advance for a murder he was implicitly inviting us to commit. Later, we spoke of one thing and another, more revolutionary than religious matters, in any case my contact knew more about the former than I did about the latter. Since we quickly became very friendly, you tell Thirteen's daughter, and besides he didn't shy away from the cognac (nor did I for that matter), laughingly I proposed that he become chaplain for The Cause. It would be a pleasure, he responded, there are souls to save everywhere, but maybe more in the Sacred College than among your comrades. What do you mean, I asked. That your colleagues' souls are more worthy of compassion, or that they have more need of it? I think you know what I meant, he says to me. In fact, God came to Earth for the sinners, not for the just.

He knocked back a last shot of cognac and took off, you tell Thirteen's daughter. What he had just told me, no matter that I'm weak in casuistry, I understood what it meant, was that by giving me a thread of information that could lead to the death of a bastard, yet nevertheless a human being, he had just committed a sin, and a really big one, from his perspective. Still, on the other hand, God didn't get himself crucified for nothing. Maybe I'm boring you with these stories, you say to Thirteen's daughter, the word *sin* doubtless means nothing to you, but watch out for this tendency today to look down on what's not cool; this word, for better or worse, has been brimming over with meaning for almost twenty centuries, it has inspired geniuses, Dante, Milton, Dostoevsky, so many others. How can you read Dostoevsky if this word means nothing to you, I wonder. She flashes me the little pink triangle of tongue, the signpost saying "Watch it, old fool"; my right hand releasing Remember's unicorn steering wheel, I make an obscene gesture for her benefit, ring finger vertical above a closed fist which in (old) Morse signifies: "OK, message received, go to hell." On the left, for maybe the tenth time, the belfries of the Grands Moulins de Pantin, which look like Hugo's chateau, then past the rue de la Clôture, wait a minute, that reminds me of something, then the Ourcq canal, a mauve line in the night that makes me think of the still warm cadaver of Rosa Luxemburg thrown into the Landwehrkanal one day in January 1919, the canal frozen and her body, tossed from atop the parapet, breaks the ice's crust, which turns red and pink, then disappears into the black water; the members of the Freikorps watch the water swallowing the body, the hair spread out a bit, the dress as well, which makes them laugh coarsely, ignobly, then the hair and dress sinking, sliding under the ice, which reforms around the red and pink blemish; the members of the Freikorps return to their armored car, lighting cigarettes; Rosa Luxemburg used to think that socialism was losing its identity by not retaining anything of sin's metaphysical profundity, I say that absolutely without any proof, for the hell of it; no matter, Thirteen's daughter will not be the one to challenge me, on the right the Zenith looking like a Zeppelin moored to its pole, the blue beacons of the Villette Park, and the shimmering green houses of the City of Science, where there once were giant slaughterhouses, ones that were never used, a notorious scandal of the Fifth Republic, NATIONAL 3, PORTE DE PANTIN, over there we used to make our false papers; the silkscreen frame was hidden under a false baby's changing table, there was even a real child to make everything more plausible; obviously the trichloroethylene fumes must not have been great for the kid's health, but what do you want, we weren't ecologists at the time, and you'd better believe it, pregnant women were smoking Gauloises and all that — now to starboard once again the grand melodic jellyfish, the City of Music, the radar housing and observatory for the music of the spheres . . . and, designed by a former member of The Cause as well, greetings on the fly, and brotherhood.

The Vichy militiaman's house was at Chambéry, or Annecy, in any case, a city in the mountains, near a lake. You recall there was a fountain there formed by four stone half-elephants, confronting each other two against two, which the locals in a bizarre tribute to Truffaut's *Four Hundred Blows* called "the four hungry bellows"; the fountain, like a good part of the city for that matter, had been constructed by an aristocratic soldier of fortune who became the general for an important Indian maharaja in the eighteenth century. He'd married someone who was going to become a famous woman of letters, the Duchess (or Countess?) de Boigne, and this bluestocking scorned her husband who was, in her eyes, merely a soldier and a thug. The idea that people find the condition of a woman — or a man — of letters superior to that of a maharaja's general struck you (and still does today) as weird. In your opinion it was only in France that such an inversion of values was possible. In England, for instance, it was unimaginable. OK, the old assassin's house was located on the outskirts of town, overlooking a little valley. You had been lucky, if this is the right word in this context; on the other side of the road was a new building with windows and balconies peering down at his digs. It hadn't been difficult to rent an apartment. All you had to do was wait: Thirteen, Fichaoui, Judith, Lock-Eater, and you. Maybe you're forgetting somebody. Of course, you had discussed all this with Gideon, just like, years before, when you had gone to the prestigious school to submit to him your plan to attack the CRS convoy. This time you were in agreement. Killing a man, even a big collaborator, was not a decision you were prepared to make yourselves. But the protection President Pomp and a part of the Church gave him made it a sort of a duty, in your opinion. So you had rented a place and were waiting, Thirteen, Fichaoui, Judith, Lock-Eater, and you. With a telescopic rifle. The days were long, the tension enormous. If suddenly you saw him get out of the car, push back the little wooden gate, and walk the short distance between the hazelnut trees that led to the front door, would you have the nerve (the toughness?) to release the safety, shoulder the gun, aim and fire? Would you be "up to doing it?" Or, on the contrary, were you lowlife enough to do it? Since after all, killing an old man . . . even if he is scum . . . and there was no doubt about that: a leader of the Vichy militia, a guy who has Jewish children rounded up, members of the Resistance executed, truly, definitively scum. I still think that today, you say to Thirteen's daughter. But was it up to us to . . . Time passed slowly, very slowly, at the window with drawn curtains, watching the intersection, standing still, smoking butt after butt, the rifle right there, loaded. You still remember orange curtains. Orange was the fashionable color back then. Smoking butt after butt behind the orange voile, asking yourself whether . . . wait, no, never ask yourself anything, concentrating on the stakeout, knowing full well that there is, right there like the rifle, a nagging question, as nagging, as present, as repressed, as the memory of wakefulness in somebody who is trying desperately to lose himself in sleep. We appeared to be brutes, but deep down we were good boys, you tell Thirteen's daughter, the remains of sensitive young people . . . In the end we did not have the chance to learn how we would have reacted if we had gotten this bastard in our sights. The cardinal's tip didn't pan out, or maybe we weren't patient enough. We waited two months in vain, and then lifted the siege. All of us pretty relieved.

Nobody could stay behind the curtain for a very long time, so we relieved each other every two hours. It was summer, so those who weren't part of the watch would leave for the lake. I don't recall which lake, maybe Lamartine's. A blue lake between mountains with crescents of white sand under the grass. It was hot, there were parasols on the grass, pedal boats on the still, blue water, which reflected the mountains and the small, dappled clouds, cafés on the edges of the lake, volleyball players, the complete vacation scene that had become so alien to us that we had almost forgotten what it was like. In a flash this image brought back our past, what we had wanted to leave, our middle-class childhoods, carefree, busy without realizing it with the creation of egotistical happiness. The long vacations on the Emerald Coast. And a few kilometers from there, behind the drawn curtains, the theater of the future that we had chosen was awaiting us: conspiracy, political violence, the death toll estimated and noted. Kill an old assassin, be killed by the police. This is the future we'd chosen, yes, it was frankly as alien to us as the past we had abandoned. The past disgusted us, the future terrified us. We were nowhere, outside of time. I'm telling you this now, at the end of the first spring of the twenty-first century, you say to Thirteen's daughter, at the time I would not have said that, not thought of things in those terms; back then our thinking and our language were cluttered, confused, but all the same we felt, and especially during those particular days at the lakeside, amid images of a former life and a death to come, amid a sort of rejected, denied happiness and a terror that was hard to get used to, that there was a flaw in us, an emptiness somewhere in us, and maybe even a taste for this emptiness. So we lived for the moment, we got high without any scruples on the modest pleasures that came our way; our anxiety was such that, extraordinary as it seems, it turned us into normal young people for several hours a day (doubtless resembling Demetrios's son who "was not like us"): happy to throw one another into the lake from the top of the breakwater, to drink chilled white wine beneath the cafés' parasols, to talk a lot of crap and then burst into raucous laughter, to kiss lying on the grass. I had probably never kissed Judith in public, so just imagine . . . Once, I remember we had rented a pedal boat, me, Judith, and Thirteen—Fichaoui and Lock-Eater were on watch at the apartment. We were in the middle of the lake, totally carefree, relaxed, happy, able to forget our troubles for a little while. I don't know what got into me, but I began to do my Red Guard number, suggesting that perhaps we shouldn't be having such a good time, that our lifestyle was going soft—all this and other moralizing mouthings. Thirteen interrupted me: Cut the shit, Martin, nowhere in the little red book does it say that people aren't supposed to rent pedal boats. And then, laughing, Judith and he threw me into the lake, me laughing all along. On the way back to the beach—we had to think about relieving Fichaoui and Lock-Eater—we improvised a little song that could have caused us trouble; Gideon demanded auto-critiques for a lot less than that: "President Mao / Enjoyed the pedalo / Like the good populo," Thirteen's the author of that doggerel, you tell his daughter, here's what I added: "If you want to be led / Read the little book red / Until you get fed," but Judith, who was sitting between us, the classic setup, came up with the most affecting strophe: "We're ready to die / But with a bit of a sigh / 'Cause we'd rather get high."

6

We had gone to the flea market looking for a large trunk in which we could put the retired general Chalais, CEO of Atofram; we found nothing that really suited us, but finally we decided on a quite spacious chest, a wooden chest like the one Billy Bones had in *Treasure Island*. After Judith gave Chalais his shot, he calmed down and we managed to get him into the chest. The head against a wall with a little pillow for comfort, feet next to each other, knees folded up. The van had been moving along for two or three minutes, thus by now the police must have been informed, so time to change mounts; a relay station was set up deep in an underground parking lot, not far from where we were. Freight-Elevator was waiting for us at the wheel of a van that was a different color and model. I don't know why I haven't spoken to you of Freight-Elevator until now, you say to Thirteen's daughter. Actually, I do know: he'd lived with Judith before. And he had caught us in the act, well not completely, but almost. Nothing ambiguous about what was about to happen. At the time I really behaved like someone in a cheap drama, had I had the time to jump into the closet, I would have done it, beet red, out of breath and disheveled; I mumbled some nonsense that we were tired, had just fallen asleep, that we were dreaming that . . . Freight-Elevator told me not to waste my breath, that he wasn't an idiot. He got his nickname because, when he was working at Citroën, he had managed along with some Moroccan workers in the middle of a wildcat strike to block all day long the freight elevator feeding the assembly line for the 2cv model. At Citroën, that was no small feat. Obviously, later they were all fired. At the time, Freight-Elevator was involved in our group with making false papers; Roger the Belgian had taught him that skill, and he did not take long to prove he was quite clever at it. After the business with Judith and me, he could have let somebody else take his place, I certainly wouldn't have given him any grief on that score, but no, he hung in there. Probably detesting me, I don't know, it's probable but not certain, in any case his attitude toward me was certainly charged with irony. So we had a curious relationship, more complex than the ones between most of us, maybe the mutual experience of ridicule — even if we were not playing the same roles — had created between Freight-Elevator and me a complicity at once paradoxical and secret, on the edge of the heroic images we usually ascribed to ourselves. And on the other hand, I admired the cool he had displayed. Besides, he had not stayed calm just on this occasion; he was one of those, along with Fichaoui, whom I trusted completely. So he was waiting for us at the wheel of a 4L van, deep in an underground parking lot in the sixteenth arrondissement. He must have been at Annecy or Chambéry as well. And it's very possible he's in the photo taken in front of the station at Guingamp or Saint-Brieuc in the summer of '69. He must have been. Anyway, in 1969 this thing with Judith and me, and him, hadn't yet happened, it would happen, I don't know, maybe a year later? Since twelve of us were in the picture — at least I'm sure about that — there is one too many among those that I told you about. I think it was Danton. At the time, he might have been already in prison. Look, you tell Thirteen's daughter, don't believe everything I say. It's not that I'm trying to dissimulate, to distort anything. It's just that these days my memory is just a pile of dissimulation and distortion.

It was when we were going down the garage ramp that all hell broke out. Chalais was coming out of his much too brief stupor. Suddenly all his energy returned; he was ready to fight. Bracing himself, with a push from his legs he broke open the chest. The wood exploded with a terrible cracking sound. Damn, we ought to have bought an iron one, said Thirteen in a sinister tone. It wasn't to save money, but because we didn't find any, asshole, I answered him angrily. Fichaoui pulled over next to the 4L van, and joined us in the back. Standing around the open broken chest, we were trying to figure out what to do when Chalais started trying to climb out. In some grotesque way, it must have looked like a Renaissance scene, get it? Still, this was a bit too much. He could have waited a little. Listen, jerk, give us some time for tranquil reflection, Fichaoui said to him, closing the lid down on his head. This "tranquil reflection" was admirable, Fichaoui at his best. But we were at a loss, there was no solution. We couldn't lock the trunk, and all Chalais would have to do was push a little for his foot to go right through the wood. There was nothing more to do than to leave him there and get the hell out. That's what we did. So while we're going up the ramp, all piled together in the van, Fichaoui suddenly exclaimed he had forgotten to lock the other van's doors, and we went back to do it. Fortunately, Chalais had not yet gotten out. Realizing that we were taking off, he gave himself a little time to rest. Then Freight-El-evator dropped us off at the metro station Porte Dauphine, or maybe Trocadéro, Thirteen, Judith, and me. In the subway car, Thirteen was seated facing us. That's when we saw his face . . . His false moustache was askew, half unglued. Hey, Santa Claus, I whispered to him, your moustache is askew. He removed it with dignity, like an old Band-Aid, and the glue left on his upper lip the sort blackish slime you find on snails. That wasn't far from being the funniest thing I'd ever seen in my life. At that time you could still run into bourgeois in the metro. There was one, on the other side of the corridor, a guy wearing a green loden coat and a little houndstooth hat; he was reading *Le Monde*, but not the "Enterprises" pages, "Financial Tendencies," or "Money," no, these pages were not yet in existence, as incredible as that may seem; he was reading the "Agitation and Subversion" pages, which were sort of the official record for agitators of all persuasions. Still, it must be said that The Cause ate up the greatest amount of space in these pages; the others were just fill-ins. This guy's eyebrow arched above the newspaper, an eye discreetly aimed at us; he was taken aback, vaguely frightened. Our gazes met; his eye, like a mollusk, quickly pulled back behind its shell of newsprint.

PÉRIPH FLUIDE PORTE DORÉE 600 METERS VOLVO LA RÉVOLUTION. that's a good one PORTE DORÉE 150 METERS METZ NANCY MR. FIX-IT, fix it yourself, how many more circumnavigations have you made, Thirteen's daughter and you, since the first time you went around Paris, that big somber ball scarred by electricity? Blue, white, red. DISNEYLAND DIRECTION METZ NANCY 32 KM, red, white, green, blue, stroboscopic streaks, maybe we should think about . . . Damn! Gas at zero. Remember is going to fall out of her orbit pretty soon, maybe I'd better think about taking you back before we break down, you tell Thirteen's daughter. Apollo 13's oxygen tank had exploded, the ship, rolling in the night and cold, had almost been lost. April 15th it entered into the earth's gravitational pull and had splashed down in the Pacific just before the American-puppet armada set off up the Mekong toward the Viet Cong "sanctuaries," the temples at Angkor Wat, and the royal way where the young Malraux had gone to saw off several pink sandstone divinities. In the end the three American astronauts returned from the moon by sitting tight and holding their breath; they were luckier than a number of their compatriots who didn't come back from the Cambodian jungles. I ought to take you home now, you tell Thirteen's daughter, otherwise we're going to break down and disintegrate in the atmosphere. A4 A5 400 METERS NANCY METZ MARNE-LA-VALLÉE, CRÉTEIL BERCY 2 CARREFOUR DARTY ÉTAP HÔTEL, smoke from the great incinerator right in front of us; we turn on the retrorockets and leave behind us the sprays of shiny iron at the Gare de Lyon, the orange and blue-gray iron hulks moistened by the dew; on the right, the phosphorescent fortress of the Ministry of Finance, the sky grows pale above the Seine, on the right, the launching towers of the National Bank of France PARIS CENTRE PORTE DE BERCY N19, 300 METERS QUAI D'IVRY, we exit after the stayed-girder bridge above the tracks of the Gare d'Austerlitz. Then it's the Avenue Maurice-Thorez, followed by a public square dominated by a gigantic piece of plumbing, a pipe bent at an angle, a chromed siphon, or something like that, it's municipal art, an equestrian statue of Maurice Thorez would have been better, but apparently less modern. At the time when the Party was unabashedly Stalinist, the members wouldn't have had any compunctions about erecting a statue of Maurice Thorez as a Roman emperor; doing him in siphon or faucet must have been expensive. You know who he is, Maurice Thorez? you ask Thirteen's daughter. No, well, it's not a big deal, you're not missing much, even if several of our great poets have written odes glorifying this dance-hall Stalin. In other countries the Communist chiefs fought against the Nazis, but our little Maurice, he spent the whole war in Moscow. Maurice Thorez-Maurice Chevalier, that's France! That's Paris! After the Avenue Maurice Thorez, there's the rue Baudin, named after a public official who got killed on a barricade, that's not such a common thing. And over there . . . It was bound to happen, Remember has a coughing fit and you just manage to get to the closest curb before the engine sputters and stalls. Shit! Out of gas. Should've been less talkative too, you must have been jabbering for five hundred kilometers . . . OK, let's not get excited, you tell Thirteen's daughter, I'm going to walk you home, is your place far? No. After that, I'll work something out, anyway, it'll be light soon. You extract yourself from the Goddess Remember who stretches out with a sigh, hunkered down on her hindquarters, her front like a predator, half lady-sphinx, half shark. You get to her street through a sloping back alley running between little gardens. Ah, all the eclectic beauty, all the broken-down poetry of an old suburb, something out of Céline, or Cendrars or Tardi in this street . . . At the corner, behind a balustrade brightened up by unsophisticated statues, there's a funny little chalet whose neorococo facade is decorated with a tracery of false branches made of cement; the whole thing's decrepit, warped, falling apart, and then there's a sort of a three-story brick chimney, spindly, an incongruous stump, a ruined tower barely higher than trees, whose tops plumed the high, black wall, pierced with vents covered with grills like a fortress. On the other side several houses, with worm-eaten shutters, crowned with dark and moss-grown tiles, transport you back to the Paris of *Les Misérables*, when Ivry was a country village, filled with lowing cows, then a steep incline, which a grove of beech trees clings to, slopes right down into hovels decked out with wash. Still farther down there's the Seine whose course you can barely make out because of the tangle of orange lights amid which slides the glowing caterpillar of the beltway, beyond that, the great incinerator sparkling like an ocean liner, its two stacks scattering braids of thick smoke in the sky, turning the mauve color to green in the east, above Charenton, Montreuil, Le Perreux, Le Raincy, above Nogent, Villemomble, and Romainville, and in the distance the teeming projects, the parking lots, supermarkets, suburban housing, workers' gardens—all of these crisscrossed, served, by highways, tracks, canals, along the Marne, which appears with the rising sun. That's where she lives, in the hills of Ivry, in this street that is like a balcony overlooking the ages of the city, a place where time expands and retracts, turns back on itself and produces arbitrary figures, like the ones on balls of crumpled papers. A street that crosses a perfect site for a battle, you point out to Thirteen's daughter: following the hillside, dominating the valley, the confluence, the east gates of Paris. Surely there were some battles fought here in 1814, during the French campaign, then again in 1870, during the Commune, there must have been some mills on the crests, some meadows spotted with little woods lower down, then the Seine, which you could see a lot better than today, bordered by willow trees between which rose the vapor from Montereau, big villages through whose center passed the invasion route, and then on the left, the barely perceptible hodgepodge of the city, smoke during the day, fires at night, behind the band of fortifications. And a constant rumbling too. Ah, you can smell the cannon powder here, you tell Thirteen's daughter with enough enthusiasm that she notices and obviously disapproves: she lives here and never smelled that. Anyway, what does cannon powder smell like? Eh, well, I don't know. Fireworks, I guess. The tricks and jokes of History.

You finish a cigarette next to her building, which, suspended as it is over Paris's bustling shadow, brings to mind a seaside casino. The suburb is waking up, the sky's turning pale, the lights are flickering, soon it will be time for the proletariat, or what remains of it, to trudge off to work. The mauve sky is turning green, then yellow; some pink filters through, the smoke from the great incinerator turns flesh colored, pearly, shades of viscera, the flesh of frogs flayed alive, gently the day seeps through the night. In the evenings during your vacations on the Emerald Coast, your mother used to take both of you, your brother and yourself, to a cliff near the house. Seated on a bench, in total silence, you would watch the sunset. The sun wasn't really setting, she explained, the earth was turning, swinging around; on the other side of the world, in that country called Indochina, the sun was rising at this very moment; this was disturbing, difficult to believe. You used to hope to see the green flash, but you never did. You would go home confused and perplexed. You take a drag on your cigarette butt. You want to say something, but you don't really know what. In Barcelona, the anarchists used to execute the bourgeois on the beach at sunrise. Look, they used to say, take a good look for the first and last time, you good-for-nothings who never saw the sunrise. Then they'd kill them. In the north, during the war, imprisoned Communists had written a song for their comrades on the way to the guillotine: "Go ahead and laugh, bourgeois, it's the break of dawn. Come one and all and see how a real fighter dies." André had told us that. You know . . . ; you hesitate. You know, I get on people's nerves a lot. I realize that. I give the impression that I despise people of your generation. That I only treat them, treat you, sarcastically. But it's not true; it's just an attitude. What I despise is the demagoguery of my generation, mine, toward yours. We don't have to look to you for love, nor to imitate you, nor to admire you. But we don't want to get old, we don't want to see the sun set on us, to see our shadows grow long, so we court you, our children. It's obscene. I prefer to pick a fight, to provoke, to run the risk of being detested. I prefer to be over the top with you. But the idea of the youth of the world, obviously that has a lot to do with the Revolution. The Year II . . . (I say the Year II, because Year I, doesn't sound right, and anyway Year II was more heroic than I). Even the idea that those who are supposed to know nothing teach those who know—it's a wonderful dream. We thought China was that. Apparently our naiveté invites laughter nowadays. Mao has a great phrase—all the same there were some: "I will freely be the child's buffalo." A Revolution is the revenge of the snotnosed: the people, that eternal child, irresponsible, thoughtless, badly brought up, rejecting the authority of its masters, the "grownups." That's why Hugo's Gavroche remains more alive than Lenin.

You flip the butt in the gutter, and light up another, you're no longer sure where you're going with all this, everything's so mixed together. Why didn't you have a child? she suddenly asks. Ah . . . well aimed. Right in the heart. Her pretty little assassin's face on the froth of dawn. Oh well . . . A long time ago, at the time of The Cause, the idea was that the future was too dangerous, too uncertain. But later . . . frankly, I don't know. You see how I'm someone other than myself. Maybe because I was marked with death's violet ink a couple of months after my birth? Or maybe stupidly hoping to escape time, to avoid everything that represented succession: generation, corruption? Escape this contingency, this power of the world on us. Refuse to surrender to realism. Our story, when we were a "we," had unfolded largely outside the constraints of the real: land right in it, up to your ankles in the real, parachuted from the region of pipe dreams—some of them could do it, most of them, but not me. I missed the target, and God knows it was big enough. The dose of the unreal was too strong, or I just didn't have any antibiotics, I don't know. Anyway, since those crazy times when Thirteen and me, and the others, for whatever it's worth, made up a team, it's odd but since then I have never taken any place seriously, or rather I've no longer been able to believe I was truly anywhere. What's called "to be," always seemed to me in the end a joke. More or less funny, but a joke. The Cause, this ship of fools, must have been my only true anchorage. Someday it will be the tomb. Between the two of them, nothing stable. I think though that I would have loved, out of simple cowardice, out of a desire to roost, to root somewhere, but not really, nothing could hold me, I was always just passing through. It might have happened with Paulina L., but she left. Because she must have felt it, that I couldn't be tied down. Anyway, she left; without a doubt I'd provoked it: when unhappiness gets into our lives, it's rare that we didn't open the door for it. So now you have it, I remained an irresponsible guy, an adult baby. Quite ridiculous. I didn't grow up. But what makes you think I despise children? you say to her as you tweak her nose. I'm not a child, she responds defiantly. I know, you say. Weird thoughts, more or less held in check up till now, start bouncing around in your head, howling furiously. I know quite well you're not a child, you say, with a sinister air. You can even imagine the ideas that gives me. Maybe I can, she responds with a laugh as she lights a cigarette. She has sat down on the little wall running along the sidewalk just above the incline, one leg crossed over the other, like at the beginning of the night, an eternity ago, at Pompabière's. Her slender silhouette, her little face in the play of the light, the ink rinsed from the sky, the smoke from the great incinerator turning pink. With rounded lips she blows the cigarette smoke away from her and in my direction. Am I dreaming or what? OK, stay calm. Something, you don't know what exactly, suggests that it wouldn't be a good idea. But without much conviction. Maybe this hesitation is just that you've been dragging around your body like an old suit, stained, misshapen, worn thin? *Caution! This program is more than fifty years old!*, as your computer would say. In the end, you say to Thirteen's daughter, I've been my own son, which is ridiculous. And if at least I'd gotten along well with him . . . But, no, I wish he'd go to hell. Let him get out of my life, the little bastard! I disown him! Naturally, I wouldn't be displeased to see this nonprogeny as the effect of a curse, I'm enough of a pedant for that, and I remember the ancient Greek authors . . . The gods have punished through me my lineage for an error committed, maybe by me, but more probably by one of my ancestors. The lieutenant died right after having fathered me, and I will die before, right before — unless I father just after my death, we'll see. Seriously, I'm really sorry not to have added someone to your group — to your generation, to your century. I have the impression . . . I don't know how to say it . . . of having betrayed, of having abandoned you. I would love to know where you'll wind up. What interests me is the depth of the future you have within you, all the unknowns you're filled with. You're still a bit simple-minded; that's inevitable, normal, and yet at the same time each of you is a facet of the only mystery that remains to us: the future. And I can't say that I admire that, anymore than there's a reason to admire beauty. But beauty, like the future, is thrilling, you tell Thirteen's daughter as you place your hand on her shiny knee, but you pull it away at once, what the hell are you doing? You're filled with stuff you haven't done, you say, stuff that doesn't exist yet — but it's a rich emptiness, the space freed up in you for the world. About us, it's all been said — and most often poorly said. There's still something enigmatic about you. Maybe you'll be adventurous, poetic — who knows? We're written in prose. And then you are infinitely more curious and tolerant than we were. We were all drowned in certitudes, and a lot of them stupid. You don't seem to like your era, she says to you. No. I despise it. And yet it's us, our generation made it what it is. Its spinelessness, religion of comfort, its conformism hypocritically disguised as various "liberations"; we were the ones, without knowing it, without wanting to do it — pathetic fools — who made it all happen. So, you're not really modern? First of all, what makes it absolutely necessary to be modern? It's not written in any constitution. OK, let's be frank: was Flaubert, who abominated his epoch, less modern than, I don't know, Paul Bourget, who was quite happy in his world? Being modern means trying to sabotage the clichés of one's era. Vast project; the spirit of the age, if one can still call it that, is a display, without beginning or end, of clichés. A little like that ring of advertisements inside of which we've been driving around all night, and inside of which the city is a prisoner. Oh and then . . . aw, shut up. Where was I?

Right. In the metro. Later, at night, we took the postal train at the Gare du Nord to go hide out in Belgium. Why this milk train that stopped everywhere? Now, I can't remember, you say to Thirteen's daughter. Maybe to arrive early in the morning at the border without having to make a change at Lille? And how come Judith didn't come with us? Don't know. It seems to me that the train was supposed to leave around eleven or midnight. In the train cars were young soldiers numb from beer, exhaustion, sadness. Their shaven heads (like criminals) knocking together as the train jolted along, cars that dated from the time of steam locomotives, you could lower the windows on top of which was a sign: "Look out for soot." "Soot," I'm not sure you know what that is, you say to Thirteen's daughter, little specks of burning coal that flew about in the locomotive's wake. If you stuck your head outside—despite the famous notice, *E pericoloso sporgersi*, which was for many children of my generation our first contact with a foreign language—if you stuck your head out the window, you had to look out not to get a speck in the eye. The train came to a clanking halt at every station; it stayed forever at the quay, loading mail, unloading mail, or both, I don't remember. Then it would start off with no warning with a fanfare of buffers, a racket of creaking noises. There used to be a romance of stations at night that's almost been lost today: lanterns swinging at the end of the arm, men wrapped in warm clothing walking along the quays, loudspeaker announcements off in the distance, the groaning of tow trains, bursts of compressed air, the distinct ring of hammers against the steel of the wheels, just like in *Anna Karenina* . . . Eventually we got under way, then stopped a little farther along; we were crossing the beet region and would soon arrive in the coal region. Busigny Cambrai Douai Pont-de-la-Deûle Ostricourt Libercourt Phalampin Seclin Wattignies Ronchin (or maybe it was Arras Bailleul Vimy Avion Lens Sallaumines). Standing in the corridor with the window lowered, Thirteen and I were smoking in silence, watching the slow progression of stations, factories, miners' housing, slag heaps, scaffolding, canals, the pale windows of a spinning mill, a road whose paving stones refract the light like fish scales, and once again brick chimneys with plumes of smoke, like the ones on the great incinerator; there, in front of us, you tell Thirteen's daughter, miners' housing, slag heaps, scaffolding, a canal under an iron bridge that the train was rumbling over. In the night, over there, on one part or another of the track, not far from here, Lucien was dreaming of derailing a TEE, maybe Winter was weeping silently, André was racked by a coughing fit; he used to drink a glass of milk trying to soothe the burning from the silica. Gustave was asleep and snoring, out cold from beer, Victoire and Laurent were printing one by one, from the "Vietnamese Roneo," tracts announcing to the "masses" what a great success had been the "arrest" of General Chalais, CEO of Atofram, the lackey of American imperialists and exploiter of the people. At the cadence that the ancient machine could tolerate (a square of tulle stretched out on a frame, a scraper), they would print the last sheet just before leaving for the "distrib," unsteady from lack of sleep, their hands black with ink. For sure their day would end in a police station.

Thirteen had one of those music-box cigarette lighters that played "The Red East," when you opened the top la la lalala lalala, the East is red, the sun is rising, lala lala lalala lalala, in *Chin-e-a* appears Mao Zedong . . . As he lighted each butt looking at the nocturnal countryside, the first measures of that ridiculous canticle resounded. Is this really necessary, I asked him testily? At that very hour there were breaking news headlines on the radio, all of them focused on the aborted kidnapping of a great industrialist associated with what we called then "the military-industrial complex"; this news was sure to be spread over the front pages of the newspapers in the morning, all the police in France must be on our heels. This was a great moment to stand out in a crowd. Thirteen chuckled silently, puffing on his butt. He hummed the words more or less in Chinese: *Dong-fan-ang hong tai-yan-ang sheng Zhon-guo chu le yi ge Mao Zedong . . .* The train remained in the Lille station for what seemed to us an eternity. Then it started off amid tremendous clanking in the direction of Croix-Wasquehal Croix-Allumette Roubaix where we got off, right before the terminus, Tourcoing. When we came out onto the square in front of the station, the sky was yellow and green like the inside of a lettuce leaf. Lights were coming on in the bistros, shop signs started blinking, Jupiler, Stella Artois, the awful moment when the proletariat trudge off to work, the sour early morning when, standing at the zinc bar, bag on the shoulder, cap lowered over one eye, people silently drink a boiled liquid, awful, dirty, filled with bubbles and smoking like dishwater. We got a tram on the industrial boulevard, Thirteen lighted another cigarette inside the tram; at the time, you tell his daughter, you smoked everywhere, especially the proles, that's not what risked surprising people, it was that little moronic music. The East is red . . . Most of the passengers just smiled wanly under the pallid lights, but it would only have taken one Communist Party member in the tram, one guy who recognized the little song and then the problems would have started. They hated the "Maos." The dumb bastard did it on purpose, to test fate, to destroy my nerves. But I couldn't say anything, just clench fists and jaw. He was silently laughing, screwing up his eyes, taking a drag from his butt. We got off in front of a large, dark-brick church with a slate steeple that crows were flying around. I gave him hell; after all, dammit, I was in charge. Then we went into the café Le Limitrophe. The boss was wiping the counter with a rag; he seemed barely awake, but he might look like that all day. We gulped down two foul coffees filled with bubbles like dishwater. I was the one who lighted the cigarettes with my Zippo. After, at the corner of Roger-Salengo, we took the road for Néchin (or Estaimpuis, I don't remember, you tell Thirteen's daughter). It was cold, steam was coming from our mouths. Beyond the cemetery fields spread out on the left and right, plowed-up black earth dusted with frost. At the bottom of the furrows, stagnant water was reflecting the purple sky. A flock of gulls were pecking away at the earthworms. On the right, at the end of an irrigation ditch, sheds from a factory cut through the vestige of the night. In front of us, dominated by a silo and a bell tower, stretched out the village with the strange name: Gibraltar. I swear it's true, the name I mean, you say to Thirteen's daughter. Look at a map, it's on the outskirts of Roubaix, on the Wattrelos side, over there. The border went right by it. Roger the Belgian was waiting for us there at the Sports Bar, rue du Congo. Just as we could make out the yellow signs with red frames containing the name of the Promised Land, *Province de Hainaut, Provincie Henegouwen*, an enormous grenadine sun sprang forth from a patch of mist atop the roofs of Gibraltar. "The East is red, the sun is rising"; we both began bellowing that, grabbing one another by the shoulders, kicking up our legs in a grotesque cancan, then kicking less and less high, bent over with laughter, "In *Chin-e-a* appears Mao Zedong," there we were, marching, or rather skipping, and pretty soon running almost on all fours in the direction of Gibraltar, our faces colored by the rising sun, right in the middle of fields sparkling with frost. "He wants our happiness, he is our savior."

The sun was also gleaming on the horizon, under canopies of purple clouds, when you entered Saigon-Ho Chi Minh, you and Driver. Driver was a little wise guy with rudimentary English and a 125 Honda; he'd come up to you at My Tho, on the dock where you were watching the traffic on the Mekong, to offer to take you to Ho Chi Minh City. *Want driver, Mister? Me best driver, not expensive. You atkouda?* (He also had a little Russian as well). *American? Phap? Fwançais very good*, and so forth. You fixed the deal for fifteen dollars. At twilight you left My Tho, the rows of hibiscus were aflame in the shadows, on both sides of the road guys were fishing, motionless in the middle of rice fields the color of green fruit preserve. At first it went pretty well. Just the normal terror that accompanies riding a motorcycle on an Asian road, rather like strolling along with hands in pockets in the middle of a herd of charging elephants. Buses with blood-red fronts, large Russian motorcycles with sidecars, swarms of cantankerous scooters, weaving bikes, saddled with long bamboo poles to skewer you, pushcarts, Chinese trucks with no brakes, rickshaws, from time to time a black Mercedes carting around at full speed a neo-Communist boss, everyone honking, beeping, hooting, backfiring—in both directions—spreading themselves out on the not very broad width of a road that had been constructed for the rare Citroën B2s or Léon-Bollés dating back to the time of the barricade against the Pacific, only to swerve at the last minute, just before the head-on collision. All this not to mention the pigs, ducks, buffaloes, old or infant lunatics crossing the road without warning, without even speaking of the rice and banana leaves strewn along the edge of the road to dry out. You were navigating amid a bombardment of screaming projectiles, a flux of enemies relentlessly attempting to pulverize you; more than a road, the scene evoked one of those video games that excites kids today. Driver was practically lying on the handlebars, his elbows raised on both sides like wings, his head with its shiny black hair just above the bike headlight. Thrust forward like a gargoyle, eating up the road. His aerodynamic position freed you to receive the full force of a burst of highly pressurized air, dust, and flying bits and pieces, probably animal parts, all of which swirled around your glasses before disappearing under your eyelids, which snapped open and shut like the reed of a musical instrument. Every so often Driver would turn around and ask if everything was fine: *OK, kharacho, Mister?* then he would take off again with a hiccupping laugh that turned into a toothless grin, screwing his head so far around that you would beg him to look in front: *vsio kharacho, no problem, but look ahead* PLEASE! It was already dangerous enough without having to drive in reverse.

However, as night was falling, in front, to the north, in the direction of Saigon, a monstrous cloud soufflé was rising, blocking the delta and the road going into it. A gigantic gratin of fluorescent cauliflowers. Blobs of spastic lightning. Damn! Spirits with scaly tails, large wrathful eyes, and warty faces with scarlet glaze, must have turned on all the electric contacts for the celestial pinball machine, up there, in front. You stopped for a moment at a bistro on the side of the road, Driver needed to get his breath in the face of what was coming. In the courtyard was a bust of Ho Chi Minh, a statue of the Belgian imp, Manneken-Pis, and a Venus de Milo. On the counter were aligned demijohns of alcohol in which dead animals were floating, mostly snakes and scorpions. These concoctions were supposed to be infallible against almost every pain, and aphrodisiacs to boot, that goes without saying. *Want boom-boom in Ho Chi Minh, Mister?* Driver asked in a bawdy tone as he poured himself a cup of this shit in which two little crocodiles were marinating. *Want girls very good?* That was not the issue for the moment. You were thinking it would be a lot better just to arrive. On the counter was a demijohn larger than the others and which appeared to be filled only with a blackish juice. However, since your attention had been caught by a sort of little clear crescent that, from certain angles, gleamed from the coal tar, you went closer and there . . . there, behind the glass, crushed against it, was the most hideous, the most obviously satanic thing you'd ever seen. What was gleaming were teeth between which hung the tip of a violet tongue. Above, white eyelids with long slashes, opening onto empty sockets. Hidden by the reflections of the glass and the blackness of the disgusting liquor, packed down, squeezed into the demijohn, seated on a coiled serpent, you could barely make out a monkey, a gibbon. His face of a blissful torture victim was framed by two white-eyed bird heads. A gecko was wrapped around his neck as a scarf. Driver, noting your horror, couldn't hold back his pleasure, he skipped around you hiccuping: *very good, very good for boom-boom, Mister; wan' a drink? Monkey-wine good for boom-boom*, he wanted to convince you to take a drink of this damn "monkey wine." No way in hell. It seemed to you that the frightful sight had something to do with why you had gone to My Tho, but what? What was locked inside the jar, this rotting carcass with empty eyes, was death, that's for sure — but what did it mean to you: that you had torn the lieutenant's shade away from death, that death was waiting for you on the road to take back what was hers and you with it, before you arrived at Saigon? As you left the bistro you had seen slowly passing in front of you, illuminated by the lightning bolts, two svelte young girls in scarlet ao dai, riding a scooter. The one driving had a baseball cap and a scarf over her nose, masking the bottom of her face, as if she was getting ready to rob a bank, the other one, seated sidesaddle, was holding above her a white umbrella. Graceful, dangerous . . . Their black hair, the driver's knotted in a chignon, plaited for her passenger, seemed streaked with sparks. Suddenly, after this infamy, all the beauty of the world.

The rain had begun to fall as you were climbing onto the motorcycle, not in one stroke, no, holding back its full force, just some pizzicato to initiate what would become, you sensed it, a Wagnerian opera. Drop after drop of tepid ink. It was completely dark now. Those who had headlights that worked had turned them on; this was not the majority and particularly not Driver's case, as you might have expected. *No lights, Mister*, he said guffawing, *too expensive.* And he further explained: *Vietnamese people no money, communists many money*, he repeated that, beside himself with laughter, *no money, many money, oh, many, many, many money*, taking his hands off the handlebars to mimic rounded forms of what were probably meant to be bags of gold, turning around to make sure you got it, *yes, yes*, you pleaded, you screamed in the night, *I understand,* BUT LOOK AHEAD PLEASE! Boats looking like junks on wheels floated in the shadows, no lights at all; some rickshaws loaded with furniture, with piles of wood, bobbed along, three or four abreast on waves of broken, swollen asphalt, scattering, pedaling frantically, when all of a sudden in a nimbus of glittering raindrops an old Desoto bus (or Dodge) dating from the Yankees appeared and tried to pass a Russian military truck, its own valves clattering wildly as it struggled to get by a Renault Dauphine (or a 203), driving on the wheel rims, a wreck dating from colonial times. Fingers glued to the roll bar of the motorcycle, knees clamped against the seat lest one of these scrap-iron Moby Dicks tear off your leg, your back rigid in anticipation of a pile-driving blow from the shock absorbers, your neck ducked down between your shoulders—your body was nothing but a bundle of fear. The vision of that hideous black face with empty eyes haunted you. Were you going to drink this thing to the dregs? Were you going to die here, on the way back from My Tho, on this road studded at broad intervals with old French milestones, white with red tops. Had you defied a prohibition in going to look for a wandering soul? The rain could still not make up its mind; every now and then you'd pass through a limp curtain of pearly drops. The sky, on the other hand, was swirling about, an orgy of lightning of all sorts, flashes, laser beams, zigzags, nets, rhizomes of fire, in every direction, even climbing into the heavens. The rice paddies sparkled under this electric hail, in the distance tiny silhouettes swaddled in candy-colored translucid plastic were scurrying along the dikes. *No need light, Mister, nié noujna*, Driver hollered in delight while he imitated the lightning with his large open hands, waving them on each side of his head. This guy was an artist.

When the monsoon's floodgates opened, you tell Thirteen's daughter, there was nothing funny about it. Waterfalls. At first Driver tried a little to struggle against it; he attacked the pools of water, sending out a yellowish spray, the cycle stalled; he paddled with his short feet, left and right, making it a point of honor, so to speak, that I did not have to put my foot on the ground. Saturated and soaking with water as we were, it was a charming gesture. We reached a little rise in the road and waited there with dozens of others, trying to smoke a cigarette sheltered in the palm of the hand, unscrewing the spark plug and blowing on it. *Many rain*, Driver was saying in somber tones, *Many many rain*. Then, to reassure me: *Ho Chi Minh not far*. Sure . . . In any case, this deluge did not really bother me at all, I would have been happy to swim back, that seemed a lot less dangerous. We started up, and the whole business began again. In the end the motorcycle had had enough. We were in the suburbs of Saigon, at the junction of the strategic road the South Koreans built during the American war. The rain had let up, but the road was completely underwater. I got into a rickshaw that was already hauling a pig. That pig was really quite relaxed. Interested, its nose in the air, enjoying the trip. Driver slung his machine across another rickshaw, just like an animal killed in a hunt. That's how we entered Saigon, through Bin Chanh, Miên Tây, Cho Lon. I had put my arm around the pig's shoulders. Poor guy. Nobody'd ever treated him so kindly. He didn't have much to look forward to. Why would they give him any illusions? I felt for him, even sensed a bit of fraternity. He had lively round eyes with beautiful blond eyelashes. Driver was shocked by my friendliness, splashing through the puddles, he came from his rickshaw to mine in order to warn me: *Pig not good, Mister: Pig*—and he held his nose to show that my friend stank. On both sides of the street, now transformed into muddy rivers, people were setting out merchandise: caps, sunglasses, sewing machines, hubcaps, batteries, exhaust pipes, table soccer games, billiards, coffins, bike tires, valises, mangos, persimmons, melons, watermelons, Frigidaires, scales, watches, etc. You tell Thirteen's daughter what you answered Driver: *this pig is my brother*. He was shocked. *Pig brother, Mister?* he asked, trying to understand, and then, since clearly he found nothing acceptable in this, he summarized his disapproval as follows: *Oh, not good . . .* As I've always done when I witnessed daybreak in one city or another, I was mechanically humming, *Paris is awakening*, but it was quite a different song that came to my lips when the sun suddenly unfurled its red flag over the mangroves on the other side of the river, over the giant signboards for HITACHI CANON DAEWOO IBM TOSHIBA TELSTRA

HEWLETT-PACKARD TIGER BEER, above the South China Sea: *Dong-fan-ang hong, tai-yan-ang sheng, Zhong-guo chu le yi ge Mao Zedong,* "The East is red, the sun is rising . . ." I still had my arm around the pig's neck, and I was singing that, *ta wei ren-min mo xingfu, ta shi ren-min da qiu-xing,* "He looks after our happiness, he is our savior." Wow. An illumination! Given the age-old love that the heroic-Vietnamese-people possess for the people of China-red-forever, Driver interpreted in his way my friendliness to the pig, a sentiment that had initially startled him: it was an anti-Chinese stunt. Well, in that case! He was thrilled. He couldn't stop laughing. *Chinese pig, Chinese pig* he hollered, *this pig Mao Zedong!* He chuckled, bouncing around the rickshaw, sending up clouds of spray. His good humor, which the motorcycle's breakdown had slightly deflated, returned now.

And it was that same stupid hymn that we were braying, Thirteen and me, that night, or rather early that morning, when we climbed up the south tower of Saint-Sulpice. This was one of our goals amid several activities that were all a bit confused that night: to see the sun rise from up there. To watch the rosy colors emerge from the darkness, to see them roll over the Vincennes woods, the distant populous suburbs of Montreuil, Le Perreux, Le Raincy, Villemomble, Romainville, the former madhouses at Charenton, and Nogent's old dance halls, because the sun rises on the past as well, you tell Thirteen's daughter. And the parking lots, the wealthy sections, the slums, workers' shanties and gardens, the bouquets of highways, tracks, and canals—all of that blue and carmine at dawn, and then the Marne flowing from the rising sun. We were, of course, completely done in. We had spent the night in the bars of the Latin Quarter. At that time, twenty years ago, we no longer did much of anything. The Great Helmsmen, the red suns shining on a radiant future, we had had our fill of that and were not interested in seconds, at the same time, we had no desire to become bourgeois, as if we had not rebelled against that, ten, fifteen years before, against this prefabricated future, as if we had never had all that anger and all that hope. Our beliefs were destroyed, but the ruins of those ideals still weighed on us, ideals from which nothing had grown, on which nothing had been rebuilt. So we were lost, nowhere really, extremely sarcastic, and heavily into drinking. Thirteen was vaguely involved with music, and I was thinking about writing a book. Yet it did not seem to us that those things would get our lives going again. I had split up with Judith. Thirteen had been with your mother; you were, what did you tell me, four years old? We were sort of derelicts, no, that's not it, not just because our bodies were still young, but especially because we still had a lot of energy, even though it was mostly expressed in despair. He used to get stoned, but that didn't tempt me, I had a kind of prudence in folly that had made me a pretty good leader, at the time of The Cause. To tell the truth, I do not think I ever did anything as well as that. I mean . . . Listen, don't be shocked, you tell Thirteen's daughter, and I hope you'll try not to get angry at me. I wasn't his damned soul; we were each other's, so to speak. Sure, he loved you, but he wasn't able to start his life over because of you, maybe because he was too tied up in our strange history, too attached to what by then had become a dead past, and then there was the memory of the future, I don't know if I'm being clear. We were not used to imagining the future in terms of a child's growth, nor reality in terms of a family, it wasn't easy for him to accept all that in the midst of our ruins.

Anyway, that morning, just as Paris was awakening, that awful moment when workers trudge off to their misery, we were wasted, also, Thirteen must have been stoned, I did not know on what, I didn't want to know. I closed my eyes and didn't see his. We got to the Place Saint-Sulpice, coming I think from the Boulevard St. Germain, from a really smelly bistro called Old Navy that was open all night (it's still there, I think, but no longer sells tobacco, probably closes at 2:00 a.m., if not earlier, the world's gotten a lot more hygienic). And there, at the Place Saint-Sulpice, we saw the scaffolding. The south tower, the beautiful and unfinished one, covered with a bunch of girders, like the launch tower for the Saturn V, and that's what got us going, that high metal ladder pointing toward the sky. We were going to slip into the Apollo capsule and head for the moon, we had nothing left to do on earth. By the way, you casually ask Thirteen's daughter, do you know why the two towers at Saint-Sulpice are so different (against them I piss, somebody once said)? No? Well, it's because of the Revolution. Initially, they were both like the south one, equally stark, equally Roman. But then the priests decided that they weren't fancy enough, and asked an architect to give them a hand—the same guy who later gave us the Arc de Triomphe, you see the likeness; I've forgotten his name, he had enough time to dress up the north tower, but at the moment he was getting ready to deal with the south tower, the one that faces Luxembourg, the game was up. It was 1789. That job could wait . . .

It was easy to knock down the fence with our feet, and we began climbing. We were incredibly strong and thoughtless. Gradually, we changed our plans as we climbed. We would take off in Apollo and start a revolution on the moon. Then we had this idea about meeting God. A roundtable up there, at the summit. We passed the doric column stage and were already in the ionic. The only theoretically true chants are the "Credo" and the "Internationale," or so I was claiming while climbing like a monkey. All the others are just cutesy little tunes. Anything that came into my head. We stopped, took a rest, lighted a cigarette, and brayed just that, *credo in unum Deum* and *Arise the wretched of the earth*. When we got to the top of the vaulted cornice, just above the top gallery, Thirteen noted: ionic motor! The ne plus ultra. We were years ahead of NASA. American technology was a paper tiger. We had ionic propulsion. We were going to fly like angels. We did not know at the time that at ground level of our launch pad there was a fresco by Delacroix showing the struggle with the Angel—and another one, Heliodorus knocked down, beaten to the earth. We didn't go inside churches; the only art we liked had to be marginal, and even then . . . Delacroix, for us, was just the name of an old friend, and a portrait on a banknote. We kept climbing. When a rusted door blocked the stairs, we went around it; we hoisted ourselves from one girder to another, like sailors on a mast. We stopped at the top of the terrace joining the two towers, above the loggia. The wind roared through the topsails; we were at Cape Horn. Dawn was coming after a tough night spent bearing windward. The albatrosses were skimming the crests of the waves. The good ship *Saint-Sulpice* was making its way, under reduced sail. We were singing: *We'll pull and haul together, we'll haul to better weather.* Soon we'd be in Valparaiso. The problem, Thirteen brought to my attention, was what do we do afterwards? That cargo of little red books we had in the hold, well, nobody would be interested. We were stuck with a load of junk, according to him. Also, there was no place to return to, no home port. We must have had one in the past; in the beginning we did set out from somewhere, but we'd forgotten from where, we even forgot the name of the place. Do you remember, he asked me. No. So we were condemned to wander. Still, while we were waiting, it seemed necessary to keep climbing to the top of the mast to get control of the topsail, which was on the brink of tearing up and making us list terribly. Swells were already sweeping across the deck. So let's go. As we were climbing and dawn was approaching, Paris below us was spreading out, wave after wave, all the way to the horizon. Swells of zinc on which twinkled golden figures, a dome, a genius, winged horses. Bell towers, Saint-Germain quite near, under whose towers we knocked the crap out of fascists from the Occident group in '68, when they'd announced their intention to hold a demonstration in favor of the puppet government in South Vietnam. The so-called Vietnam, sneered Thirteen. On the other side of the river, the tower of the Saint-Germain l'Auxerrois church, which rang out for the St. Bartholomew Day Massacre, Saint-Eustache just above what was at the time still a large hole, as if a meteor had hit there, the barbed harpoons of Notre Dame, and the Sainte Chapelle, the Saint-Jacques tower, Saint-Etienne-du-Mont where Racine and Pascal rest in peace and to whom we paid homage from a distance, there was the tower of Clovis on top of which Angelo raised the red flag. The khaki pylon over there, shepherdess, oh, Eiffel Tower. Thirteen and I had only gotten to the first level. We had gone up there one day to unfurl large banners celebrating "the victorious struggle of the Vietnamese people." This was during Nixon's voyage to Peking . . . Was it before or after his great trip to Peking? It must have been before, Thirteen assured me, because it was during the Peking voyage of the head paper tiger that Pierre Overney was killed in front of the Zola gate at the Renault factory in Billancourt; and that was February 1972, he still remembered. One of these days we will have to climb to the top of the Eiffel Tower, he said to me. Now we have nothing to do there, just look, like everybody else. Now we'd just become gawkers. At that time, you say to Thirteen's daughter, we were not yet used to the sight of that sort of giant comb case, the Montparnasse Tower, no more than to the Zam Tower or the Science School. We didn't like the President Pomp style. It was under the Zam Tower that we had an unforgettable scrap when classes resumed in '68, but this time with the "revisionists," with a table dropped from the fourth floor; Thirteen nearly flattened like a crepe a guy who one day would be the director of *L'Humanité* . . . To the south, the blue tops of the Luxembourg Gardens broke through the fleecy clouds, ten years later I would be walking there, arm in arm with Leïla L, whose name means "my little night," and now I walk by myself all alone; that's life, you tell Thirteen's daughter, it's the approach of death, the black butterflies we chase. The white breasts of the Observatory. The hills coming out of the shadows, the Butte-aux-Cailles where Chloe has a little studio, Chaillot where we grabbed the retired general, the CEO of Atofram, Montmartre where we kept our stuff for wiretapping the police. Once again it was the snipe hunter who had patched the equipment together, but it worked better than the transmitter. The girl who handled the equipment, what was her name? She was the one who used to work at Gévelot where she would rip off ammunition? Later, when it was all over, she joined a sect. Suzanne. The heights of Belleville where I had lived with Judith, the lady notions seller and her son's place. The Seine was almost discernible behind a ridge of milky mist. To the left of Montmartre were the roofs of Saint-Lazare where we had tried to dump Chalais. On the right the Gare du Nord where we'd caught the postal train. Do you remember your lighter that played "The Red East," I asked Thirteen, and we began to squeal together: *Dong-fan-ang hong, tai-yan-ang sheng* . . . Through the girders of the scaffolding the sky was mauve just above Père Lachaise and Nation. Some planes were passing over them, trailing an icy pink wake. I asked him if he remembered the part in Victor Serge's *Memoirs* where he's on the roofs in Petrograd, rifle in hand, but that instead of shooting at the White Russians, he just contemplates the city in the brightly lighted night. Golds and pastels reflected in the canals. Thirteen didn't remember. At that time Victor Serge was not a recommended author. Trotskyist, leftist: petit-bourgeois revolutionary. Toward the west, at the end of the big trench made by the rue de Sèvres and the rue Lecourbe, to the left of the Invalides Dome, you could make out the Citroën plant; it had been several months since the smokestacks last spewed smoke over the Citroën factories on the quai de Javel. Behind all that, invisible, the Point-du-Jour where we explained the advantages of the people's war to housewives. Above us, obviously upset by our presence, the falcon couple who nest in the tower took off, screaming, beating their wings like dragonflies; suddenly they banked and headed toward the trees in the Luxembourg Gardens. Swells of roofs bathed in blue toward the east, then shading to a feathery gray in the west. There's a passage in Victor Hugo, I tell Thirteen, I don't know where, but it was Victor Hugo, when as a kid he climbs into the lantern room at the top of the Sorbonne's cupola (or maybe it was the Val-de-Grâce) to see the king's pathetic army enter Paris after Waterloo, and on the staircase he's quite dazzled by the sight of the prancing legs of the little girl in front of him. I no longer know where I found that passage, but I know I love that scene: the grand panorama, Paris, History, the end of an era, the defeat, and then, most of all, the girl's legs. Doubtless tanned, doubtless with some little scratches, little girls' legs are always like that. I think her name was Rose. I haven't read this Victor Hugo either, Thirteen says to me, but from what you've just told me, I think he must have been a Trotskyist too. Anyway, Rose's legs had to have been more exciting than yours, is what I answer. Her name was Rose, she was beautiful, she smelled good like a new flower, he sings. We were very high up now, above the circular pediments, at the last level of our rocket. Thirteen inspects the lunar module, he feels the stone, he looks inside the shaft. Everything seems OK Suddenly he changes his mind. What about God? Where'd he go? Didn't we have a meeting with him? Weren't we supposed to have a talk with him? Is he late? Or hiding? Maybe he's scared of us? You're afraid, One Ball? One to my two. He roars with laughter in a way that seems to me a little excessive. As if he had just said the funniest thing in the world. He appeared to be getting more and more excited, while me, on the other hand, I was becoming more and more reasonable, as usual. Fatigue and cold were getting to me, and with them some dizziness. What the hell am I doing here? The Pindar circus offered me $100,000 to capture Him, Thirteen went on with his index finger across his lips. Can you imagine the glory this would bring their menagerie? Next to the elephants, the lions Hector and Andromaque, Mimi, Fifi and Riri, the seals, the Divine One Ball! The primordial hermaphrodite! He went to the edge of the scaffolding, whirling what must have been an imaginary lasso at the end of his outstretched arms. Windowpanes gleamed far to the west, at the top of the towers in the new Défense quarter. The sun raised its rosy head above Nation, the distant working-class suburbs of Montreuil, Le Perreux, Le Raincy, Villemomble, Romainville, the slums, the workers' gardens, the parking lots, the highways that went around the malls—all that was coated in a raspberry sauce. The signposts flickered and went out on the road around Paris. The grenadine sun rose above the black trees in the Vincennes woods, *gong-chan dang, xiang tai-yang* bellows out Thirteen, with the exaggerated accent of a Chinaman in an operetta, high pitched and nasal, *zhao na-li, na-li liang*, the Communist

Party is like the sun, where it shines, light reigns. He'd already forgotten about capturing God. He bursts into laughter, but not the laughter that marked our lives, like the time we buried the dynamite, for example, that was, I don't know, six years ago; he's laughing for himself and didn't expect me to share in it, a whistling laugh, ringing out from a depth of sorrow, a spasm that has nothing to do with joy. It even seems to me that it's not him laughing, not the guy I knew all my life, my eternal friend, but something else, a power that possessed him. The sun rises on the Vincennes zoo; the monkeys must be putting on their sunglasses right now, is what he brays, he pulls out sunglasses and flicks them on his nose, and there he is, careening about on the scaffolding as fast as he can, screaming that President Mao is the king of monkeys, the golden monkey, and that he wants his people's happiness, *ta wei ren-min mo xingfu*, the happiness of the monkey people, Kipling's Bandar-Log. That's exactly how it happens, Marie, you say to Thirteen's daughter. Then he falls.

That's it, all done. You don't know what to say, you're uncomfortable, you light a cigarette. The sun has risen, the smoke from the big incinerator is black in the dawn, lights flicker, like a ship on fire. Anyway, you knew all that, you say just to say something, I'm not telling you anything new. Yes, but do you think that . . . No. I don't know, but I don't think so. He was loaded and he fell, that's all.

You both smoke in silence. The advertisements along the highway flicker and go out. One of the first suburban trains glides by, in the midst of lightning, down there, in the valley, toward Austerlitz. You pat her neck, under her hair. You think that in several days it will be the first solstice of the twenty-first century.

And later? Later, nothing. We went our separate ways. Nothing to worry about.